REFINING EARTH

ELIZABETH KNIGHT

Knight, Elizabeth
Refining Earth

Editing: Swish Editing & Design
Cover artist: RYN KATRYN BOOK COVERS
Formatting: Creative Wonder Publishing

CHAPTER 1
LAILAH

A loud crack of thunder pulled me out of the blissful dream I was having. Not wanting to let the dream slip away, I snuggled deeper into my bed and relished in the warmth it was radiating. Oh God, this detergent is heavenly. I don't remember my laundry smelling this good. Too tired to care, I nuzzled my nose into the fabric to get a better whiff. All of a sudden, the fabric under me moved. My eyes popped open, and I discovered that I was shamelessly smashing my face into someone's chest. Slowly, I lifted my face and looked up to find Brayden's warm hazel eyes greeting me.

"Good morning," Brayden said, brushing his hand down my back. "Did you sleep well?" I could feel his words rumbling through his chest, which I was still splayed across.

I lurched away from him so violently that I fell off the bed and onto the floor. In addition to my uncoordinated behavior, my body felt sore, but I couldn't remember why. *Wait! Where am I? Why was I in bed with Brayden? And why can't I remember what happened last night after the party?*

I could feel my face burn with embarrassment as I realized I'd koala-ed him in my sleep. I panicked for a second and wiped the back of my hand across my mouth, making sure that I hadn't been drooling on him all night. Thankfully, my wild mass of curls shrouded my face, keeping me from having to look at him.

Brayden slid off the bed and crouched in front of me. "Hey. It's okay, Lailah, you're safe. We brought you to our place after everything went down last night."

Momentarily distracted, I took in his handsome face. His soft, dark brown hair was mussed, when it was typically styled perfectly in that *Mad Men* slick look. Brayden's eyes were filled with worry as he watched me—it was as if waiting for a reaction of some kind.

Wait—what did he mean by *we*? I tried to grasp for anything about what happened after I left the guys outside the event hall. Suddenly, the memories came crashing back, and I gasped at the force of it.

"That was real?" I whispered, wrapping my arms around my legs, trying to keep myself from freaking out.

Brayden sat on the floor next to me and pulled me close, putting his arms around me. When he touched me, a wash of calm flooded through me and brought me back from the edge of a panic attack. "Tell me what you remember after you left us to go to the bathroom."

I paused, sorting through the fragments of the night and trying to put them in order. "Someone smashed my head, knocking me out . . . Oh, God. It was Mallory."

Brayden nodded, encouraging me to continue.

"When I came to. I-I was in a field, and there was a demon . . ." I stopped as I watched the scene replay in my brain, and the nightmare unfolded before me once again. "She's dead, isn't she?"

"Mallory's been dead for some time. I don't know when the demon fully took her, but there was nothing we could have done for her last night."

"The demon wanted to kill me. He kept saying that his master would be so pleased that I was killed. Why would someone want me dead? He said something about not knowing what I would be like with powers." I looked up and met Brayden's steady gaze. "He called me Synergy. It's true, isn't it? I'm the sixth element."

Not saying a word, he just nodded his head and took my hand in his. All I could do was take a deep, shaky breath and squeeze his hand like he was my only lifeline.

"We did something special last night, didn't we?" I asked, vaguely remembering a talking bright light. "Something made me use my powers, but I can't remember what it was for."

"You helped us renew the protective wards around the school. You even made them more powerful than before. Now there's no way a demon can try a stunt like that again."

"I did what? How could I do that? I don't even know what the hell is going on!" I said as the panic began rising again.

Brayden stood and pulled me to my feet wrapping me in a comforting hug until I stopped shaking. "Why don't you take a shower and change? I know that helps me when I feel like life gets to much. Then I can show you downstairs and get you some breakfast. I think this is going to be better explained by someone else."

"But I don't have anything to change into."

"Cami brought some stuff for you when we told her what happened. She stayed here last night too." Brayden still hadn't let go of my hand and led me to a half-open doorway. He flicked on the light to reveal the bathroom. "Everything you need should be here for you. Beth made sure it was stocked for when you needed it."

"Beth?" I think I'd heard the guys mention her before...

"She's our resident director, or as Parker likes to call her, the Den Mom. She makes sure we're looked after while at school. She'll be the best one to explain things to you after breakfast. If you need anything, my room is to the left of yours."

"Thanks, Brayden. If you hadn't been here, I think I might have lost it," I said, smiling.

"Anytime."

He surprised me by kissing my forehead before leaving to get ready.

As I pulled myself together for the day, it gave me a sense of normalcy and kept me from letting the panic close in. It could also be that the bathroom I was using belonged in some million-dollar home, and that never failed to perk a girl up.

Once I was dressed, I pulled my hoodie over my tank top and smiled at the words written on it—*Feed me and tell me I'm pretty*. The need to feel warm and safe was at the top of my list, but as I walked out of the bedroom, I was unsure of what would happen outside of these walls.

I opened my bedroom door and discovered there was a large open sitting room with a giant TV and an assortment of armchairs and couches. This looked like a place the guys would hang out in a lot. There were large bookcases on either side of the TV that were filled with movies and video games. As I walked closer, I scanned over the movies and was surprised by how many I hadn't seen.

"I'm thinking you have the right idea, Trouble. We should totally have a movie marathon and do nothing all day," Parker said from across the room.

I turned and saw him leaning against a doorframe to a bedroom that I could only assume was his own. He had his signature goofy grin aimed right at me, and I couldn't help but return the smile. I also couldn't help but notice that his t-shirt was tight across his chest and showed off his linebacker physique. His vibrant red hair was, of course, spiked and wild just like him. A day lounging with him sounded amazing.

"Sounds good to me, but I'm going to need food first," I said.

"Follow me. I was just about to head down."

"Is it just you and Brayden that have rooms up here?" I asked.

"Nope. The rest of the guys are here too. Micah is on the other side next to Brayden, then Jay and Hudson."

"Oh, you're all right here," I said, surprised. I figured in a house this big they would be spread out.

"Yeah, it's easier for Miss B to keep track of us if we're all in the same area," Parker said with a wink as he led me down the short hall to the main staircase.

"Miss B?"

"It's the horrible nickname that Parker has given me," a woman answered as we reached the bottom of the stairs. "Hello, you must be Lailah. I'm Beth."

Beth was not at all what I pictured when I heard the guys talk about her. Her warm brown eyes welcomed me and were framed by a sleek shoulder-length bob of dark brown hair. She was smartly dressed in a soft lavender button-down, paired with a pencil skirt and heels. Beth gave off a very capable air that gave me no doubt she ran this house well and always kept the boys in line.

"It's nice to finally meet you," I said, grasping her hand. She gave me a firm handshake and smiled.

"Don't trust a thing these boys say. It's all lies," Beth said, giving Parker a knowing look.

"What? I didn't say anything," Parker said, raising his hands in defense. "Not this time anyway."

I laughed, enjoying the way Parker was squirming under Beth's gaze. My stomach growled loudly to let everyone know that I was hungry. I blushed and clutched my stomach as if I could tell it to shut up.

"Come on, let's feed the poor girl," Beth said, turning and heading further into the house.

She led us to a large dining room that had a massive table with twelve chairs. Jay, Hudson, and Cami were already at the table with food in front of them.

"Take a seat wherever you'd like, Lailah," Beth instructed.

I slipped into a seat next to Cami, thankful that she was here for all this. As close as I had gotten to the guys, I still needed my best friend. Once I was seated, a lady came out of a side door with two place settings that she set in front of Parker and me. Breakfast was laid out on the table, and without even asking, Jay and Hudson began to pass trays of food in my direction, ignoring Parker.

"Hey!" Parker said as Jay pulled a plate of sausage away from him. "I wasn't done with that."

"There would be nothing left after you," Jay said, sliding it my way.

I couldn't help but smile at the banter between the guys. It was different to see them in their own environment where they were more relaxed. Even though I really hated breakfast meats, I took one sausage so as not to be rude. Cami, knowing better, slid over the large bowl of fruit, and I took a big scoop. Then I plucked one of the large cinnamon rolls and took a bite.

"You really shouldn't eat that much sugar in the morning," Hudson pointed out.

Cami snorted. "I wouldn't get in the way of Lala and her sugar, especially her sugar cookies. If you ever see any lying around and you value your life, I wouldn't eat it."

"I'm not that bad!" I said, gaping at her.

"Supposedly, I'm your best friend, and I've only been allowed to eat one of your cookies," Cami challenged.

"I've eaten one," Jay said, and everyone froze to look at him.

"What!?" Parker said, slamming his fork down on the table. "You let him have some of your cookie?"

With the looks I was getting from Cami and Parker, I wanted to crawl under the table and hide.

"I think an explanation is in order," Parker said, crossing his arms.

I looked over at Beth to see if she could help me out of this. Shockingly enough, she was reading the newspaper and sipping her coffee like nothing was going on.

"Trouble?" Parker insisted.

I hesitated, but then couldn't take the pressure anymore. "Jay and I went on a long run, and while taking a break, I found out he'd never eaten a sugar cookie before, and Parker just happened to send some along, and—"

"What the actual *fuck*. You gave him one of my apology cookies?" Parker shouted.

"Not a whole cookie, just half," I said, not understanding why he was so upset.

Jay just sat back and watched the whole thing, his eyes shining with humor. It made me linger on him a moment, because typically he never showed that much emotion. His head was freshly buzzed, so his hair was just a faint black hue over his scalp. He was taller than most Asians I had met before, but even though he was lean, he was buff. Guess that comes with the territory of working with a father who owns the largest private military organization in the world.

"Fine, I won't share my cookies with anyone ever again," I huffed, rolling my eyes. "Happy?"

"No," Parker snapped. "I want you to share your cookies equally. If you're going to give Jay some, then you have to be fair with the rest of us."

"Wait, are you still talking about cookies?" Cami piped up.

My gaze snapped back to Cami with my mouth open in shock at her suggestion. "Cami."

"What?" she replied.

"If that's the case, then Cami, you can never have another cookie," Parker said, laughing so hard he almost fell out of his chair.

"Parker," I yelled.

"Oh, come on, that was too good to pass up," he said, smiling.

I just blushed and ducked my head while stuffing my face with the cinnamon roll.

"Well, look who's up before noon," Hudson said as Micah joined us and sat next to Jay.

Micah's thick chestnut hair was in a haphazard messy bun, and he wasn't wearing a shirt. My eyes lingered on his tan skin and muscular chest, which led me to notice the fact that his sweatpants were low on his hips. His sapphire gaze wandered over the table, taking in the food and people around him with a scowl on his face.

"With you assholes being so loud, how is anyone supposed to sleep?" he muttered.

Hudson put down his book and looked at Micah, running a hand through his honey blond hair. Normally he had product in it to keep it there, but it was nice to see him so relaxed for once. "Studies have proven that sleeping longer on the weekends throws off your whole sleep schedule." He pushed his glasses up, drawing me to his blue eyes that shone with intelligence.

Micah didn't answer and poured himself a cup of coffee.

"Seems like I'm late to the party," Brayden said as he sat on my other side.

"If you want to call it that," Micah muttered, loading up his plate.

"Well isn't this nice having everyone here for breakfast," Beth said, smiling at us. "Lailah, I'm sure you must have lots of questions about what happened last night. If you feel up for it, we can chat about it when you're done eating."

"Thank you, I do have lots of questions," I sighed, glad that I wouldn't have to beg for people to explain.

"Lovely. Cami can show you to my office when you're done," Beth said, rising from her seat and heading out of the dining room.

"Would you like any of us to come with you?" Brayden asked.

I smiled at him and shook my head. "No, I'll have Cami with me, but thanks for offering."

"When you're done with Beth, you better not run off. You said you'd have a movie day with me. I might even be talked into teaching you how to play Call of Duty," Parker said.

"What's that?" I frowned.

Parker's eyes widened in shock. "You're joking. You have two brothers, and you've never heard of Call of Duty?"

"My brothers were never into video games. Our parents told us that if we wanted that stuff in the house, we had to buy it ourselves," I explained.

"This is something we will have to rectify. I, myself, am not in favor of wasting brainpower on video games, but it does help with hand-eye coordination," Hudson interjected.

Grinning, I looked at the rest of the guys, and they all seemed to be in favor of teaching me how to play. "Okay, I'll give it a try."

Parker whooped as he shot up from his seat, mumbling about having to hook up the second unit for more players as he left the room.

I turned back to Brayden. "Should I be worried?"

"No, I think you just became Parker's dream girl. No one else likes to play video games with him . . . he gets a little intense."

"Come on, Lala. The sooner we talk to my sister, the faster we can get this shit show started," Cami said, nudging my arm grinning at my shocked face. "Told you I had two sisters, guess I forgot to tell you who the second one was."

CHAPTER 2
LAILAH

Cami led me to a set of wooden French doors and opened one without knocking. I followed her in and gaped at the stately office. It was warm and inviting, but it had a polish that let you know everything in here was expensive. Beth was working at a contemporary wooden desk with bookshelves and a large tapestry of some crest as the backdrop.

"Come in, please, have a seat," Beth said, standing and motioning to two love seats framing a low coffee table. "Do you want any coffee or water?"

"I'm fine, thank you," I said as I took my seat.

"She hates coffee; Lala is more of a tea drinker," Cami shared.

"Good to know, I will make sure we have tea stocked. Do you have a preference for a particular type?"

"Um, I'm a bit of a chai addict, although I'm fine with most tea," I answered, feeling awkward that she was being so accommodating, like she thought I was going to be here a lot or something.

Beth just nodded and typed something on her phone before setting it down and crossing her legs to look at me. "Now, I'm not sure where you want to start this conversation, so let's just start with your questions."

This whole thing had been feeling so surreal that I didn't really know what I wanted to ask anymore. I took a deep breath and sorted through my thoughts and what happened last night.

"Demons," I said, looking up at Beth. "One wanted to kill me, and I don't understand why. I didn't even know that demons really existed other than in books and religion."

"Our world has been in a fight behind the scenes for a millennium. Since the fall of man, demons have been hidden in plain sight, doing their best to keep the world in chaos," Beth said, smoothing her hands down her skirt. "The angels have been doing what they can to balance out the attacks, but they are limited because they are truly unable to interact with the human race. God's blessing of free will is not to be affected, even if it is for the greater good. So the angels created a handful of blessed warriors gifted with abilities to help them battle the demons."

Realization slammed into me; Beth was talking about the Elementi. "That story is true?"

"Tell me what you know, and I can fill in the blanks," Beth said, nodding for me to share.

"Five Knights of the Templar were blessed by an angel with powers to battle evil in the world. When the Knights started to die out, a group separated and became known as the Elementi. They helped those in need, but as time went on, they disappeared from society and became more legend and rumor," I said.

"That is all correct, but we didn't fade from the world. We went underground, literally. We have a whole training facility under the school and this house. The Elementi are still active to this day, we just needed to become invisible. The demons got smarter and started hiding in places and positions we couldn't get to them. We could no longer fight out in the open like the Templar days.

Nowadays, demons place themselves in a spot where they

can influence someone of a higher power. A secretary to a military general, wife to a politician, advisor to a king. Without the right place in society, we couldn't enter the world they were a part of. That's when the Elementi came up with the idea of this school. Its founder, Aiden Ryevick, was a member of the Elementi and our registrar. Most of his records are kept in the protected records room Mr. Phillips let you have access to," Beth said.

My head was spinning with the information Beth was sharing with me. "Wait! Is Professor Phillips part of the Elementi?"

"Yes. So is Nona, Professor Whittemore—our sister," Beth said, glancing at Cami to give me a moment to connect the dots.

I turned so I could look at Cami, and the guilt in her eyes told me everything I needed to know. "You knew this whole time the Elementi were real?" I whispered.

Cami opened her mouth to say something, but Beth cut her off. "I was the one who instructed Cami to keep this information from you. I wanted you to be protected while at school, and since Cami is one of our best warriors, the task fell to her."

Whipping back around, I narrowed my eyes at Beth. "Are you telling me *you* knew who and what I was this entire time?"

I felt the betrayal of my best friend like being stabbed in the heart. I'd survived it once before in high school, but I thought Cami was different. She understood what it was like to feel used and different. Knowing that her sister made her keep this from me did not help the situation, since I didn't trust or know Beth.

"Lailah." Beth spoke in a calm, steady voice, like you would to a small child. "Please understand, we wanted to ease you into this world. I didn't want to take away the chance for you to have a normal college experience, if I could help it. I placed you with teachers who could direct you into finding out about the Elementi on your own. We in no way were trying to manipulate you or to harm you."

"Did the guys know too?" I snapped. I wasn't sure I could handle that on top of everything else.

"No, I didn't tell them about you. They figured it out on their own about a week ago. They came to me as upset as I can see you are now. From this point on, there will be no more secrets between us. There are no locked doors to you here, and I will answer any question you can think to ask. The Elementi is founded on truth and honor; we would not have been sent you if we had betrayed the angels," Beth tried to explain, holding her hands out in surrender.

I took a shaky breath, relieved to know the guys hadn't lied to me this whole time. Then another thought popped into my head. "Did I actually get into this school on my own merit or was it because you knew I was Synergy?"

Beth stilled, looking down at her hands. "Do you remember the ancestry test we had you send in?"

"Of course—it was such an odd thing to ask for."

"If you hadn't been Synergy, you wouldn't have made it into our school on your ACT score alone," Beth admitted.

I shot to my feet, fury surging through my body. "So you're telling me that NOTHING about being at this school has been real. All of it has been a manipulation to get me to come here so I can be a part of your cult!"

"Lailah, that's not true —"

"Name one thing you haven't twisted for your own needs," I demanded.

"The boys. I wanted to keep them away from you. I never wanted them to meet you until you understood what you were," Beth said, slumping back against the couch, letting her perfect shell crack a little. "I should've known better than to keep them from you or to lie to you all. You are made for them; there's no way they wouldn't be drawn to you."

"Explain," I bit out, my hands shaking at my side in frustration.

"When the angels blessed the original five warriors, they

were told if they stayed true to their task, they would be gifted with the sixth element. This element was to be the turning of the tide, the weapon they needed to win against the Dark Lord."

"What does that have to do with the guys?"

Beth stood as well and began pacing around the room, trying to ease the tension that was thick around us. "You are the sixth element, Lailah. No one was ever told what Synergy would be, but Aiden, our school's founder, said he had a vision showing him it would be a human. He went so far as to write down this vision in his journals, one that we could read, but the second journal was sealed away from us until Synergy's power unlocked it. Even though the council didn't believe him, we knew better than to ignore the information. That is when we started to test people who seemed to be drawn to the Elementi. None of us imagined you would be born in the States. You are the first American we have ever let enroll in our school, and do you know why?"

"How could I, you're not very good at sharing information," I grumbled.

"It never happened before. In the hundreds of years our school has been around, no one from the US has ever applied, until you. I knew even before we had you tested who you were. Nothing was going to keep you away from the boys. The six of you were always meant to be together," Beth said, pausing to stand in front of me and giving me the full weight of her gaze. "Synergy's power is to combine all the elements to become stronger. To bond and become one unit, with you at the center."

My anger washed away, but was replaced by terror as I sank back onto the couch. Nothing about my life was what I thought it was. My mind raced trying to process this new revelation. *Did this mean the guys were drawn to me because of what I was, not because they really liked me? Could this be why I was so comfortable around them? What does this all mean, now that we all know? Will they reject me now that they understand?*

"Lala, breathe. It's going to be okay," Cami said, rubbing her hand up and down my back.

I turned to her, feeling my eyes welling up with tears. "Are you drawn to me too because I'm Synergy? Is our friendship real, or was it all an act?"

Cami looked at me like I slapped her. "How could you even ask me that? Of course our friendship is real. I never once pretended with you. It killed me every time you talked about the Elementi and I couldn't tell you everything. Hell, I even encouraged you to connect with the guys against Beth's instructions."

I blinked at that in surprise. Cami ignored her sister's orders to help me get closer to the guys? When I looked over at Beth, I could tell she didn't know about Cami's rebellion.

"Thank you. I don't know if I could handle losing my best friend through all of this," I said, pulling her into a hug.

"Oh, silly Lala, you can't get rid of me that easily," Cami teased, hugging me even tighter.

Feeling my emotions settling down, I took a deep breath and looked at Beth. "What now?"

"We start your training. Now that you have come into your power, we need to make sure that you can control it. Typically, the Five Warriors' power presents during puberty, which is helpful to hide it happening because your emotions are already more volatile. For this reason, I am going to ask that you move into the house with the others."

"Um, you want me to what? Why would I move into The Manor? Do you have any idea what that would do to me? I have enough trouble with the other girls just being friends with all the guys. If they find out that I've moved in with them, I might just get murdered in my sleep."

"That wouldn't happen if you stayed here. We have the best security on campus," Beth said, unbothered by my concerns.

"Beth, don't be like that. You know how much trouble the girls have been," Cami snapped, glaring at her sister. "If we do this, there needs to be a plausible reason for it, and right now there isn't any."

Suddenly an idea came to me. "What if I finish the semester out in my normal dorm, and then when we leave for holiday break, we can change things up. Lots of people make changes during that time. This way they don't need to know I'm living in The Manor; they'll just know I'm not in Ashfall anymore."

Beth considered this for a moment, tapping her fingers on her chin. Coming to a decision, she pinned me with a look as she leaned forward. "I will allow you to give it a try, *but*—if anything goes wrong or you lose control, then you're coming back here, no arguments."

"Deal. I can work with that."

"I expect you to still attend classes here, on top of your current load," Beth said, narrowing her eyes at me. "After this semester, we will change your schedule so these special classes take more of a priority."

"What kind of classes are they?" I asked.

"Elementi history, demon theory, element manipulation, combat, and physical fitness, to start off with."

"And you want me to add this all to my current class load?" My mouth fell open in disbelief.

Beth stood and grabbed a tablet off her desk, and with a few swipes, looked over something before she answered me. "Hmm, it seems that you changed what I had originally set your schedule up with."

After I'd been accepted, I'd received a pre-filled class schedule that was far too easy for me to waste my time taking. "They were all easy classes; I knew I could push myself more."

"As much as I admire that, I did have it arranged so that when you came into your powers we could easily add to your schedule. Now it seems I'll have to wait till next semester to add them all," Beth said, making notes on her tablet. "There are a few areas we can't neglect. I am going to inform Professor Phillips and Nona that you will not need to complete the finals for their classes. I need you to work with them on different subjects right now. Nona needs to work with you on elemental manipulation, and Professor Phillips will catch you up on Elementi history. We also need to add in some physical training to help you deal with your new powers."

"That makes sense to me. I don't want to hurt anyone because I don't know what I'm doing," I agreed even though dropping my favorite class would suck.

"I'm glad you realize that. When an Elementi Warrior has a meltdown, it can have catastrophic effects. To make sure that doesn't happen, I want you to keep one of the guys around you as much as possible. They are the only ones who can handle it if your power gets out of control."

"Can't I just have Cami with me? I don't think this will help with my mean girl situation," I mused before I glanced over at Cami with a questioning look.

"Oh, I'll be around, but when shit gets real, I'm ducking for cover. The power you have will make me one crispy critter, and I like my pasty-ass skin just like it is." Cami smirked.

I laughed, relieving some of the fear that was building about me hurting people.

"Do you have any more questions for me?" Beth asked.

"I'm sure I do, but I don't think I could handle any more information right now. That was a lot to take in," I answered, rubbing my temples.

"Fair enough. Feel free to ask the boys or Cami if anything else comes to mind. They've grown up in this world, so they might not notice doing or saying things that seem weird to you."

Nodding, I stood and followed Cami out of the office and back upstairs to the common room, where we found the guys throwing cheese puffs and yelling at each other. Cami looked at me and wagged her brows.

"Aren't you a lucky girl to have all that to look forward to for the rest of your life."

I laughed, drawing the attention of the guys, who changed from yelling at each other to waving us over.

CHAPTER 3
BRAYDEN

"Trouble, you are truly terrible at this," Parker said as Lailah cheered after she killed Jay again. The problem was, he was on her team.

She stuck her tongue out at him and turned back to the game. "I can't help it! I see someone and I just get so excited I forget to check who it is."

"That doesn't bode well for us on a mission," Micah grumbled. "If you fucking shoot me, I will burn all your hair off while you sleep."

Cami chucked a pillow right in his face. "Shut the fuck up, asshole."

"God damn it, Cami, look what you made me do," Micah yelled as he blew himself up walking over the landmine that he just placed.

"Serves you right for being a dick to my Lala."

I smiled to myself, watching the chaos before me. Little did Lailah know, us all hanging out like this hadn't happened in years. Typically, we all did our own thing, and if we did hang out, it was just two or three of us—never all five. Cami had grown up around us, and she was the annoying little sister who always wanted to play with us. Now she was going toe to toe with Micah, and I wasn't sure who was going to win if they really had it out.

My phone buzzed in my pocket, and I looked down to see it was one of my little sisters. I frowned. She never called me. I answered it as I walked into my bedroom, away from all the noise.

"Kayley, what's wrong?"

"Why would anything be wrong?"

"Kayley."

"Fine, I need you to come get me, but our parents cannot find out about this."

I scowled. Kayley was always the wild child, but she'd never called me to bail her out of a problem. "Where are you?"

"Jail . . ."

"What the fuck, Kayley, what happened?"

"Look, I can't explain it over the phone. I was only given five minutes. I'm only three hours away from you, in Enderton. When you come get me, I'll explain everything, I promise."

"Know that if what you tell me isn't a good enough reason, I will tell our parents," I threatened.

"Whatever you say, big bro. See you soon."

I looked down to see she'd hung up on me. "Fuck!" I said, running my hands through my hair.

Things with my family had been strained after my brother died three years ago. Before that, we'd always been a very close-knit unit, always together. Now I was lucky if I saw them all at the holidays, which wasn't helped by the fact I avoided going home if I could help it. My mother didn't take Michael's death well; it changed her into a hollow shell of a woman.

A soft knock sounded on my door, and I looked up to see Lailah poking her head in. "Hey, you okay?"

I didn't even know how to answer that, so I just shrugged my shoulders. Lailah slipped in, shut the door, and walked over to me, her crystal eyes filled with concern.

"I don't mean to intrude, but I've noticed that unlike the rest, you're not one to swear unless you're mad about something."

I blinked at that, surprised she'd picked up something so subtle about me. "I got a call from my little sister. It seems she has found herself in trouble and wants me to go get her."

"Oh no, is she okay?" she asked, resting a hand on my arm. "I think I would react the same way if my little brother called me in trouble. Do you need to head out right away?"

"Yeah, she's about three hours away, so I should get going if I want to get back at a reasonable time."

"Are you going to bring her back here?"

I shook my head. "No, her boarding school isn't too far from where she's at. If it's not serious, then I'll just get her back in time for school."

"Drive safe. Will you text me when you get back?" Lailah asked, her cheeks blushing as she looked down at her hands. "Just so I know you're safe."

I smiled, loving that she didn't even question me needing to go. After my brother died because of me, I shied away from having a deep connection with anyone outside the four guys. Even in that, we failed at having any kind of meaningful relationships like most of the Elementi Warriors before us did.

I leaned down and placed a gentle kiss on her forehead. "Of course. I promise you'll be the first to know."

I made good time, since it was a Saturday and there was hardly any traffic. When I pulled up to the police station, I sighed and headed in. What could Kayley have possibly done to end up here?

"Hello, how can I help you?" the officer at the front desk asked.

"My name is Brayden Dolton, I believe my sister, Kayley Dolton, is here."

The officer typed something into the computer and scanned the screen. "Looks like she was detained for starting a fight and assaulting another female while in a clothing store. Because she's still a minor and this is her first offense, we're letting her out on bail in the amount of ten thousand dollars."

"Wait, you said this was her first offense, why is the bail so high? She isn't a flight risk, and like you said, she's a minor," I challenged, frowning.

The officer just gave me a bored look. "Look, if you don't want to pay, then I can file this paperwork here and she will have a record. As of right now, we've held off putting anything in permanently. The choice is yours. How much is it worth to you not to have this arrest in her file forever?"

"Can I pay with this, or do I need to get cash?" I asked, holding out my card.

"This will do fine," the officer said, swiping the card without hesitation. "It will take us a few minutes to process her out; there's a waiting area over there where you can take a seat."

"Do I need to sign anything?" I asked.

"Your family owns Dolton Plant Sciences, right?" I nodded, seeing where this was going. "Then we thank your family for this donation to our department. It was lovely having your sister stay with us. Did you want the official story to go differently?"

"No, that won't be necessary, officer. I'm sure my sister was in the best care," I said, trying to keep from rolling my eyes.

I sent Beth a text letting her know what Kayley was in trouble for and what happened with the cops. She agreed with Kayley about not letting my parents know, since I could handle the situation. Who knew what would cause my mother to spiral, or what drastic measures she would use toward my sister. I found out that she once ran away from home when she was twelve, and when they found her, Mother locked her in her room for weeks to make sure she stayed safe. The thought of my mother possibly losing another child made her react irrationally, so my dad and I worked to get Kayley out of the house and into boarding school.

"What up, big bro? Long time no see," Kayley said, pulling me from my thoughts.

I looked up to see her in her school uniform, which was torn and wrinkled with a little blood splatter on a sleeve. The little girl I'd seen at Christmas two years ago was long gone. Now stood a young woman of fifteen, with the same stubborn jaw as our father. Clearly, she had taken after him in more ways than one if her temper was anything to go off of.

"Kayley," I replied as I stood, wanting to give her a hug but knowing she wouldn't want one. "Come on, let's get you back to school."

"Yeah, that's not going to happen."

"Why is that?"

"Because the girl I beat the shit out of goes to school with me. I'm sure she's informed the headmistress about what happened, and fighting is grounds for expulsion."

"Of course. Why did I think you would make this easy?" sighing I rubbed a hand across my forehead before deciding the next step. "Looks like you're going to have to come back with me, and we can ask Beth where we can get you into another school this late in the year. But we'll at least have to go back and get your things if you don't want Dad to notice you spending money."

Kayley punched me in the shoulder and grinned at me. "Whatever. Come on, big bro, this is going to be fun. Some good old sibling bonding time."

I sighed as we got into my car, trying to remind myself that I was the oldest and it was my job to look after her. "Care to share why you beat up the girl?"

"No."

"Well, isn't that a great start to our bonding time," I huffed, pulling out of the parking lot.

CHAPTER 4

LAILAH

The house was quiet as I wandered through the rooms. It seemed that I was up before anyone else. Granted, it was five a.m. on a Sunday morning, but I couldn't sleep. I kept having nightmares of that demon's face chasing me. This time the guys didn't come to my rescue, and I was left to fend for myself. The adrenaline rush when I woke up was enough to keep me from falling back asleep. I have to admit, I was glad to be alone as I explored the rest of the house, settling my nerves.

So far, I'd discovered a game room filled with a pool table, foosball, ping-pong, and even a few arcade games. Apparently having one hang out room wasn't enough for these guys, but I noticed it didn't look very used. A workout room was next door to the game room, filled with all kinds of weight machines, treadmills, and stationary bikes. I didn't think it was possible for me to be more impressed with what was going on in this house until I found the pool with an attached hot tub. There was no reason to ever leave this house—it had everything you could possibly want or need. Finally, I found the kitchen, and there were already two people cooking and getting things ready for breakfast.

"Good morning, Miss Lailah, can I get you anything?" the woman who I saw yesterday at breakfast asked. She set her work aside and walked over to me with a soft smile on her face.

"Um, if you could just point me to where I can find the hot tea," I said, taking in the huge intimidating industrial appliances. It reminded me of what my mother always dreamed she could have one day at the diner.

"Of course. Did you have a particular tea in mind? Ms. Whittemore mentioned you enjoy chai teas, so I made sure to have a selection for you," the woman said, leading me over to a small three-person table.

She was older, her graying hair wrapped up in a neat bun on the back of her neck. As she smiled, her eyes seemed to disappear under the wrinkles around them. For some reason, it instantly made me like her.

"That would be lovely. I'm sorry, I don't know your name."

"Goodness, look at me, forgetting my manners. My age must be catching up to me," she chuckled. "I'm Sarah, and that handsome-looking man over there cooking is my husband Garrett. We've been working in the Aiden House for nearly forty years, along with Garrett's brother Larry. He takes care of the grounds and maintenance-type things."

"It's nice to meet you." I smiled as she handed me a good-size basket full of thirty different tea packets. As I looked through the selection, Sarah set down a small tray that had a mug of hot water and little containers of sugar and cream.

"Can I get you anything else? Breakfast should be ready soon; we're not used to someone being up this early on the weekends."

I shook my head, plopping in a teabag. "No, I can wait, I just couldn't fall back asleep."

"Can't say I'm surprised. You've had quite an upheaval in your life," Sarah said, going back to the cutting board.

I watched the tea bloom in my mug, the brown infusion slowly taking over the water, morphing it into something completely different than what it once was. In a matter of minutes, this simple cup of water would be transformed entirely until you couldn't even recognize it anymore. Was I any different? I thought I knew who I was, but then all of a sudden, along comes this flood of power, and I'm transformed. Now my whole future is changing from what I had planned. I was no longer in charge of my fate. I was a part of a bigger plan, according to Beth, but what about *my* plans? *My* dreams and aspirations?

"That must be some fascinating tea."

I jerked up from my hunched position to find Hudson sitting across from me at the table. I'd been so lost in thought I didn't even notice him sitting down. He watched me with bright blue eyes that were only enhanced by his black-framed glasses. His blonde hair was tousled, and he even had some scruff on his jaw. I was surprised by how much I liked seeing this rugged side of him.

"Just lost in thought."

"Would you like to talk about it? I find it helps me process a problem if I verbalize it."

I smiled. Hudson was ever the practical one. Sarah set down a full coffee cup for Hudson, and I sighed as she patted him on the shoulder before walking away.

"I was thinking about how everything has changed now. All the plans I had for the life I thought I was living are now going to be thrown out the window. There's a bigger purpose for me, and that is the path I have to follow." I paused as I took the teabag out and mixed in the milk. "How am I going to explain this to my family? Can I even tell them? Did they have any idea what I am? What the hell am I going to do now?"

Hudson reached out, placing a hand on mine, making me realize how tightly I was holding onto my mug. I'm surprised it didn't shatter in my grip. These feelings were overwhelming, and I didn't know what to do with them as they built up inside me.

"You're looking at the big picture. No problem can be solved unless you take it apart piece by piece to make it more manageable."

"How do I do that? It's my whole life that's changed; everything I thought I knew isn't true anymore."

"Wrong."

I looked up at the tone in that one word. Hudson was rational; he didn't do dramatic, but that one word was filled with such emotion, it took me by surprise. "What?"

"You said everything you thought you knew isn't true anymore. That, Lailah, is incorrect. You're now the person you were always meant to be. Will it change a few things, sure, but that isn't the same as everything not being true. Your parents may not know about this, and we will have to come up with a way to explain it to them, but that won't change their love for you. Sure, they will have questions and be shocked, but who you are at the core, the daughter they raised, hasn't gone anywhere."

I sat stunned at the words that were coming out of Hudson's mouth. Never would I have guessed that he would be the one sitting there telling me in the most rational way possible that I was overreacting.

"As for what you're going to do now, you're going to take it one day at a time. We're all here to help you through this. The five of us have been where you are now. I remember how volatile my emotions were after I came into my power—it made me feel like I couldn't control anything. That will change in time. The more you learn, the more your confidence will grow. Never feel like you can't talk to us about what you're feeling. You're part of the team now; we have your back."

I felt something wet hit my hands that were folded in front of me, and when I looked down, I realized I was crying. Hudson had literally said exactly what I needed to hear. He stood up and walked over to me, wrapping his arms around me as I hid my face against his stomach. Without saying anything, he just stood there, rubbing my back, letting me feel the emotions that had been building over the past twenty-four hours.

"Can I get a hug too?" Parker asked.

Pulling away from Hudson, I smiled, wiping away the last of my tears, and stood. "Sure."

Returning my smile with his signature grin, Parker pulled me against his chest, almost squeezing me a little too tight. He placed a kiss on the top of my head and set me back on my feet, pulling me away from him but still not letting me go. "Why the waterworks so early in the morning?"

"Just trying to figure out this new version of my life and what it means for the future."

"Whoa, that's a little heavy for first thing in the morning. I would cry too."

I giggled, wondering if Parker could actually survive a serious emotional discussion.

"Goodness me," Sarah said, pulling my attention. "This is a sight, seeing you up so early, Parker. Should I be expecting the rest of the boys joining us here in the kitchen?"

"If Lailah stays here, then I would say there's a strong chance you'll have us all underfoot soon enough," Hudson said.

"Off with you then, to the dining room. I'll bring out what we have ready now, and then everything else when it's done," Sarah said, shooing us out of the kitchen.

Parker slung his arm around my shoulders, guiding me out and across the way to the dining room. Hudson pulled out the chair at one end of the table for me, and I sat as he pushed it in. They settled down on either side of me, sipping on their coffee, making me realize I left my tea untouched back in the kitchen.

"Here you are, love," Sarah said, placing a fresh mug of water and a tea packet at my elbow. Bless that woman.

Soon, the table was full of delicious-smelling food, making my mouth water. Hudson took my plate and filled it with a little of everything. I opened my mouth to tell him I wouldn't be able to eat that much, but before I could, he cut me off.

"You'll find that with your new powers, you're going to eat a lot more for the first few months. It's a side effect of your body adapting to the high rate you will burn calories."

I took the plate and decided it wasn't worth arguing about when they were more familiar with the changes that would be happening to me. As we ate in a comfortable silence, I was surprised when a teenage girl came waltzing into the dining room and sat down. The guys both had frowns on their faces but didn't seem alarmed that she was there.

"Kayley," Hudson said, pulling her attention from her plate of food. "To what do we owe the honor of your visit?"

"Hey, Hud, Parker." She smiled, waving her fork at them. "I just needed some bro time, so I called Brayden to come and get me from school for the day."

Hudson's frown deepened, and Parker's eyebrows raised at her words. I had to admit that my curiosity was through the roof. I was about to ask her a question when Brayden made his entrance, pausing when he saw us all staring at him.

"Oh, good morning. I didn't think anyone would be up so early," he said, sitting next to his sister.

"So, are you going to introduce me to your girlfriend?" Kayley asked, her keen brown eyes looking over at me.

Brayden sighed as he poured himself some coffee. I wasn't sure what caught me off guard more—that she assumed I was his girlfriend or that Brayden wasn't denying it.

"Kayley, meet Lailah. She is a good friend of ours. Lailah, meet Kayley, one of my little sisters."

"So, she isn't your girlfriend? You made such a fuss about getting back so late and not knowing if she had stayed up last night waiting that I just assumed."

"Kayley," Brayden groaned, hiding his face in his hands, not looking at me.

"This is why I'm glad that I don't have siblings that bother with my personal life," Hudson interjected, pulling the attention away from Brayden.

"As a fellow younger sibling, Kayley is only doing her sisterly duty in embarrassing Brayden," Parker said with a wide grin.

"What the hell is the pint-sized menace doing here?" Micah interrupted.

"Micah," Kayley said, jumping up from her seat and racing over to hug him.

I sat stunned, watching Micah hug her back with a hint of a smile on his face. I don't think I've ever seen him happy to see anyone before. Though I had to admit, even the ghost of a smile transformed his face into something breathtaking. Micah caught me watching the exchange, and the warmth fell from his features, shuttered behind the cool blank expression he normally had.

"What the fuck did you do this time?" Micah asked, holding her away from him.

"Language," Brayden snapped.

"Yeah, yeah, yeah. Young virgin ears present, my bad," Micah grumbled.

Kayley rolled her eyes and looked back at her brother. "Seriously, it's not like I haven't heard it all before. Even some of the teachers swear around us. I'm not a little kid anymore."

"Oh, so ending up in jail has made you an adult now, has it?" Brayden asked, glaring at her.

Micah spun Kayley back to face him as he scowled at her. "What the hell is he going on about? Did you really land yourself in jail? I will spank you myself if you pulled some crazy stunt."

Now there was the Micah I knew well; the disapproving look she was getting that I had become well accustomed to.

"I was just defending myself. I wasn't going to let that snobby bitch talk about my family that way."

"Explain," Micah bit out.

"This girl at my school found out about Michael and said that the reason I was sent to boarding school so young was to keep Mom from killing me too. That Mom wasn't stable, and she's the reason that Michael killed himself."

Everyone in the room froze at her words. I flicked my gaze over to see Brayden's reaction. The shame and hurt that washed over his face told me there was more to this story. Kayley started to cry, and Micah pulled her against him and let her cry it out.

"Goodness, what happened here?" Beth asked, walking in with Cami.

"Just a typical day in the Dolton household," Brayden said as he passed Beth on the way out of the dining room.

I was torn whether to follow after him or to worry about his sister. Hudson touched my elbow and gave me a look that made the choice for me. Pushing my chair back, I hurried after Brayden. I really wasn't sure where he would run off to when he was upset. My instinct was to try his room.

When I knocked on the door, I didn't hear a response, so I opened it and peeked inside. Empty. Then I remembered seeing a library on the first level and headed off in hopes he would be there. When I reached the library, one of the wooden sliding doors was partially open, and I could see Brayden hunched over in an armchair. I slipped into the room and closed the door the rest of the way.

Brayden looked up at me with tears shining in his eyes. Seeing him so vulnerable made my heart break as I walked over to him. I wrapped my arms around him, holding him close, his head resting on my chest as he wrapped his arms around my waist, pulling me onto his lap. With anyone else, it would feel far too forward, or I'd worry that they would take advantage, but this was Brayden. Not wanting to push him to talk, I just held him and showed him I was there for him. Brayden had been my safe place through all this, and I wanted to be that for him.

"Michael was my older brother," Brayden said, breaking the silence. "We were eighteen months apart, and we were inseparable. He was the other half of me, but he always struggled with some mental health issues. He was diagnosed with bipolar disorder at the age of ten. His only dream in life was to be the next Earth Elementi. He talked to my uncle incessantly about it."

Brayden pulled back to tuck me under his chin as he contin-ued. "Michael and my father had many arguments, being so similar, with strong opinions and even stronger tempers. My father knew that the chances of Michael becoming the next Earth Elementi were five to one, so he didn't want my brother pinning all his hopes on that one thing. He tried to get him inter-ested in the business side of things, but nothing would deter him. When his thirteenth birthday came and passed with no powers, he became despondent and inconsolable."

"The final straw was when I turned thirteen and inherited the earth element. Michael wanted nothing to do with me after that, telling me that I stole everything from him. We had to have him admitted into a mental health facility because he kept trying to kill himself. He made it another two years before he finally managed to find a way to end his life. He wrote me a note telling me that if he couldn't be an Elementi Warrior, then he didn't want to exist in the world, couldn't watch me have what he longed for. After that, my mother became depressed and started to do odd things trying to keep us safe. It became too hard to be around the house, so Micah and I moved into this house a year early with the other guys and started training as Elementi Warriors. As you can see, that has worked out well for us."

I waited a few moments before I said anything, just absorbing what he told me. I had never lost anyone in my life—both of my grandparents were even still living. There was no way I could even imagine the pain of losing a sibling and having them blame you for it. Sitting back, I looked him in the eye and saw that a few tears had escaped and trailed down his cheeks. I cupped his face in my hands and wiped away his tears, pulling his head down so I could kiss him on the forehead.

"I am so sorry you have to live with this pain. I can't even begin to know the burden that you hold on your shoulders. Just know that I am here for you, and I will be by your side, however you need me," I whispered, leaning my forehead against his.

"Thank you, Lailah." Brayden sighed, holding me close again. "You have no idea how much it means that you're still here. Most people would run away from a mess like this."

"Can I assume the rest of the guys know about this?" I asked. "I just don't want to say anything to people who have no business asking."

"They know, not all of it, but they know enough. Well, except for Micah, who lived through it all with us. He came to live with us when he was twelve and his parents died," Brayden said, surprising me once again at the loss they both suffered.

"Now I know, and I'm not going anywhere. You're stuck with me, so get used to it."

I leaned back so I could see his face, and his lips landed on mine in a gentle kiss. My surprise quickly faded, and I melted against him, threading my fingers through the hair on the back of his neck. With my reciprocation, Brayden deepened the kiss, one hand on my lower back holding me tight while the other swept into my hair. I was lost in his lips and emotions, letting all else fall away from my mind.

"I thought she wasn't your girlfriend?" a voice I didn't know asked, and we jerked apart.

Feeling my cheeks burn with my blush, I peeked to see Cami smiling at me with a knowing look and Brayden's little sister gaping at us.

"Kayley, could you mind your own business just this once?" Brayden sighed as he let me slip off his lap to stand next to him.

"Whatever. Just so long as she doesn't get any ideas about my Micah," Kayley said with a sniff.

I blinked at her, totally taken by surprise at her words. Micah was definitely attractive, but once he opened his mouth, everything changed. Apparently, Kayley having grown up with Micah, allowed her to see a different side of him. I might have seen a glimpse of it here or there, too.

"I just wanted to say I'm sorry that I got kicked out of school. I know how hard it was for you to convince Mom to let me go,"

Kayley said, dropping her eyes, her shoulders slumping. "Please don't tell Mom and Dad. I can't go back to the house. I know you haven't been home in a long time, but Mom has gotten worse. It's almost like she is starting to get dementia or something."

"What do you mean?" Brayden asked as he stood and pulled his sister to sit next to him on the couch.

I made to leave, wanting to give them space, following after Cami when Brayden grabbed my hand.

"Stay, please." Nodding, I settled in the open spot next to him as he turned back to Kayley. "Is everything okay? Ms. Tabitha is still there caring for David and Hope, right?"

"Yeah, but I think she's part of the problem. She keeps making Mom drink this weird tea that's supposed to help with her memory loss. But I think it's making it worse, not better."

"Is Charlotte still doing classes at home?"

"Yeah, her school is all online, so she does it in Dad's office. Charlotte told me Mom is working on some new project, but she won't tell us anything about it. I don't understand how she can forget to turn the water off after washing her hands but still do complex physics. It doesn't make any sense."

"Mom has always been the brain of the family, you know that. If she is having dementia problems, it's always the short-term stuff that goes first. She has been a scientist for a very long time; it will take longer for that to be affected," Brayden reasoned. "Has Dad taken her to get checked out by a doctor?"

"That would mean that he'd have to take time off of work to get her to the doctor," Kayley said, frowning. "No, Ms. Tabitha took her to get some tests done, but they couldn't find anything wrong with her. They changed her meds, but that's about it. I'm telling you, Brayden, there is something strange going on. You just have to see it for yourself."

"Okay, what if I came home for Christmas? It's not that far off, and I can stay for two weeks with everyone," Brayden asked.

"Are you bringing Micah?"

"You know he always comes back with me. Who knows, I

might even talk Lailah into coming," Brayden said, grinning at me.

I smiled at the idea. "We'll see, I'll have to check with my parents about that."

"Come on, let's sit down with Beth and see if we can find a new school for you to finish out the year at."

CHAPTER 5
LAILAH

Spending the weekend with the boys was great, but it made for a rough return to reality on Monday. I looked over at the books and new assignments that Beth had given me to start working on in addition to my current workload.

Of course, this needed to happen while I was gearing up for finals. It's not like this has been hard enough already, why not add more to the list? A knock sounded on my door, pulling me out of my inner grumblings.

I opened the door to find Cami with two coffee cups, one of which she handed to me as she walked in and flopped on my couch.

"What's wrong?" I asked.

"Why would you think there's something wrong?" Cami asked, frowning at me as she gulped down more coffee.

"For starters, you're awake, dressed, and got us both our morning kick-start, and it's only seven-thirty."

Cami leaned her head on the back of the couch and groaned. "Don't remind me what time it is."

"Out with it. Trust me, after everything I learned this past weekend, I'm pretty sure I can handle whatever you have to tell me," I said, placing my free hand on my hip and glaring down at her.

"It's nothing major, Lala, really," Cami said, waving off my look. "Beth, in all her wisdom and overbearing ways, thought that I should be here in case you had a meltdown."

"What? Why would I have a meltdown now? If I was going to have one of those, I would have done it already."

"That's what I told her, but of course she didn't believe me. Like seriously, does she not think I know my best friend enough to judge how you're taking all this in? Which, by the way, you're kicking ass at," Cami said, grinning.

I smiled back and sat beside her, finally giving in to the piping-hot chai latte she had provided.

"So, if you're going to have a breakdown before your first class, then you have exactly fifteen minutes before you have to leave." Cami looked down at her imaginary watch and then back at me. "Times a tickin'."

I shoved Cami with my shoulder, laughing. "Stop. I promise, as of right now, I'm good. If that changes, I'll let you know. My plan is just to take this all one day at a time. There's nothing I can do about it, so now I just have to learn this new part of my life."

"So you're telling me that I did all this for nothing?" Cami said, dramatically collapsing against me. "What will I do with all this extra time in my day that I could have been sleeping?"

"Why not take your girlfriend out for breakfast? I'm sure it will shock the hell out of her, and you didn't get to see her this weekend because of everything that went down."

Cami popped up from the couch and grinned at me. "That's a great idea! Breakfast in bed sounds amazing!"

I rolled my eyes at her as I gathered my stuff for the day. "You're worse than Parker."

"Gasp! You wound me; how could you say something like that to me?" Cami said, faking being stabbed in the heart. "I have my Maggs, and she is enough for me. I don't need five people to satisfy my needs, unlike someone I know." Cami gave me a pointed look.

"I'm leaving now. See you later." I waved as I walked out the door, not falling for her tricks.

All it took was one kiss with Brayden, and suddenly I was in a relationship with all the boys. Brayden and I hadn't even talked to each other about that kiss yet. Not letting myself get carried away with my emotions like I had with my ex, I chose to lie to myself and believe it wasn't a big deal. I jogged my way to class, knowing I was cutting it close.

"Lailah," Brayden called out.

Had I summoned him just by thinking about him? Can I do that with my new powers? I stopped and turned to see him coming out of the coffee shop on campus.

"I'm glad I caught you before class. I just wanted to see how you were doing?" he asked once he reached me, giving me a soft smile that made my heart melt.

"I'm good, but I have to run. My class starts in five minutes. I'll text you when it's over and see if you're free," I said, returning his smile.

I did not want to have a talk about our kiss before class. If he was going to tell me it was a mistake, then I didn't want to be a basketcase during a lecture. Better to wait for me to have some time to hide in my bed and ugly cry.

"Okay, sure. I'll be around," Brayden said, his smile fading a little at my brush-off.

I stopped, hating to see the doubt in Brayden's eyes. He had opened up to me and told me about his brother, had shared his pain. Deciding to trust that even though my world changed in the past few days, he hadn't, and he wasn't going to use me like my ex did, I walked back up to him and kissed him on the cheek, letting it linger for a moment too long.

"See you after class," I murmured into his ear and stepped back to see his shocked face and his cheeks blush slightly.

Laughing to myself, I raced off to class, feeling the heat on my own cheeks. Never was I the one to initiate things with a guy, but when it came to Brayden, I had always felt comfortable. I tried to focus on class and what Professor Phillips was saying about our final project... that I didn't need to do anymore. But instead, all I could think about was the spark in Brayden's eyes as I walked away.

"Miss Mackenzie, could you please stay a moment," Professor Phillips called as we filtered out of class.

Nodding, I walked over to him, and he just stood there waiting until everyone left the room.

"I wanted to touch base with you on the changes Ms. Whittemore informed me of," he said, leaning against his desk.

"My psychology teacher?" I questioned, surprised that he would be interested in my other schoolwork.

"Ah, no, I meant Beth. I forgot that you had Nona as a teacher as well. I know Beth told you that I would be doing all the teaching on Elementi history," Professor Phillips said, handing me a sheet of paper. "Here is what I would like for you to work on for the remainder of the semester. Also, on the sheet is the code to get into the special records room where these books are. If you have any questions, please feel free to reach out or even email if it's after office hours."

I was excited to be learning more about this new secret history. I had a weak spot for history in general, but getting to study an underground ancient society was a whole new level of awesome. Even though I didn't have to do the final, the list of books to read was long.

"Thank you, Professor, I will definitely reach out," I said, grinning and waving as I left the classroom. I immediately pulled out my cell and texted Brayden.

LAILAH:

Done with class. You still free?

BRAYDEN:

Yes. Checking out at the library. Meet you at the quad?

LAILAH:

On my way!

Taking my time, I texted Cami to see if she met up with Maggs, or if she was free. When I didn't get a response by the time I reached the quad, I had my answer. Cami always answered her texts, except in rare moments when she didn't have her phone with her.

"Hey," Brayden said, drawing my attention to him as he shoved two books into his messenger bag. "How was class?"

"Nothing too exciting, just going over the project we have to complete for finals. Thankfully, in that class, I won't be working on anything but the reading list Professor Phillips gave me. Adding on these new studies is going to take over what little brain power I have," I sighed.

"Take a walk with me and give yourself a break for a few minutes," Brayden said, holding out a hand to me.

Shrugging my shoulders, I took his hand, and we headed out to the gardens by the reflecting pool. We walked in a comfortable silence, allowing me to just enjoy watching the fall leaves swirl around us and breathing in the crisp fresh air.

Tugging on my hand, Brayden pulled me down beside him on a bench near a small water fountain. "I know I already asked you this, but how are you doing—truthfully?"

"I can't tell if I'm just in shock about the whole thing, or if I truly am feeling totally fine about all this. Hudson and I had a good talk before breakfast yesterday, and that helped. I was feeling a little lost, like my whole life was a lie. He made a very convincing case that I was being overdramatic." I chuckled, remembering his scolding.

"If you ever need someone to point out the facts and keep a level head, he's the one you can always count on," Brayden nodded with a small smirk. "Beth was worried that since you had a night to think on things back at the dorm, you might run for the hills."

"Yes, I gathered that when Cami showed up at my door this morning before class. Poor thing was rudely pulled out of bed for nothing."

"Cami needs to learn how to live like a human, not a vampire."

"Wait," I said, grabbing Brayden's arm. "Are vampires real? What about werewolves and other mythical creatures?"

Brayden smiled and looked like he was holding back laughter. "I hate to crush your hopes, but as far as we know, there are no paranormal creatures besides us."

"Bummer. I totally would've thought Mr. Creed was a vampire, or something equally creepy," I mused, remembering the strange teacher I'd seen around campus.

Brayden burst out laughing. "Mr. Creed is our demonology specialist; you will be working with him next semester, I imagine. He also teaches religion classes to the normal students."

"Seriously, I didn't make such a great first impression on him."

"Oh?"

"I ran into him and knocked him and all the books and papers he was carrying to the ground. I don't think I'm his favorite person."

"Lailah, no one is his favorite person. Actually, I take that back—Micah and he seem to be amiable, bordering on friendly."

"Of course they are, that seems so fitting," I said, tossing my hands up in defeat. "Oh, did Kayley end up finding a school to finish out the year with?"

"Yes, thankfully. We're running out of schools that she hasn't been kicked out of. So here's hoping this one will last her longer than the previous school."

We both laughed and fell into a comfortable silence. I was so relaxed I didn't even realize I was resting my head on his shoulder until he shifted to wrap an arm around me.

"How would you feel about me taking you on a date? A real

one this time, off campus. No more coffee dates that others crash."

I smiled at the memory of our first attempt at a date that Parker and Hudson crashed. Turning, I looked up at him and searched his face a moment before answering.

"I would like that very much."

Pulling me closer to him, he brought his lips to mine in a soft kiss that made me curl my toes. Wanting more, I reached out and pulled his head closer to deepen the kiss. More than willing, he shifted me so I was straddling him. My arms wrapped around his neck, and I lost myself in our connection. I could feel my new powers humming under my skin, alight with the emotions I was feeling. Brayden's hands gripped my hips and pulled my body flush with his, and I could feel his body vibrating, trying to contain his power from leaking out.

Finally, I pulled away and looked down at him, his lips swollen and his eyes blazing with elemental power. I could feel my face heating with embarrassment at my wanton actions and dropped my gaze.

"None of that," Brayden said, tucking two fingers under my chin, lifting my face so I was looking him in the eyes again. "I don't want you to ever feel like you need to hide from me."

Brimming with emotions I couldn't express, I pressed my lips to his again, hoping to show him how much his words meant to me.

"Well, this would explain why neither one of you is answering your texts," Micah snapped, causing me to jump and pull back from Brayden.

I tried to move out of his lap, but his hands held me firmly in place as I watched Micah approach over my shoulder.

"What's up?" Brayden asked casually.

CHAPTER 6
MICAH

Thank God she didn't run.

When I got the text that she didn't show up for her psych class with Nona, I feared the worst. Brayden had told me he was going to check in on her to make sure she was really handling things okay. I just didn't picture that would involve her on his lap and his tongue down her throat. Jealousy roared in me at how easily he could be around her. How he was just letting his power draw her to him without a worry. I had decided long ago I wasn't going to be attached to someone, especially if I didn't know if I could be with them forever. Out of everything that we've told Lailah, our little gift from the angels, we didn't go over the most important part.

"We all got a text from Nona when Lailah didn't show up for class. Apparently, they were supposed to meet about the new elemental classes assigned to her. So when she didn't show up, Beth freaked and sent us all out to look for her," I said, letting my irritation sharpen my words.

"I didn't miss class; it was on the syllabus that today was an optional day. Beth never told me I was meeting with Professor Whittemore," Lailah said, tugging at Brayden's arms to let her go.

I could tell from his face he didn't want her to move, but he gave in when she insisted. *Look how everyone is blind to the hold she has on us. I may not have been able to avoid being around her now that we needed to train together, but I wasn't going to be her lap dog. She had Brayden and Parker for that.*

"Yeah, well, Beth is on high alert when it comes to you, so why don't you make it easier on all of us and just stick to the normal routine. I don't have time in my day to keep hunting you down when you decide to get frisky."

Lailah stomped up to me, her crystal eyes alight with anger. For reasons I couldn't explain, I loved to see the fire in her, so I pushed her buttons just so I could see it. My need to push people away by pissing them off seemed to have the opposite effect on Lailah, drawing her to me even more.

"Fuck you, Micah. It's not your life that just imploded two days ago, so shut the hell up. Brayden was kind enough to check on me and give me the chance to feel like my world isn't crumbling around me. He's supposedly your best friend, so maybe you should get your head out of your ass and see he's taking the time to look out for someone besides you. Stop getting jealous over it and leave. You found me, so just back off," Lailah snapped, her chest heaving with the exertion of her tantrum.

"You think I'm jealous because he's spending time with you?" I asked, scrunching up my face at her accusation. "I'm not a twelve-year-old girl. Brayden is allowed to do whatever the hell he wants. What I have a problem with is the fact that you can't seem to stay out of trouble, and we keep having to bail you out."

"Forgive me for not knowing that I was being targeted by demons because I'm a Blessed Warrior from the heavens. I didn't get a training manual like some people, or grow up around people who knew what was really going on in the world," she huffed as hurt flashed across her face before her anger covered it. "From now on, I will try to be less of an inconvenience for you, so that I don't disturb your life further."

My anger at her words flared. I balled my hands into fists, trying to keep from letting my power take over at my volatile emotions.

She didn't understand how I was feeling at all.

I needed to walk away, or I was going to do or say something that I was going to regret. Spinning on my heel, I stormed away, ignoring Brayden calling after me. I pulled out my cell to text everyone that she was fine and with Brayden so they could call off the search.

CHAPTER 7

LAILAH

Watching Micah storm away hurt me more than the words he'd hurled at me. I knew that Micah and I had a very tenuous friendship, if you could even call it that, but I didn't mean to lash out at him like that. For some reason, every time we were around each other, he seemed to always be picking a fight with me. Something about him brought out my need to fight and prove myself.

I started to follow after him, but Brayden grabbed my hand and pulled me into a hug. "Let him be. When he gets like this, no one can talk sense into him. Once he cools off, he'll realize he was being an asshole."

"If you say so. You know him better than anyone," I said, taking in a deep, calming breath of his fresh, earthy scent.

"You also have to keep in mind that you'll be much more emotional for a little while as you adjust to your powers. One reason it goes unnoticed for us is because it typically hits around puberty."

"So, you're telling me that for the foreseeable future, I'll be PMSing?" I asked, leaning back so I could see his face.

"Ah . . ." Brayden said, shifting uncomfortably, not wanting to look me in the eye.

I laughed, seeing how the mere mention of a woman's cycle made him cringe. "Seriously, you have sisters, and you're freaking out about this?" I teased.

"My mom dealt with all that, I just stayed out of the way. You're the first female to have an elemental power, so I really have no idea how it's going to affect you, honestly."

"Fair enough," I said, blowing out a breath and feeling calmer. "We should probably head back—wouldn't want to miss my next class or Beth might send out the search party again."

The rest of the day went smoothly. I even had another quiz in Organic Chemistry, and thanks to Hudson, I felt much more confident in my answers. I swung by the cafe and grabbed a chai before heading to the dorm to get some homework done. Sometime later, my phone chirped, letting me know I got a text. After what happened this morning, I figured it was best to leave the sound on just in case.

BETH:

Can you come to the house tonight? I have a few more things I would like to discuss with you.

LAILAH:

Sure, when did you want me to come over?

BETH:

Are you free now? I don't want to keep you too late.

LAILAH:

Okay, I'm on my way.

BETH:

Lovely. You can join us for dinner if you'd like.

My mouth watered at the thought of Sarah and Garrett's cooking. It'd only been a weekend, but I was already spoiled, and nothing from the cafeteria could live up to their cooking.

Stretching from sitting for so long, I grabbed my jacket and headed down. Not having been running for the past few days, I decided on taking the stairs so that I could get my blood pumping a little. Bursting out of the stairwell, I spotted a group of girls crowded around the front entry looking out at something. Peeking over the shoulder of one of the girls, I saw what caught their attention.

Now I understood the gawking. Jay was leaning against his Jeep, arms crossed over his chest, showing off his muscles. I'm sure he had no idea what a stir he was causing, but I took a moment to appreciate him. I can't say I'd ever been that drawn to an Asian guy before, but there was something in the mystery of Jay that did it for me. I pushed my way through the crowd and exited the door. I could feel Jay's eyes on me the moment I stepped outside, even if I couldn't see past the lenses of his aviators. Jay couldn't help the soldier vibe he gave off; it was truly in his blood. His hair was freshly buzzed, and as always, he was clean-shaven. This was the first time I'd seen him in black fatigues—he must have come right from working with his dad.

"Hey, what are you doing here?" I asked, knowing the answer but fighting back my grin.

Pushing away from the car, he opened the door for me. "Beth."

"Figures. She probably thinks I'm going to get lost on my way over to the Manor," I said, grabbing the handle to help pull myself up into his car.

"That's because you would."

I paused at his words and giggled as he jumped into the driver's seat. "Did you just make a joke at my expense?"

"It's not a joke when it's true."

This caused me to burst out laughing, and Jay just gave me a raised eyebrow. "The fact that you guys know me well enough to send an escort is killing me. My own family still forgets this flaw of mine anytime we go somewhere new. I could regale you with so many stories of family vacations where I got lost and they spent half the day trying to find me. I think the only reason I got a cell phone so young is so they could just call me to find out where I'd wandered off to."

"You sound close to your family."

"Yes, I'm very blessed to have amazing parents and some overbearing brothers. What about you? I don't really hear you talk about anyone besides your dad," I asked, turning my gaze towards him.

"My parents had an arranged marriage, and I am their only child," Jay answered succinctly.

It was moments like this that I couldn't tell if he didn't want to talk about it or if it was just his normal tendency to just give the facts. I didn't press the issue, since we'd already pulled into the large underground garage where the guys kept their vehicles.

Jay waited for me to hop out of the Jeep before he led the way into the house. We walked up a short flight of steps to the main floor of the house back near the kitchen. As we walked through, I waved at Sarah, who was busy getting dinner ready. She smiled back and gave me a wink.

"Ah, Lailah, perfect timing. Thank you for picking her up on your way back, Jalen," Beth said as she met us in the foyer.

Jay nodded once, a quick, sharp movement, and started up the stairs, leaving me with Beth.

"Let's have a seat in the library. It's more comfortable than my office, and I don't want you thinking you're in trouble."

Is Beth a mind reader? How did she know that I was concerned she was going to yell at me for what happened today? Letting her lead, I followed her into the library, and we both settled into armchairs next to each other.

"First, I wanted to apologize." She paused, seeing what I'm sure was a shocked expression on my face. "These boys are like my own children, and even though you haven't known me that long, I view you that way as well. I have been keeping an eye on you since I got your application last year."

Frowning, I opened my mouth, but she held up her hand to stop me. "Please, I promise I will answer any questions you have, but let me explain myself first."

Deciding to give her that, I settled back in my chair, ready to listen.

"The world of demons is new to you, but I've grown up knowing about them and what lengths they will go to in order to plunge this world into darkness. As you have seen, almost no one around you is safe from their tricks. We of the Elementi are smart and well-educated to see the signs around us, but we are only human and will fail from time to time." Beth paused to let that sink in. "Knowing that your family has no idea who and what you are, or of the darkness that is around us all the time, I couldn't leave you unprotected. I had a few of our best men and women watching you from afar to make sure you got here to us safe and sound.

"Now that you are here and know that you're Synergy, it only makes the world more dangerous for you. I trust the boys to take care of you, but they are also still learning and have more growing to do. Today when you didn't show up to class, I chose not to listen to Cami and Brayden when they told me you were okay. I assumed the worst. It's my job to assist them and you in this battle, but ultimately, it's the six of you who are going to change the world. I need to let you guys grow, fail, and get back up again." Beth sighed heavily like she was releasing a weight from her shoulders. "So, I hope you can forgive me for doubting you and the others."

All the irritation I had towards Beth melted away at her explanation. This was something I'd seen my mother have to go through with my brother when he went off to college. They got into arguments all the time when my brother would do things without telling her, or do things she didn't agree with. Beth and

I didn't know each other very well, and we were going to have the same bumps in the road as we figured things out between us.

"There is nothing to forgive; hearing your side of things makes sense. I appreciate you looking out for me," I said, giving her a smile.

Beth smiled back and reached out to squeeze my hand. "Thank you."

A knock sounded on the door, and Sarah popped her head in. "Dinner will be ready shortly, but I can hold off if you need more time."

"We're ready when you are, Sarah," Beth answered, getting up from her chair.

"Lailah, are you joining us for dinner?" Sarah asked.

"Absolutely. I'll never turn down the opportunity to eat anything prepared by you and your husband."

"Lovely, I'll set a plate for you. Looks like everyone will be home tonight but Micah."

I wanted so badly to ask why Micah wasn't home, but decided to leave it alone. I wasn't sure I could handle it if I found out it was because we got into a fight. Making my way to the dining room, I picked a random spot and sat down.

"Well this is a nice surprise, I didn't know you were coming for dinner," Hudson said as he entered the room and sat across from me.

"Uh-oh, Trouble in the house," Parker called as he plopped down next to me.

"Stop embarrassing her or she might never want to come have dinner with us again," Brayden said as he walked in.

I grinned as the guys sat down, loving the dynamic of them all together. "Wait, where's Jay?"

"Here," Jay said, from the seat on my right.

I jumped and swore under my breath to see him sitting there as calm as could be. His eyes shimmered with humor, pleased with catching me off guard.

"One of these days I'm going to put a bell on you," I grumbled.

"Still won't hear me. I control air," Jay pointed out.

"I'm pleased to see that I'm not the only one he does that to," Hudson said, winking at me.

Conversation paused as dinner was set on the table and we all dished up our plates. Everything looked delicious, and I was afraid to run out of space on my plate for everything. It was like eating a holiday dinner with all the options.

"You know, I don't think we've actually told Lailah what element we each have," Brayden mused.

My ears perked up at this. The guys all knew what I was, and I had a hunch as to what each of them could be, but I didn't know for sure.

"I think we should make her guess first. It's more fun that way," Parker said, wagging his brows at me with an excited grin.

"Does everything need to be a game, Parker?" Hudson said, frowning.

Parker shrugged his shoulders, then looked at me expectantly.

"Fine, I'll take a guess. Jay just told me he controls air, so that one I know. Brayden I know is earth, so there's three left. My guess is Parker fire, Hudson spirit, and Micah water," I guessed.

Parker looked down at me, mouth gaping like a fish. "Wow, you suck at this game. Why did you think I was fire? How in the hell am I anywhere close to being like Micah?"

"Unfortunately, none of those were right," Hudson said. "I am water, Parker spirit, and Micah is fire, if you couldn't already guess that."

"This is why we should have just told her. You're offended, and now she feels bad," Brayden said, giving me an apologetic smile.

"Whatever. Being spirit is way cooler than fire anyways," Parker pouted.

Racking my brain, I tried to think of something that could

get us off this subject. "What is everyone doing for Thanksgiving? It's a few weeks away, the holidays are coming fast."

The guys paused and gave me a strange look, then looked at each other as if silently trying to communicate with each other.

"We don't do Thanksgiving," Jay said, breaking the silence.

"What? Who doesn't celebrate Thanksgiving? It's all about food and being grateful. Who can't get behind that?" I questioned, utterly confused.

"What was the original purpose of Thanksgiving?" Hudson asked.

"Well, the pilgrims left England . . ." I started to explain when understanding hit me like a brick, and I dropped my head in my hands. "Oh God, I'm such an idiot. Of course you guys don't celebrate Thanksgiving, it's an American holiday."

Parker, unable to hold it in any longer, started laughing, causing me to follow and then the rest of the table, Beth included.

"Oh man, Trouble, that was amazing. I needed a good laugh."

CHAPTER 8

LAILAH

"Okay, Lailah, I need you to focus within to find your power source," Nona said as I sat across from her in the yoga studio.

I took a deep breath and closed my eyes once more, trying to do as she asked. We had been at this for nearly two weeks now, and I still couldn't find my power source. My power flowed around me readily, but I couldn't pinpoint the center of it, which is how I was supposed to control it better.

"All I see is blackness, and I can't feel a damn thing," I grumbled, gritting my teeth.

"Don't focus on your outer senses, you need to delve deeper than that. Your power is a part of you. Like your heart, it controls life running through you. All you need to do is tap into it once, and you will be able to find it again easier," Nona said. Her voice soothed me as my irritation flared.

Fidgeting on the pillow I was sitting on, I tried to push all the other emotions in my mind out. I needed to be calm and centered. Every other Elementi Blessed Warrior had managed to do this, so I could figure it out too. The ticking of the metronome in the background wasn't helping me regulate my breathing, though—instead I wanted to chuck it against the wall. Snapping my eyes open, I got to my feet and started pacing, feeling too wired to sit and do this.

"Tell me what's going on right now. The only way I can help is if I understand," Nona said.

Being half-sisters, Nona and Cami shared similar features, but Nona had this eccentric free spirit thing going for her. Nona's honey brown hair was in a big messy bun, and her large glasses were sliding down her nose, which she pushed up for the hundredth time. Even though her outward appearance didn't impress, the intelligence in her green eyes told a different story.

"I'm pissed, Nona," I ranted, spinning to face her. "Sitting here on a cushion with the new-age meditation crap is just making it all worse. All I want to do is smash that damn metronome and get the hell out of this stuffy little room."

Getting to her feet, she walked over to me and grabbed my shoulders, stopping me from pacing. "This is exactly why we do this; your emotions are going haywire, and this will help you gain some control over them. We can't start working with your power until you can manage to keep it contained."

Glaring at her, I brushed off her hold of me. "It's been contained for twenty years. It's done being put in a box or whatever it is you want me to visualize. Nothing I do right now will work."

"Are you telling me that you can feel that your power is upset with being locked away for so long?" Nona asked, her eyes full of curiosity. "I had always hypothesized that Synergy would need to be around the boys to be triggered. Now knowing it was a person all along, it gives my theory even more ground."

For some reason, hearing Nona talk about me like I was one of her case studies made me lose it. "There is more to me than being Synergy! I am a human being who is just as frustrated and angry as her power. Stop turning me into one of your experiments! If you can't help me, then just leave me the hell alone!"

Nona looked at me, shocked, her eyes wide and mouth hanging open. I could see her gearing up to address my disrespect to her as a teacher and as someone older than me, but Jay's appearance in the room drew our focus.

"I think it might be best if we take Lailah out for a little while," Hudson said from the open doorway. "Come on, we're going on patrol of the school grounds."

My first reaction was to argue, but Jay took hold of my arm and dragged me out of the room after Hudson.

"This isn't optional," Jay said, pushing me towards the elevator.

"Just what I wanted to do on my Saturday night—go hunting for demons," I muttered as I waited for the doors to open, bringing us back up to the Manor.

When Beth told me that the Elementi went underground, she wasn't kidding. Under the school and the house was the hub for the secret society. It was something out of a science fiction novel with a dash of James Bond. I had fingerprint access to the whole facility, and it was where I spent many of my nights, working with Professor Philips and Nona. All I wanted was to go back in time before Halloween when I didn't know about any of this. That night my life had changed, and I thought I could roll with the punches, but the way my emotions had become so volatile, I didn't even know who I was anymore.

"The plan tonight is to patrol the border of the school to make sure the wards are still functioning as they should," Hudson explained as we exited the elevator in the oversized pantry of the kitchen. "I think it might be best to take your Jeep tonight. The south pastures are still wet from the rain we've had the past few days."

I hopped into the back jump-seat without further protest. I would much rather spend my time with the guys than any of the other Elementi at the moment. They understood what I was going through and didn't hold my nasty temper against me . . . for now, that was. Jay took us out to a dirt road that was far from the used part of the campus.

"How can you tell if the wards are working or not?" I asked, peering out into the blackness.

"Bring your power up to the surface and let it coat your vision," Jay said, glancing at me in the rearview mirror.

"Personally, I think of it filling my eyes with my energy, but it's whatever comes naturally to you. Water is more fluid, and air is more external, so that is how Jay and I use it. For you, it could be completely different," Hudson said, seeing the question mark in my expression. "Don't think of your power as something separate; it's an important part of you. Just like your blood flows through your veins, so does your power."

This had been exactly what Nona was trying to explain to me, but for some reason, hearing it from Hudson it made more sense. Like a cat brushing itself against me, it surrounded me as I reached out to it. Unlike what they were talking about, it seemed my energy was more sentient. This time, I tried asking it to show me the wards, instead of trying to demand it to bend to my will.

Suddenly the world around me lit up, and I could see the dome the wards created around the school property. "Holy shit!"

"Pretty cool isn't it? Like we have our own private aurora borealis here at school. Before we boosted the wards, they were just a faint glimmer, but now they're holding strong," Hudson said, twisting to grin at me.

"If they're strong, then why do we still need to patrol?" I asked, my head smashed to the window, trying to see the top of the dome above us.

"Everything has a weak spot, even magic," Jay said, slowing down at a dim spot in the shimmering wall of light. "Just because demons can't get in now doesn't mean they won't scope out another way to make it happen."

Stopping the car, we all got out and walked up to the weak spot in the ward. It was low to the ground, and it looked as if on the other side someone had etched something into the ground.

"A demonic rune will cause a crack in our defenses over time," Hudson explained. "Runes like this could take days, weeks, or years to work, depending on how strong the demon who cast it was."

Reaching out, I ran my fingers over the magical wall, feeling it send tingles of energy down my arm. My power pooled in my hand as if it was just as curious as I was about this blemish in our creation. It tried to fill the spot, but it was missing something to bind the powers together.

Turning to the boys, I held out one hand. "Hold on to me, I think I can fix this spot."

Hudson's eyes grew wide, and he looked at Jay, then back to my outstretched hand. Tentatively, he placed his hand in mine, with Jay grabbing my wrist. Shifting my attention back to the shield around us, I placed my hand back on the weak spot, and this time, I could feel the difference. I was pulling from both Jay and Hudson, their gray and blue energy mingling with my golden power before it seeped into the shield. The spot glowed and became more solid than it had been, but still not as bright at the rest.

"That's incredible," Hudson cried out, letting his hand slip out of mine to examine the ward more carefully. "I wonder if the rest of the guys had been here if it would have repaired completely. It would only make sense since it took all of us to make the shield."

I glanced over at Jay, who was still holding my wrist, and grinned at Hudson's excitement. Jay gave me a ghost of a smile before his typical stoic expression returned, and he removed his hand.

"Still a lot more ground to cover," Jay said, heading back to the Jeep.

We stopped twice more to patch up spots, and we were only halfway done with the route. Being able to bleed off some of my power this way helped me feel a little more like myself. The next half would be closer to the school and would be more populated.

"I think it should be late enough that no students will be lingering around campus," Hudson said as he looked down at his watch. "The library is closed, and they lock down the buildings on Saturday nights for us to do our scouting. If they're still awake, they'll be at a party or in their dorm."

Suddenly, I was slammed into the back of Jay's seat as he slammed on the brakes. Tossing open his door, he leaped out of the car and started running. Hudson quickly followed, leaving me to scramble out of the car and catch up with them. Luckily, I was a fast runner, so I was right on their heels once I had my feet on the ground. Running in a forest with hardly any moonlight to go off of was tricky, but I wasn't going to be left behind.

I still had no idea what we were chasing after, but I could feel the wards as we passed through them. Jay was like a heat-seeking missile—he didn't hesitate for a second, and he never took his eyes off whatever it was we were chasing. Whipping out a hand, I saw him swirl his wrist and cast it out like he was holding a lasso. Wind burst out from him, trapping whatever we had been chasing against the trunk of a large tree.

Having caught the creature we were chasing, we all slowed down to a walk. Hudson's hands glowed an icy-blue color, and two pistols appeared, one in each hand. Jay's silver energy glowed, and he had a bow in his hand with a quiver of arrows on his back. I had so many questions, but I knew now wasn't the time.

"Stay behind us. Until you can manage your own powers, it's not safe to have you use them," Jay said, casting a quick glance back at me.

As much as I wanted to argue, I couldn't. I had no idea what I was doing and didn't want to hurt either one of them. Hudson and Jay slowly approached the creature, weapons at the ready. Jay dropped his wind trap, and Hudson shot a stream of water at the creature's feet and legs while Jay sent a gust of cold wind, freezing the water. The toddler-looking thing trapped before me could only be a demon. Its gray-looking skin was sunken, showing every bone in its body, eyes glowing red with tiny rows of razor-sharp teeth. Knowing it was trapped it suddenly let out a high-pitched scream that made me wince.

"Shit, we need to kill it now before it calls more to his rescue," Hudson said, lifting one of his guns.

Jay snapped out a hand, stilling Hudson's movement. "We need answers first. There's been no other sign there are more minor demons around."

"You really want to take that chance while we have Lailah with us?" Hudson argued, frowning at Jay.

Jay just stepped away from him and closer to the little demon. "What demon has been carving the runes? You're not powerful enough to do that with the holy wards so close."

The demon hissed at him, spit flying out of his mouth like a rabid animal before it answered, "The Dark Lord knows Synergy has awoken, he is coming for her."

"That's not what I asked you," Jay snapped, placing an arrowhead flat on the demon's body, causing the skin to smoke like it was burning.

The demon started his keening cries again, squirming to get away from the pain. Feeling sick to my stomach, I turned my back to what Jay was doing. I knew the demon was our enemy and that it wanted to hurt us or others—that wasn't what bothered me. It was the fact that Jay seemed so calm and practiced about the whole thing, that he had obviously done it many times before. The demon started ranting in another language, but by the tone, I didn't really need someone to translate it.

"Speak if you want us to end this, and we will banish you back to the furthest gates of Hell," Hudson cut in over the demon's tirade.

Something in the shadows caught my eye, and I moved away from the guys to get a better look. I could see movement in the forest, but it was hard to tell if it was just my mind playing tricks or not. It might just be animals in the woods, scurrying away from all the noise the demon was making. But... the glimpses of movement were getting closer, not further away. Then, as if my nightmares over the past few weeks had come to life, a demon much like the one that had killed Mallory appeared out of the darkness.

Its tall, skeletal frame moved in a strange, disjointed way. What little flesh it had was black and charred, falling from him like ash. The face, just like last time, had no eyes and a gaping mouth with rows of teeth. I froze at the sight of it, a scream clawing its way out of my throat.

"Lailah," Hudson yelled, and I could hear feet pounding in my direction.

I hadn't wandered that far from them, had I? I wanted to peer over my shoulder to see how much longer it would take them to get to me, but I couldn't force myself to move. What I thought were animals in the dark had been other small gray demons that now popped out on all sides and rushed past me to attack the boys.

"Goddamn it, Jay, I told you there would be more of them! They never work alone," Hudson growled as I heard shots going off behind me.

The soft twang of a bow and grunts from demons being killed was the only sound in the forest, aside from my wildly beating heart. The larger demon approached me slowly, letting my fear eat away at me. A clawed hand reached out to me, the tips oozing black liquid that sizzled when it reached the ground.

"Synergy . . ." it rasped. "Dark Lord . . . wants . . . must . . . bring you."

I gulped, trying to get my body to do something, anything, that would keep me from being a sitting duck. There had to be something I could do to protect myself that wouldn't endanger anyone else. My power flared to life, swirling around me, agitated at the sight of the demon. I could feel something solidifying in my hands, and I looked down to find two golden weapons. Never had I seen anything like them before. One long, sharp point came out of the middle of the handle, while two shorter points framed it. They were like tridents, only smaller and handheld.

Having no idea what to do with them, I clutched them for dear life and lifted them just in time as the demon took a swipe at me. The impact of the hit broke me from my frozen state, and I dodged to the left as it sliced at me again. Man, was I glad that I was tiny and fast while the demon was large and cumbersome. Not knowing how to really fight put me at a disadvantage, but the kickboxing I had done kept me light on my feet and out of harm's way. Deflecting another attack with my weapons, I stumbled, not having my legs under me to withstand the impact. Leaping out of the way, I fell to the forest floor and scrambled away like a crab on the beach.

"You guys, I could really use some help here," I called out, having lost track of where they ended up in my effort to stay alive.

Stabbing pain roared through my leg as two of the demon's claws punctured my skin. It felt like liquid fire had entered my bloodstream, and I screamed and screamed and screamed until my throat was raw. I could feel my body convulsing on the ground, but there was nothing I could do to stop it. Hands latched onto my arms and legs, and I kicked and fought against them. I was not going to be dragged to Hell.

"Lailah, it's us." I stopped fighting as Jay's voice penetrated my panic. "We need to get you back to the house and get this wound looked after."

The relief of knowing I was safe allowed me to let go and blackout at the pain.

CHAPTER 9

HUDSON

Scooping Lailah up, I noticed the weapons in her hands had dissipated into golden light, staying hidden until she needed them again. I had wondered if she would be given her own set of blessed weapons, and now I had my answer.

"How the fuck did we not sense a greater demon?" I growled as we made our way back to the Jeep.

Beth was going to be furious; she hadn't wanted us to take Lailah with us tonight. I'd thought it would help to get her out and see the other side of what we do as Elementi. We were warriors, but they had been treating her more like a lab experiment, keeping her in controlled environments. That wasn't real life, and we lived in a far more dangerous world than anyone was telling her.

"It had to be cloaked somehow, there's no other explanation," Jay said, opening the passenger door for me and holding Lailah until I got seated. "It's a trap."

"That's what I was thinking as well, but how would they know that we had Lailah with us?" I mused, holding her tightly against me.

Her body still shook with the poison running through her, but I had managed to flush a large portion of it with my water power. I just hoped that I had gotten to her fast enough that there wouldn't be any after-effects. In a normal person, demon poison could make them go mental and start attacking people for no reason. In some cases I had read, it changed the way they thought and would cause hallucinations.

"Beth, you need to call Mr. Creed. We got ambushed by demons, and Lailah got poisoned," Jay said into his phone. Not waiting to get yelled at, he hung up and tossed the phone on the dash.

"How mad do you think she's going to be?" I asked, brushing stray hairs out of Lailah's face.

Jay didn't answer, and a couple minutes later we pulled up to the front door. It was tossed open, and Brayden came rushing out to meet us. I knew the two of them had gotten super close lately, but the panic in his eyes told me just how much she meant to him. Ripping open my door, he pulled her from my arms and cradled her like she was the most precious thing to him.

"Get her to her room, Mr. Creed should be here any second," Beth instructed. "Do you know what kind of demon got her?"

"It was a greater demon, seeker class, just like the one that took over Mallory," Jay answered.

Taking the steps two at a time, I was on Brayden's heels. Guilt for endangering her gnawed at my stomach, seeing how pale she was. How had I not noticed she had wandered off from us? I should have just ended the lesser demon's life, ignoring what Jay wanted. This was all my fault; I let my quest for knowledge endanger Lailah. Some guardian warrior I was.

Brayden laid her out on her bed and formed one of his blessed daggers to cut open her jeans on her wounded leg. Two long gouges circled her calf. They weren't bleeding, instead looking almost like they had been charred. The black-colored poison still seeped out of it a little bit, but with holy water and a blessing, it would be fully cleansed.

Jay stood by the door, his eyes fixated on Lailah. I knew that

Jay felt protective of her—he had since the first time he found her lost on a run. Even though he would never voice it, I could see the disappointment in himself, letting her get hurt by forcing himself to keep distance between them.

"What the fuck happened to Trouble?!" Parker asked, bursting into the room with Micah and Mr. Creed right behind him.

Parker made right for the bed and sat near her head, looking over the sight before him. Anger flashed in his eyes as he reached out to touch her but then thought better of it. Micah carried the items Mr. Creed would need, setting them on the nightstand before he turned his gaze to Lailah. He was another one that was holding himself back from being close to her. Jay, I understood—he didn't ever interact with people outside of a select few. Micah, on the other hand, seemed to be irritated that she even existed, using his anger to drive a wedge between them.

"If you're going to stay in the room, I need you to step away from the bed and leave me room to work," Mr. Creed instructed, pulling off his suit coat and laying it over the back of one of the armchairs in her room.

Mr. Creed smoothed his black slicked-back hair as he undid his cufflinks and rolled up his white shirt. I often wondered why a more rotund man would wear a three-piece suit when it didn't really flatter his shape. Everything about him reminded me of a pig, especially his squashed nose and his small round eyes. He was the best at his craft and knowledge of demons, which was why he was here at the moment.

Mr. Creed turned to look at all of us standing in a semi-circle around Lailah's bed. "No matter how painful it sounds, I need you all to stay out of my way. Removing demon poison is not a pleasant process, but it must be done. I need your word you lot won't try to stop me from healing her."

The five of us all looked at each other and nodded. Looking back at Mr. Creed, I placed my hand over my heart and bowed.

"We give you our Knight's oath that we will not hinder you from your work."

Mr. Creed huffed and turned back to his ingredients. Holy water, myrrh, and olive leaves were placed in a bowl, where he ground them up into a paste. Sliding a thick towel under her leg, he took the concoction and drew a series of runes around the wound, each one glowing with her golden power once it was complete. I could see her stirring, her head turning from side to side, her fists and jaw clenching. No sound came out of her, even if it was obvious to us how much pain she was in. Once he was done with the runes, he grabbed the vial of holy water and poured it over her wounds.

This time she sat up, screaming and fighting against Mr. Creed's hold on her. "Micah, come hold her down for me; her body is fighting me more than I anticipated."

Micah walked over and slipped in behind her, holding her tightly to his chest. He turned to look out the patio doors, not wanting to see the pain written all over Lailah's face. Everything in me wanted to toss Mr. Creed out of the room and pummel him for hurting her, but my oath kept me rooted. It was the only thing keeping any of us from acting on our need to protect Lailah.

"Not much longer now; it would have been much worse if Hudson hadn't cleaned out as much as he could," Mr. Creed muttered as he poured more holy water on her skin.

The blackened, charred look of the skin was gone, along with the black matter oozing out of the wound. Now it looked pink and raw, as if it was a burn that was weeks old instead of minutes. Eventually, Lailah's cries turned into whimpers, tears streaming down her face as she clung to Micah's arm.

"Brayden, I need you to place the blade of your blessed weapon on the wound so I can see if it's been purified enough," Mr. Creed instructed, stepping away from her.

Dagger in hand, Brayden slowly lowered the weapon to her skin. When nothing happened, we all took a deep breath. Apparently, I wasn't the only one who had been holding it in; all of us were a nervous wreck.

"Very good, my work here is done. She will need lots of sleep and food when she wakes up. Don't be surprised if she doesn't remember any of this—the effects of demon blood present as memory loss most of the time," Mr. Creed said, wiping off his hands.

We continued to stay silent as he packed up all of his things and left the room. Unable to hold myself back any longer, I approached Lailah. She lay there, passed out, sweat beaded on her brow, her curly hair damp from the pain. Micah looked torn between not wanting to move and knowing that he couldn't stay there. Brayden saved him as he cradled her, freeing Micah to leave. I pulled back the covers so we could get her tucked in.

"We should have Beth or Cami clean her up," Parker whispered and gestured to the state of her clothes covered in mud and other substances.

"Good call. I'll go get one of them," I said, needing to leave the room while I still could.

CHAPTER 10

LAILAH

Feeling the sunlight on my face, I rolled over and groaned as my body protested the movement. I felt like a piñata after it had been attacked by children and split open. Slowly, I opened my eyes and then quickly shut them. The sunlight that filled my room was too much for my eyes to handle, sending sharp pricks of pain into my brain.

"What happened?" I rasped, slowly rubbing my face with my hands, trying to clear the cobwebs.

My bedroom door opened, and someone came in, but I wasn't willing to open my eyes again.

"Can you close the blinds? The light is giving me a migraine," I asked.

"No problem, Lala. Maggs, can you do that for me since my hands are full?" Cami asked, sounding close to my bed.

I could sense the room darkening through my eyelids, and when I felt like it was safe enough, I cracked them open. The now dusky-lit room was much easier on my eyes. Opening them all the way, I looked up to find Cami setting a tray of food down on my nightstand. My stomach growled at the smell of whatever she'd brought me.

"Come on, let's get you sitting up so we can feed the beast," Cami said, sitting on the bed and supporting me as I moved.

Maggs stepped up on my other side, pulling pillows behind me so I could lean on them. Gingerly, I settled into the new position and took a few deep breaths, cataloging my body. Nothing seemed to hurt too much, more of a stiffness that ached with each muscle movement. Although my right leg ached deeper than the rest, almost bone-deep.

"What the hell happened to me?" I asked, looking at each of them in turn.

Maggs sat next to Cami, nudging her as if to make her explain. Maggs and Cami had been dating for a few months now, and they had fallen hard for each other. Maggs was much more grounded and even-tempered, where Cami was the wild child. I loved Maggs's sense of style—true rockabilly pinup, complete with flaming-red hair and soft-green eyes outlined in cat-eye makeup. She also led one of the off-campus sororities that hosted the best parties.

Cami took a deep breath and grabbed her hand before looking at me. This worried me. Cami never had a problem telling me things like it is—why would she be worried about this?

"Yesterday, Hudson and Jay took you with them out on patrol off the campus grounds," Cami started.

Memories came back in flashes; we had fixed some weak spots in the wards. Then we'd discovered something and chased it into the woods. I remembered fighting, me screaming, the sound of Hudson's guns going off. Then the haunting face of the demon hung before my eyes, causing me to lock up once again.

"Lala, it's okay; you're safe," Cami said, reaching out to take my hand, grounding me. "You got hurt, and the boys brought you back to the house. The demon that attacked you has venom that runs through its claws, and it scratched you. The wound needed to be cleansed."

I flashed a worried look between Cami and Maggs, gripping her hand to stop her from saying more.

Cami smiled, then nodded her head towards Maggs. "She's one of us, Lala. Maggs works in our IT department, tracking those demon cockwaffles."

Just when I didn't think I could be surprised anymore, Cami had done it again. If I hadn't felt like roadkill, I'm sure I would've been more upset, but right at that moment I just wanted to eat and go back to sleep.

"I'm sorry I didn't say anything sooner, but I felt like you had enough on your plate to add me to the list. Cami didn't want to keep this from you, but I asked her to wait until things settled down; seems like that isn't going to happen any time soon, though," Maggs said with a smile and a wink. "You sure seem to find adventure wherever you can."

"Trust me, I would love to have things quiet down," I said, giving her a grin before I turned back to Cami. "What did you mean by having it cleansed?"

"Mr. Creed came and did a ritual to cleanse your wound and purify it so it would heal. He did warn that there might be some side effects to the poison, though. You will be extremely tired and hungry for the next day or so, and the wound might ache more than usual. Less likely repercussions are that it could make you hallucinate or hear voices. But Mr. Creed seemed to think that being a Blessed Warrior might keep that from happening, especially with you being Synergy," Cami explained.

I leaned my head back, looking up at the ceiling, absorbing what she told me. Not only were my emotions on a hair-trigger; I could also start hearing or seeing things. I could only imagine the delightful things that demon venom might induce to torture me.

"Let's not dwell on that right now," Maggs interjected. "We should let you eat so you can go back to sleep. I can already see you're struggling to stay awake."

She carefully set the tray on my lap, and I looked over what they brought me. A large bowl of creamy soup and a hunk of fresh bread that made my mouth water.

"I asked Sarah to make you potato soup since that is what your mom used to make as a comfort food," Cami said, grinning at me.

"Thanks, I could use some warm comfort food right now," I said, digging in and slurping down the first spoonful. It tasted just as amazing as it smelled, but I would expect nothing less from Sarah.

Cami and Maggs chatted about things going on around the school as I ate, keeping my mind off darker thoughts. By the time the meal was gone, I could barely keep my eyes open. A warm, full belly did little to help me stay conscious enough to lay back down. Cami and Maggs got me situated and tucked in before leaving the room.

"One of the boys will be around up here. If you need anything, just give a shout, okay?" Cami said as I gave into my desire to sleep.

I slept the day away and didn't wake until the next morning, and my stomach demanded that we get up. This time as I moved, my muscles didn't hurt so bad—it was more of a mild ache, like the second day after a tough workout. When I opened my eyes, I had to blink a few times to remind myself where I was. My head pounded, reminding me what it felt like to be hung over. I stretched in bed, letting my body work out some kinks. I took a moment to look around the room that apparently was mine to use whenever I needed it.

The bed was huge—three people could fit comfortably. The cream sheets were soft against my skin, which made it even harder to get out of the bed. The whole room was in tones of golds and soft cream, making it very soft and feminine. To the left of the bed was a set of French doors that led to a small balcony with two chairs and a small table. In front of the bed was a large fireplace with a simple sandstone mantel that had decorative knickknacks on it. Two comfortable armchairs faced the fireplace with a coffee table in front, a perfect place to curl up and read on a winter night.

Did all the bedrooms have fireplaces? I guess that would make sense for how old it is, even though they remodeled it for updates.

To the right of the bed were two doors, one I knew led to the bathroom, and the other I could only assume was the closet since I didn't see a dresser anywhere. After a hot shower and some more stretching, I was back in action. My right leg still had phantom pain, but every time I felt around the area, nothing seemed to be amiss. There were two pink scars that hadn't been there before, but I was thankful that was all it was. If something worse had happened and I'd lost the ability to run, I didn't know what I would do.

It took me longer than usual to get dressed because I was sorting through my T-shirts until I found the right one to fit my mood. The challenge was deciding what my mood was, but I knew when I saw the right one, it would click. And it did. Pulling the shirt off the hanger, I grinned. This would do nicely. Slipping it on, I looked in the mirror, making sure of my choice: *Do you see my personal bubble? Pop it. See what happens.*

Stepping into my slippers, I headed out of my room and down to the kitchen. I had no idea what time it was, but I knew I could find something to satisfy my demanding tummy. Passing through the common area, I saw Hudson asleep on the couch. He must have been there in case I needed him. Not wanting to wake him, I tiptoed my way past and jogged down the steps. The rest of the house was quiet, so that meant it was either super early or everyone was out. Reaching the kitchen, I glanced at the large clock on the wall, and it halted me in my tracks. It was three in the afternoon. Either I had only slept half a day, or I had slept a full day and a half.

My stomach grumbled louder, as if it knew that we were

close to finding food. Opening the fridge, I skimmed over what leftovers there were and what would catch my stomach's attention. Spotting the tell-tale signs of spaghetti and meatballs, I grabbed the container and tossed the whole thing into the microwave. Minutes later, I was elbow deep in some pasta, not even bothering to sit at the small table, opting to lean against the counter. That's how Brayden found me when he walked in from the garage.

"Feeling better?" he asked with a humorous glint in his eyes.

Grunting, I continued stuffing my face while he set his bag down and walked over to me. Gently, he grabbed my arm and escorted me over to the three-person table and pushed me into a chair.

"Let's eat like the civilized human I know you are," Brayden teased, but I just rolled my eyes. "Let me get you some water to wash all that down. We can only save your life once a year, and you have already used up two years' worth."

Will he just shut up? Why is he harping on me about this? He's acting worse than my mother, and she's half a world away, I mused, the thoughts popping into my head as I glared at his back, watching him move about the kitchen.

I couldn't place why what he was saying was rubbing me the wrong way, but many odd things were happening with my emotions these days. Having powers was cool, but the side effects were rough to get a handle on. I envied the days when I only had to deal with a week or so of these crazy feelings.

Brayden sat across from me, placing the glass of water down next to my dish of pasta. "How are you feeling? Mr. Creed warned us that you would be hungrier than normal."

"I just slept for almost forty-eight hours, you would be hungry too," I grumbled, gulping down some water, not happy he was pointing out I was eating a lot.

"Fair point. Cami told me that you don't have much memory about what happened after you were attacked. Do you have any questions? It was only me and the other guys in the room when

Mr. Creed did the cleansing." Brayden leaned his elbows on the table as he waited for my answer.

I paused, thinking as I chewed my food. "The only real question I have is why do the demons want me? I thought once my power came that I wasn't going to have to worry about them coming after me."

Brayden sat back, his frown growing deeper by the second as he thought about my question. "You're right, it doesn't make sense. Unless we were wrong on the reasoning for why they wanted you from the beginning."

This thought seemed to make Brayden more agitated than I was. He chewed on his thumbnail, something I had never seen him do before, as he became lost deep in thought. I just continued to eat my food, watching until he decided to share. Finally, he looked over at me, holding my gaze, determination radiating off of him.

"You can't go back to the dorms. It's not safe. It would be best if you lived here where we can keep an eye on you. Better yet, one of us should be with you at all times. If something like this happens again who knows what could happen," Brayden said, finality in his voice.

I slowly set down my fork, not wanting to stab him with it as my anger burst forth. "Who the hell are you to decide that for me? Beth and I already came to an agreement on me living in the dorms until after winter break. Now that I know the demons are after me, I will be more aware of what's going on."

Brayden scoffed. "You don't even know what to look for to avoid demons. Two high-level seeker demons have gotten the drop on you, and both times, it almost killed you. Hudson told me what kind of blessed weapons you have. Sai are meant for police to disarm and block attackers. It's not an offensive weapon, it's defensive, and they are no help to you unless you know what to do with them."

Shooting up from my seat, I slammed my hands down on the

table. "Then I'll fucking learn! Why are you being such a dick about all this?"

Brayden's eyes softened and I could see how scared he was for me. "That's not something you can learn overnight. We've been training since we were thirteen, and you can't handle your own powers. You're not in control, and that's okay. It's barely been a few weeks; just let us help keep you safe. That's what a team does. We work together to protect the weaker members until they are stronger."

His words were like a slap in the face. He didn't think I could do this. Brayden thought I was the weak link in the group, that I wouldn't be able to catch up to them in time to be useful.

"You know what, Brayden? Fuck you and the high horse you rode in on. I don't need this shit from anyone, least of all you, so back the fuck off. I'm doing the best I can. Sorry that's not good enough for you!" I snapped, fists clenched and chest heaving as I tried to control my anger.

Unable to look at him any longer, I stormed out of the room and headed back upstairs to my bedroom. Hudson was now awake, watching me silently as I slammed the door to my room. I could hear Brayden running after me, so I twisted the lock in place and started to gather my things.

"Lailah, open the door. We need to talk about this," Brayden said through the locked door.

Ignoring him, I continued what I was doing and grabbed the last few things and stuffed them in my backpack. I slipped into my shoes and pulled on my puffy winter coat. When I yanked the door open, Brayden was still waiting on the other side, arms crossed, mouth tight with disapproval.

He opened his mouth, but I held up a hand. "If you don't want me to practice my kickboxing on you, I wouldn't say anything right now. You have already expressed your opinion loud and clear."

Shoving past Brayden, I jogged down the steps to the front door without looking back.

"Lailah," Hudson said as my hand grabbed the door handle.

Turning to look over my shoulder, I saw him at the foot of the stairs, giving me my space. "What?"

"Let me take you home, the temperature dropped a lot last night," he offered.

I sighed, knowing I should take his offer, but in my head, it just seemed to show that they couldn't even trust me to walk back to the dorms without their help. "Thank you, but I think the walk will do me good."

Hudson gave me a soft smile and a nod as I left.

CHAPTER 11
LAILAH

The next week, after my fight with Brayden, I didn't spend much time with the guys. I was locked away in a library study room or in my dorm. If demons were going to come for me, then I wasn't going to make it easy for them. Weak link or not, I was going to prove I didn't need the guys hovering around me to keep me safe. Not having been this alone since I got to Ryevick, I was becoming homesick for the first time. Sure, my parents and I talked on the phone or emailed when things were crazy, but it wasn't the same as being with them. As Thanksgiving loomed closer, my outlook grew darker. This was one of our favorite holidays as a family. We always cooked crazy amounts of food and would host whoever didn't have a place to go at the diner.

I knew that everyone was noticing my spiral, but I just didn't know what to do about it. I had never suffered from a gloom like this before. Even after my ex and I broke up, and I found out everything about my best friends, I just pulled away. This was different. I was getting angry over silly little things and habits that people couldn't fix. I felt like in some ways I was going crazy. Beth was certain that this was a direct correlation with coming into my powers and couldn't tell me if it would get better or worse. On the edge of my emotions, I could feel something else eating away at me, but I just couldn't seem to put my finger on it.

"Knock, knock," Cami said, cracking the door to the study room I was using. "Is it safe to come in?"

"To be determined, but I think you're fairly safe," I responded, setting down my pen.

"Well, that's an improvement over throwing your textbook at the door like the other day," Cami teased, pulling a chair out from the table and sitting on it.

"Oh God, I did do that, didn't I?" I groaned, dropping my head on my arms. "Why do you keep coming back? I would just cut my losses and run."

"Nope, not gonna happen, Lala. You're not in control of yourself like you normally would be. How can I blame you for that?"

"Have I told you lately how amazing you are?" I asked, looking up at her with a smile.

Cami tapped her chin. "Wow, I can't even remember the last time you told me that, so clearly it's not often enough. I'm going to need you to step up your quota on that, like stat, little missy."

I chuckled at Cami's antics, making me smile bigger. I couldn't remember the last time I'd done that. "This is killing me. I know I'm acting like a crazy person, but I can't seem to do anything about it. Even Nona tried to help me with some tricks to calm my anger before I lashed out at someone, but it clearly didn't help."

"Yeah, I heard about that. Brayden is fine, by the way. He doesn't hold it against you, and neither do the other guys."

"Oh, even Micah? I haven't seen him around since we argued that day Beth thought I ran away," I grumbled, scribbling on one of my notebooks.

Cami leaned forward and started flipping through one of my textbooks. "So, about that. We might have all told him to stay away if he couldn't keep to the Thumper rule."

"The Thumper rule? What the hell is that?"

"You watched *Bambi* as a kid, right? Remember the bunny that he's friends with, Thumper? There's that part where he makes fun of the skunk for being called Flower."

"Okay..."

Cami waved me off as she was getting to her point. "His mother told him that if he couldn't say anything nice, don't say anything at all."

I froze as understanding washed through me like a tidal wave, bringing me to my feet. "You're telling me that he's keeping away from me because he has nothing nice to say to me?! That asshole treats me like shit all the time, and the one time I stand up for myself like he always bitches at me I should, he runs away?!"

"And... I owe Parker fifty bucks," Cami muttered.

"Get out!" I snapped.

Cami looked at me blindsided. "What?"

"I am following the Thumper rule. Now, get out," I said, pointing at the door.

The look of hurt in Cami's eyes made me pause and gave me a moment of clarity in my blind rage, but I knew if she stayed, I was going to say something I would regret even more. Cami didn't say anything, and the click of the door was the only thing that told me I was alone in the room once again.

I picked up my phone to see what time it was back home. Being nine hours apart made trying to connect challenging. Seeing as it was still early in the morning, I decided to chance it and see if my mom would answer.

"Hey, Ladybug, everything okay?"

I couldn't hold in the sob when I heard her voice. "Mom."

"Luke, I need to step into the office, Lailah called," I heard my mom tell Dad before the noises of the diner faded away, letting me know she was alone. "Oh, Ladybug, what's wrong?"

I tried to answer her, but all the sadness and chaos I'd been feeling fell away at the sound of my mother's words. I just let myself sob while she tried to soothe me and tell me everything would be alright.

After I'd cried myself out and felt like I could catch a breath, my mom tried again. "Tell me everything, young lady."

It broke my heart to know that I couldn't. I hadn't figured out a way yet to tell my family that I wasn't the same daughter that they sent off to school. I was blessed by an angel to hold the element of Synergy, and I was training to fight demons that were hidden everywhere in our world.

"I'm sorry, Mom, I didn't mean to lose it over the phone like that."

"Don't you dare. I'm your mother, and that is exactly what I'm here for. To be honest, I'm surprised it hasn't happened sooner. Did you know it took your brother only three weeks to call me crying on the phone because things were harder than he thought they would be? Look at you, making it almost four months."

I smiled, wiping my tear-stained face off with the sleeve of my sweatshirt that just happened to be from the brother in question. "I had no idea."

"Of course not, because I never told anyone but your father. Some things are meant to stay between parents and their children, just like this will."

"I don't know what it is, but all of a sudden, it hit me that Thanksgiving is in two days, and they don't even celebrate it here. Then it made me think of you guys and what it would be like at the diner, and here I am studying my brains out for finals."

"I'm sure this makes me sound like an ignorant American, but it didn't even cross my mind that they wouldn't celebrate Thanksgiving," my mom said, making me feel better that I wasn't the only one who forgot that. "Would your friends be up to celebrating it with you? What if you did your own version? You said that the group of boys all live in a house, right?"

I could just picture it now, Sarah and Garett letting me take over their kitchen for the day to make our traditional Thanksgiving foods. All the while, the guys trying to help and ending up just arguing amongst themselves, causing more work.

"That's actually a great idea. I've been a bit of a bear to them all lately."

"Ladybug, you know when you get too stressed out it's never good for you. It's one of the reasons you started running," my mother reminded me.

Rolling my eyes, I sighed. "Yeah, Mom, I know. The weather here turned this last week, and they're saying it might snow soon. I haven't found a place to go running inside, so I've been slacking off on that."

"Seems like you might need to find a new outlet then. Do they have any fitness classes you can take? Anything to help drain all that stress out of you? I know you also used to cook, but seeing as you don't have a kitchen, that puts a kibosh on that, doesn't it?"

"You're right, I need to be better about finding a way to manage my stress. My friends have been trying to help, but I keep scaring them off. I don't know how I'm going to make it up to them."

"Sounds like a home-cooked meal might help smooth things over," Mom said with a chuckle. "If they're still coming round with you acting like an ogre, I don't think you have too much to worry about. Not all friends are like Clara. To me, it sounds like these friends are not the type to give up on you so easily."

"Mom, have you always been this smart?"

"Where do you think Kyle got his smarts from? It certainly wasn't your father, Lord love him."

We both laughed at that and took a few minutes to catch up on other things that had been happening before she had to head back to work.

"Ladybug, I love you more than fresh brownies with ice cream."

My eyes welled with tears at her words. My parents and I

had always played this game when we were young, trying to show how much we loved each other by saying they were more important than our favorite thing.

"I love you more than sugar cookies, Mom."

"Oh, that's a tough one to beat, Ladybug. Fine, you win. I'll talk to you later."

After hanging up with my mom, I felt better and more in control of myself. It's amazing how one conversation with the right person can change everything.

LAILAH:

Hey Beth, what are the chances that I might be able to take over the kitchen this Thursday?

BETH:

Depends on why you need it.

LAILAH:

Two reasons: an I'm-sorry dinner that I want to surprise everyone with and it would be Thanksgiving in the states.

BETH:

Let me talk to Sarah and Garett and see how they feel about a night off. I'll get back with an answer soon.

LAILAH:

Thank you Beth. I appreciate it.

Setting aside my homework for the evening, I pulled out a clean sheet of paper and started writing down all the things I would like to make for the holiday if I got the kitchen. This was going to be as traditional as I could make it. Getting lost in my planning, I didn't realize the time, and when the door opened and someone flicked off the light, I yelped.

"Oh gosh, I'm sorry! I didn't know that anyone was still in this room," a gentleman in a janitor uniform said, turning the light back on for me. "I do have to ask you to pack your things up though, because the library is closing for the night."

"Sure, no problem. Let me clean my stuff up and I'll be on my way. Didn't realize it had gotten so late," I said in apology, shoving books and papers into my backpack while waiting for my computer to shut down.

"It happens more than you think, especially this time of the year. Everyone's cramming," he said, holding the door for me as I exited and he locked up the room. "Have a good night, and try to get some sleep."

I thanked him and headed out into the chilly night air. *I must look awful if he told me I needed to get some sleep.* Sniffing myself, I grimaced. *A shower might be a good call too. Man, when was the last time I ate?* I mused as my stomach grumbled at me. Learning from Jay, I kept a few power bars in my backpack for cases just like this. *How major of a fog have I been in this last week?*

The campus was quiet this late in the evening and the moon was high, giving me enough light to see by as I crossed the campus to my dorm building. Swiping my keycard, I yanked open the front door and made my way up to my room. When I got there, I noticed that my door was slightly ajar, which was strange. I always made sure to keep my door closed, since I didn't have the best relationship with the girls in the building. Apparently, being close with all the most wanted men on campus made you a target and not friend material.

I pulled out my cell, Cami's number ready to dial if I needed it, and nudged open my door the rest of the way. Flicking on the light, I took in the room before me, and it made my blood boil. All the calm that I had gained from talking to my mom was blown away like a leaf on the wind, replaced with an erupting volcano. The first thing that hit me was the smell of rotten milk and garbage. My clothes had all been pulled out from the drawers and left in piles on the floor, where it looked like someone had emptied the trash from the cafeteria on top of them. My bed was also covered in garbage, but the final straw was to see Elle, my stuffed elephant, covered in eggshells and a brown banana peel.

Written on the wall above my bed in black spray paint was:

TRASH LIKE YOU ISN'T WELCOME HERE.

Ever since the Halloween party, the mean girls believed that I was the reason that Mallory had left school, and hideous rumors spread. None of them came close to the truth, but they did not paint me in a good light. I'd been surprised that the other girls of her squad had left me alone, but it seems that they were aiming for a bigger hit than normal.

My rage flowed out of me, causing me to shake, my hand crushing whatever was in my grasp. All else was forgotten, except for the fact that my sacred safe place of a room had been violated. I could take their snotty comments and petty tricks, but this was going too far, and I wasn't going to stand for it.

"Lala, what the hell is going on?" someone said behind me, but I didn't respond.

I heard more words, but I blocked it all out and plotted my revenge on those who'd dared to act against me. I was Synergy, I was the most powerful weapon on Earth, and they dared to defile my sacred space?

You're more powerful than them. It's time they learned what it means to fuck with a Blessed Warrior.

Cami appeared in front of me, pulling me from the voice inside my head, fear making her eyes wide as she took me in. I could see her lips moving, but I couldn't hear what was being said. My gaze flicked from her back to the words written on the wall, the words that were now seared into my brain. Turning on my heel, I started to make my way out of my room to exact my revenge, but something stopped me.

Blocking my exit was Brayden—but this wasn't a Brayden I'd ever seen before. Green power flickered across his skin, his eyes alight with determination, and it brought me to a halt. My power lashed out at him, but he brushed off my attack with the flick of his hand, not backing down. My golden power surrounded him, checking for any weaknesses, but found none, which only irritated me further.

Crush him. He is weaker and does not deserve to stand in our way.

Just as I was about to lash out another attack, his voice rang through my head, clear as a bell and capturing all my attention. "Lailah, I am not your enemy."

CHAPTER 12

BRAYDEN

As I walked out of the bathroom, getting ready to turn in for the night, I noticed my phone light up and vibrate across my nightstand. Grabbing it, I noticed it was Cami, so I swiped to answer immediately, knowing this wasn't a good sign.

"Cami, what's wrong?"

"You need to get to Lailah's dorm right now! She's going to lose it, and I'm afraid she'll take everyone with her."

"Slow down, tell me what happened."

"Brayden, you're not understanding me, there is no time to explain. You need to get here *now*." With that, the call was cut off, and I flew into action.

I thought about telling one of the others since Lailah still wasn't really talking to me, but I didn't think I had time for that. I threw on sweatpants over my boxers and grabbed a zip-up hoodie, then raced out the door. Needing to get there as fast as I could, I grabbed the keys for Parker's motorcycle off the wall. He would forgive me later when he knew what it was for.

Racing out of the garage, I decided to avoid the main road. I took the walking paths instead. Since it was so late, I was betting on there not being anyone out. As I got closer to the dorm, I could feel the waves of power pulsing from somewhere inside. It didn't take a genius to know it was coming from Lailah. Watching her adjust the last few weeks made me appreciate my parents and Beth so much more. Lailah was volatile and could turn on a dime between her sweet, normal self and the wicked witch of the west. It killed me not knowing how to help her through this, but I knew it would pass in time—we just needed to survive through it first.

All the guys decided to give her some space after she and I had our blow up. Micah avoided her at all costs, knowing that the two of them were like oil and water, setting each other off. This alone showed me, in his own way, how much he really cared about Lailah—because if he didn't, he would do as he pleased, damning the consequences.

I pulled up right on the sidewalk in front of the steps leading to the dorm entryway. Thankfully, I thought to grab the master keycard that we had so I could get into the dorm without having to get someone to let me in. Not wanting to wait for the elevator, I flew up the steps, taking them two or three at a time, my heart beating wildly in my chest, knowing I was running out of time. Lailah's power vibrated around me, zapping across my skin, causing my own to flare up around me and seek out the owner of the golden energy.

Finally, I made it to her floor. *Why did she have to be on the tenth floor, of all places, at a time like this!?* Running down the hall, her doorway was the only thing in my sight. It was open, and I could see a glowing, golden light that flickered like flames. Anger and violence pulsed through the energy, giving me a heads up on what I would be dealing with. Skidding to a halt in her doorway, I growled at the state of her room and the words plastered across her wall. This was the perfect thing to set anyone off, but little did they know they'd pissed off the one person who could take out the whole school with one flick of a finger.

"Lala, listen to me. I know you're upset, but this is not the way to handle this. You need to take a deep breath, or your power is going to take down the building with you in it," I heard Cami beg, but Lailah didn't seem to hear her.

Turning on her heel, she stalked to the door, where I was standing. I don't think she noticed me at first, but her power did. If I had any doubt about who Lailah was, or how powerful she would be, the sight of her right now would erase that. Golden power swirled around her, pulling at her loose curls as if there were a breeze. When her eyes finally met mine, they were no longer their normal crystal blue color, instead, they were like liquid gold.

Finally seeing me, she paused, taking me in, and yet not really *seeing* me. As if testing me, her power lashed out, but I had been ready, knowing she wasn't in full control. Creating a shield with my power, I wrapped it around myself and braced for impact. I didn't let it show how hard her attack had hit, not wanting to seem weak. When her blow glanced off my shield, she frowned, her energy wrapping itself around me, seeking out any place it could wiggle its way in.

"Enough," I said, putting power into my words. "I am not your enemy, Lailah."

Her body jolted as if I had struck her, and I could see in her eyes that she was fighting to gain control.

"Lailah, I need you to take my hand. Let me help you. I know you're angry, and you have every right to be, but this isn't the way you want to handle things. Not really," I said, trying to keep my voice calm but still backing it up with my power.

I could see Cami behind Lailah, tears streaming down her face as she fought against the staggering amount of power echoing in the room. Humans, for the most part, could never feel or see our powers—unless an overwhelming amount was being used. At this moment, in this tiny room with two of us letting our power loose, it was. I couldn't imagine how suffocating it must be for Cami, but she wasn't going to abandon her friend.

I turned my attention back to Lailah, who I could see struggling for control. Her breathing was erratic and panicked. I took a step closer to her, seeing that she couldn't do it herself. I grasped her hands in mine, and she sucked in air like she could finally take a deep breath. Her power no longer fighting mine, I was able to twine our powers together and attempt to bleed off some of hers by sending it into the earth. The floor beneath our feet started to shake as the earth below tried to disperse her immense power. This was not going to work. I was going to need to do something else.

"Lailah, take a deep breath for me, and when you let that breath out, send your power away from you. Let it go like sand through your hands. You're safe, and I won't let anything happen to you. I promise you no one will harm you," I said, reassuring her by rubbing my thumbs over the backs of her hands.

She took a deep, shuddering breath, closing her eyes, and the energy in the room lessoned, making it more manageable. When she opened her eyes, they were that mesmerizing clear blue once again. Seeing the fear, sadness, and lingering anger flicker through her gaze made me pull her close to me.

"How could they do this to me, Brayden? They broke into my room, my safe place," Lailah sobbed, wrapping her arms and power around me.

This time, I noticed the golden wisps didn't try to fight with mine; instead, the gold and green energies mingled. I could see them intertwining, swirling, and cocooning us in their protective hold. My heart broke for the woman in my arms. So much had happened to her in the past few weeks, and then to add on this petty girl shit seemed so pointless. It also made me mad. I was one of her guardians, and we had failed at our job to keep her safe. If random twenty-somethings could break into her room this easily, then who or what else could?

My protectiveness reared up, and I held Lailah even tighter as I said, "I promise you that I'll do everything in my power to make sure this never happens again."

With those words, the world around us began to glow in a pure, white light. Then I realized it wasn't something around us —it was Lailah. Her whole body burst into a blinding beacon that forced me to let her go and drop to my knees before her.

Then she spoke.

CHAPTER 13

LAILAH

Hearing Brayden's promise flipped a switch in me, and my body exploded with a new power. It was almost like someone else was using my body as a conduit for them to funnel their essence through. Something about it made me think about the night my power first manifested and I talked to the angel.

I opened my eyes and found Brayden on his knees, his body glowing with green energy, and two daggers in his hands that glowed with the same pure white light. As I looked at him, it was almost like I could see a shadow of another figure flickering deep within him, dressed like a medieval knight. Power drew me in, and I was a puppet in my own body.

"Brayden, Knight blessed with Earth's power, Warrior for the angels. I find you true of heart and mind, upholding the agreement given to your ancestors. Do you accept the eternal bond to protect the people of this world, and vow to cherish the vessel that holds the gift of Synergy, who has been placed in your protection?" I heard myself ask Brayden with a voice that echoed with another.

"I, Brayden Dolton, Blessed Elementi Warrior gifted with Earth's power, vow to cherish and protect this world, my fellow brothers, and the one bound to us as Synergy; or my life be forfeit," Brayden whispered, bowing his head and presenting his daggers to me.

My hand reached out and touched him on the shoulder. "Rise, faithful one, and seal your Oath."

Brayden rose to his feet, his daggers disappearing from his hands as he cupped my face between his hands. "I have been waiting for you all my life, even if I didn't know it."

He placed a gentle kiss on my lips, causing our power to burst forth and whip around us like a tornado as a tether snapped into place between us. I could feel a new flickering power resting in my soul, a piece of Brayden to be with me forever.

Brayden stiffened at the exchange, but only for a second. Next thing I knew, his hand wrapped around the back of my head, holding me steady for him to kiss me more thoroughly. I melted into his kiss, letting him lead as I felt his power flow into me and mine into him. I couldn't tell where I ended and he started. He moved his other hand to my lower back, pulling my body to mold against his. He pushed us till I bumped against the wall, but that only gave him the leverage to deepen his kiss.

His hand moved to my side, sneaking under my shirt so that his powerful grip held my waist. I could feel the calluses on his palms, rough against my skin, sending tingles up my spine. I let out a small moan, reveling in the feeling of our power and his touch. My approval caused his power to surge through us and around us till I felt the foundation of the building begin to rattle.

Brayden broke the kiss first, shoving himself an arm's length away, panting, "If you keep making sounds like that, I'm going to bring this building down around us."

Snapping out of my haze of power, I felt my cheeks flush, embarrassed at what I'd just done. Brayden's face glowed, seeming more than happy with how things had turned out.

"If I'd known that bonding with Synergy would be that amazing, I would've led the search party to find you sooner,"

Brayden said, dropping his hands from me and running them through his hair, causing it to stand on end.

"Is it safe to look now?" Cami's voice called out from behind me.

"Oh my God, Cami, when did you get here?" I asked, shocked, my cheeks flaming deeper with embarrassment.

"Um, Lala, I've been here the whole time. You called me but didn't say anything. So I came up to find out what was going on and discovered you on a rampage to kill every bitch in this building," Cami explained, wiping at her red eyes.

"I didn't hurt you, did I? You've been crying!" I gasped, rushing over to her and squashing her head on my boobs.

"Not that I don't appreciate your hug, but don't you think this is a little inappropriate to do in front of your boyfriend, who you were just climbing like a tree?"

"Ugh, you're totally fine," I let Cami go and gave her a little shove.

"I'm just looking out for you, girl. I don't want lover boy over there to get the wrong idea about us," Cami said, grinning from ear to ear. But her smile faded as she looked around the room again. "I think it might be best if you stay with the boys tonight. It's going to take a few loads of laundry and a shit-ton of air freshener to get this place back to normal."

I didn't want to look over my room again, afraid that it would trigger me into another rage. Strong hands grasped my shoulders and pulled me back against a solid chest. "Come on. I'm sure I can lend you something to sleep in, and we'll figure this out tomorrow. You need to rest. It may not have hit you yet, but using that much power is going to wipe you out," Brayden said.

Letting out a heavy sigh, I settled back against Brayden. "You're right, this will still be here tomorrow, no reason to stress about it now."

Brayden took my hand and led me out of my room, leaving Cami, who was on the phone. My money was on Beth—she would be the first person any of them called when there was a problem.

"How did you know what was going on?" I asked Brayden once we were in the elevator.

Brayden slipped his hand around my waist and pulled me close. Our powers hummed against each other in a comforting way, reassuring me of the Bond we now shared.

"Cami called me demanding that I come ASAP because you were about to bring down a building. Thankfully, I was home and could get here fast enough."

"What else would you be doing on a Tuesday night?" I asked, curious but also a bit jealous.

Typically, I was never one to be jealous of others, but now that Brayden was bonded to me, the green-eyed monster reared its ugly head. I shook myself out of it. I had no right to be jealous for any reason. We may have made out a few times, but we'd never talked about what that meant. He didn't answer me right away as we stepped out into the lobby and made our way down the steps to Parker's waiting bike.

"Lailah," Brayden said, grabbing my hand and turning me to look at him. "Do you remember what I asked you at the Halloween party when you apologized for being a cock block to us all after your declaration to Mallory?"

I frowned, trying to think back to that night, but many of the little details had been lost to me. "There are a lot of things that I can't remember from that night. I'm sorry, you're going to have to remind me."

"I said 'What if we were all yours and not interested in anyone else?'"

I was struck dumb at his words. *He can't really mean that. There is no way that all five of these guys liked me that way, let alone them all being okay dating the same girl. How could this ever work? Wouldn't they get jealous and fight even more than they already do? There is no way that Micah would ever see me as anything more than a friend he merely tolerates. He can't even talk to me right now because he has nothing nice to say. Parker is practically my other best friend, but he wouldn't be interested in more . . . would he? Jay and I are close, but I don't ever get a romantic vibe off of him, same with Hudson.*

"Stop. I can see your mind running a million miles per hour," Brayden said, taking my head in his hands as if that would slow down my panic. "What I'm trying to say is that I, personally, am all in, whatever that looks like for us and this new bond. As for the others, I'm not saying this is going to happen overnight, but I just wanted you to know it could be a possibility. There are a few aspects to being Synergy that we haven't quite gone over yet." Before I could ask what that was, he held up a hand. "We are not going over that tonight. A lot has already happened, no need to add more to the plate that's already full. Come on, let's get you back to the house."

I hopped on the bike behind Brayden and snuggled into him like I had always wanted to do to Parker. It was definitely helping to settle my nerves. There was something about Brayden that always seemed to ground me, keeping me calm. I felt safe with all the guys—even Micah—but with Brayden, there just seemed to be a different level of trust. He was my rock and always stood by me. Even after I lashed out at him last week, he'd raced over here to help me, not even knowing what really was going on.

As Brayden drove, I settled into myself and found that the new connection between the two of us glowed in the darkness. It was a pale green light, and when I touched it, it filled my body with warmth and love. Could I feel Brayden's emotions? Or was I just projecting my own? Then the warmth turned hotter, setting my skin on fire, flooding my body with need that I'd never felt before. It reminded me of that dream I had of Brayden and Parker on the dance floor and how they made my body burn for them.

Brayden shivered as I felt the heat seep into his skin. He parked the bike close to the door and yanked me off, cradling me to his body. He ushered us inside and then kicked the door shut with his foot, tossing the keys on the counter of the kitchen before racing to the stairs. Surprised at his need to rush, I looked up and saw his eyes filled with desire. The urge to drag his face down so I could kiss him was overwhelming. Taking the stairs two at a time, we made it to the second floor in record time. Darkness filled the rec room, but that didn't slow Brayden down at all. Kicking open his door, he stalked over to the bed and placed me gently on it before he turned and shut the door, locking it with a soft click.

Laying on his bed made my body hum with excitement at what I could only hope was going to happen next. Flicking on a lamp near the bed filled the room with a soft glow, setting the mood further. I didn't get a chance to take in his room, having only been in it once before, because Brayden unzipped his hoodie and tossed it aside. He didn't have anything on underneath, and I was blessed with the sight of his bare chest.

Brayden was fit in all the right places; he took care of himself, but he didn't look like a guy who lived in the gym. The soft light set off his golden skin, making it almost impossible to look away. He climbed up on the bed, straddling me but keeping his body above mine, not letting anything touch. His hazel eyes were alight with need, his breath coming more quickly, as if he were having to hold himself back.

"Lailah, I need you to tell me right now if you're not ready for this," Brayden said, his voice strained.

I gave myself a moment and made my decision. I reached up and pulled him to me so I could kiss his perfect lips. He moaned and let his body cover mine, careful not to smother me beneath his larger body. I could already tell this was going to be a far different experience than the one I'd had with the one other guy I'd gotten this far with. Never had I felt the need to have my naked skin on someone else's. With Brayden's help, I peeled off my shirt, and he helped to unhook my bra. Not needing my encouragement, Brayden slipped me out of my jeans, pulling my underwear with them. I was now bare under him, and the heat of his gaze on my skin set me alight.

"Lailah, you are stunning; you could make angels weep." I could feel my face begin to heat with embarrassment at his words and inexperience of what to do now.

As if sensing my insecurity, Brayden pulled me to him, nipping and licking at my lips until I let him in, and he swept me away from my worries. I let myself surrender to him and the intensity of our feelings. He gently kissed down my neck, using his teeth ever so slightly, causing me to gasp under his attention. When he made it down to my breasts, he held one in his hand and looked me in the eye as he let his tongue flick over my nipple. Sensations I'd never felt before rocketed through my body, directly to my core. I shifted under him, needing friction between my legs.

"Liked that, did we?" Brayden asked before doing the same thing again, only this time after the lick, he latched his mouth on my nipple and swirled his tongue around the pert bud.

"Brayden, please," I begged, but I didn't really know what I was asking for or how to get it. I just knew my body was pleading for him.

"Patience, my Angel. All in good time," Brayden said, moving to my other breast, causing me to arch under his attack.

My blood was singing and breath quickening with the onslaught of sensations as he used his other hand to flick the nipple that wasn't in his mouth. I let out a sharp cry as he bit down gently on one nipple and pinched the other. I bucked, trying to get away from the stimulation, but his body kept me in place.

"I am going to erase any other memory you have of someone touching your body. I want you to think of me and only me right now," Brayden said, whispering along my lips before he kissed me hard and pulled away to slide further down my body.

"That won't be hard to do," I panted, knowing that the space between my legs would be soaked with my desire for him and him alone.

Brayden chuckled along my stomach, driving me crazy with his nips and fingers trailing closer to where I needed them to be. Lost in all the sensations, I didn't notice that he had finally gotten to where my need was pulsating until he languidly let his tongue make his presence known. Gasping, my hand latched onto his hair, and I felt myself bolt into a sitting position with him between my legs. He gently put a hand on my stomach and pushed me back so he could have better access between my legs.

I'd never had anyone go down on me before, it had me wondering what other amazing things I'd been missing out on. Brayden's tongue swirled around my clit, causing me to dig my nails into the sheets so I could have something to hold onto. He shifted, and I felt one of his fingers rubbing between my lips, wetting his finger before he began to nudge at my opening. For all intents and purposes, I was a virgin, and I wasn't sure if Brayden knew this or not, but I couldn't find the mental capacity to tell him.

Slowly, his finger entered me, and I groaned. "Oh God, *yes.*"

Brayden just let his finger sit there, and he wiggled it along the top of my channel. I writhed under his assault as he timed his tongue to what he was doing with his finger. Just when I wasn't sure I could take anymore, he added another finger, sending me off the cliff. I cried out his name as he drew out every ounce of pleasure, making my body shake. Slowly, he slid his fingers out, and he crawled back up my body, scattering kisses as he went.

"That was amazing," I panted.

I rose up and kissed him, letting our lips linger and taking my time. I could taste the saltiness that I could only guess was myself. I thought I would be grossed out, but hey—it came from me originally.

"You are the sexiest woman I've ever seen," Brayden said, a pleased smile on his lips.

"Is that what sex is supposed to feel like?" I asked, still trying to catch my breath.

Brayden chuckled. "No, Angel, that was just foreplay. Think you're up for the real deal?"

"Oh, hell yeah," I said, causing his grin to grow wider.

He slid off the bed and slid down his sweats and boxers, revealing what he was packing. My eyes widened when I took in all his glory. I didn't have much to go on, only having seen one other dick up close, but I had no doubt he was above average. While not overly thick, he was long and had a slight curve. Crawling off the bed, I had the strongest urge to touch. Kneeling in front of him, I let my finger trail over the length of it. Brayden hissed at my touch, and his dick bobbed with my attention. Getting braver, I grasped him firmly, feeling how silky and soft the skin was.

"Angel, if you don't let go, I am going to come here and now. That is not how I want this to go down tonight," Brayden said, pulling my attention back up to him.

Yanking me to my feet, he then bent down, cupping my ass and pulling me up so I could wrap my legs around him as he walked back to the bed. He flopped me down so that my ass just made it onto the bed. Standing over me he looked down at me with such tenderness and desire, my heart was bursting. Bending my knees, he pushed them back till they were hugging my chest, leaving me utterly exposed to him.

"I could feel how tight you are, so I'm going to take this slow at first. I don't want to hurt you. This is all about your pleasure too, not just mine."

I could have wept at his words, and I relaxed even more knowing he wasn't going to just use me like my ex had. The sensation of Brayden's dick gliding across the outside of my vagina caused me to throw my head back and let out a moan of pleasure. Doing that a few more times, Brayden gently pushed the head of his dick in with a steady pressure, letting my slick-ness guide him in bit by bit. I knew he was doing this for my benefit, but at this pace it was pure torture. My hips bucked, trying to get him to move faster, but he ignored my encouragement and kept at his lazy pace.

Finally, he was in as far as my body could take, his cock butting up against the end of the road. He started to pull back just as slowly until I latched onto his wrist.

"If you don't start fucking me like you mean it right this moment, I am going to lose my mind," I snapped.

"Seems my little angel has a dark side," Brayden commented.

Then, giving me a wicked grin, he pulled all the way out, causing me to cry out in ecstasy as he plunged all the way back in seconds later. He did that two more times before I started to break out in a sweat as my body burned with pleasure. Seating himself deep in me, he got to work plundering my vagina, letting out his own grunts of pleasure to accompany my own. Reaching out for him, needing to feel him closer to me, he leaned forward and captured my lips as he kept up his steady rhythm. Pausing, he picked me up and moved us both farther onto the bed. My legs, now free, wrapped around his waist and clutched him to me, our bodies molded together.

As I could feel my release building, my power started to as well. I could feel Brayden's response as well, both whirling around us in a torrent of heat, passion, and power. My breath quickened, as I knew I was teetering on the brink of an orgasm, and I noticed that Brayden's rhythm was becoming more erratic. Unable to hold back any longer, I let myself fall over the edge, letting it take me, and Brayden was soon to follow behind.

Power burst out, causing us to float a few inches above the bed, knocking things off the wall. Our pleasure bounced off one another, dragging it out further, both of us lost in our ecstasy. The bond that I felt earlier glowed brighter, and stronger emotions flowed between us as if a curtain had been pulled back. I could feel Brayden's joy at having me in his arms, the contentment of having shared this experience together, and a fierce protectiveness over me. As I basked in his emotions and the warmth of his body around mine, I let myself drift.

Until the sound of a door getting kicked in broke us out of our stupor.

"Brayden, wake up! We're under attack!" Micah's voice bellowed as he flicked on the main light to the room. "What the *fuck*?"

CHAPTER 14

LAILAH

Brayden scooped me up and wrapped me in his comforter before he turned to deal with his best friend. Micah stood there with only a pair of boxers on and red headphones around his neck. The shocked look on his face as he absorbed what he had walked in on was priceless. I had to cover my mouth so I wouldn't burst out laughing and make his embarrassment worse.

Brayden, unbothered by the fact that he was still naked, stood up from the bed and grabbed his boxers off the floor. "What the hell are you talking about? No one is under attack."

"I felt a power surge, and the walls rattled, I assumed . . ." Micah said, trying to justify his actions.

"Bro, you're going to need to tell me what kind of headphones those are if you couldn't hear the noises that were going on in there," Parker said, leaning against the door jamb.

Oh my God. They heard me. I am going to die of embarrassment. Please ground, open up under me so I can just hide in a hole deep underground.

"Shut the fuck up, Parker, you're freaking Lailah out," Brayden snapped.

Parker looked as shocked as I was. Brayden never yelled at the others; he was always the last to get riled up about things. *Wait, could he hear what I was thinking? Can he understand what I am thinking right now?*

Turning, Brayden walked over to me and wrapped me in his arms, and I buried my face into his neck. "Angel, you're going to need to calm down. Your panic is driving me crazy with the need to fix it."

"You can feel her emotions?" Hudson asked.

Is everyone awake? Did I keep everyone awake with how loud I was during sex? Kill. Me. Now.

Brayden pulled back from me to look at the others, but I continued to hide behind his chest. "Yes, now you all need to leave before her embarrassment chokes me to death. God, guys, show some class and go back to bed."

"You try going back to bed with the worst case of blue balls ever," Parker muttered.

The sound of shuffling feet and the slam of the door brought a flood of relief.

"They're gone now," Brayden confirmed.

I sat back and searched his face, feeling his irritation at the guys for barging into the room like that. Then his gaze met mine, and I was flooded with warmth at being so cherished.

"I'm sorry our first night together ended so poorly."

"How could we know that sex would send off a power burst like that? I guess we can't fault him for jumping into action," I said with a smile.

"True, but still. He and the others didn't need to linger after they knew everything was okay. Parker most certainly didn't need to bring up how vocal you were."

I slapped a hand across Brayden's mouth, glaring at him. "Which is something we are *not* going to bring up ever again."

He just nodded his head under my hand before licking it. "Gross."

"That's not what you said when I was licking you before . . ."

Blushing furiously, I grabbed a pillow and slammed it into his face. "That's it, I'm going to sleep in the other room by myself."

"Yeah, that's not gonna happen, Angel," Brayden said, grabbing me around the waist as I tried to hop off the bed. "You're going to stay with me all night. Who knows, if you're lucky I might remind you how much you liked my tongue on you."

My body tingled at the thought of him giving me a repeat. "Fine, but I need to use the bathroom first. I can't sleep feeling so . . . sticky."

"Shit," Brayden muttered, letting his head fall to my shoulder. "I feel like such a dick."

"What? Why?" I asked, feeling panicked. *Did he regret what we just did?*

Brayden looked up at me, his lips thinned and worry creasing his eyes. "I didn't put on a condom or even ask you if you were on birth control. God, that makes me such an ass. I'm also clean by the way I haven't been with anyone in a long time."

"I appreciate that you're worried, but we're all good. I got the implant before coming to school. My mother insisted that you never know what could happen, and it was better to be safe than sorry," I said, feeling my cheeks flush.

He let out a heavy sigh and kissed my lips before lifting me to my feet and giving me a swat on the butt. "Go get cleaned up. We both need to get some sleep."

I could feel Brayden's heated gaze as he watched me walk to the bathroom, making me feel sexier than I ever had before in my life. The connection between us warmed me, letting me know just how much he liked the view. Quickly washing up, I made my way back to him, and he lifted the covers for me, inviting me in. As I slid in, he wrapped his arms around me and hummed his contentment. Wrapped up in strong arms and nestled against his warm chest, it was easy to drift off to sleep.

The late-night and early morning classes weren't the combination I wanted after the amazing night I'd had with Brayden, but there wasn't much I could do. Letting him sleep in, I borrowed a t-shirt and made my way into the room they had set up for me. I found a pile of clean clothes on the bed with a note from Beth letting me know that the rest would be cleaned and brought over along with all my other things. As much as I wanted to argue with her, I was going to need to put a pin in that for later. I quickly showered and sorted through the clothes on my bed. I smiled when I found the right shirt to pair with my jeans. This one said *Physically, I'm here. Mentally, I'm in a galaxy far far away.* It would fit my mood perfectly. Swiping the hoodie I took from Brayden's room, I tossed my backpack over my shoulder and ran down the stairs to the kitchen.

"Oh good morning, Lailah. I heard about what happened last night. How awful is that," Sarah said, reaching out to hug me.

"Thanks, Sarah. It definitely was not a college experience I was expecting to deal with. I have to run to class, so I'll just grab something at the cafe between classes. I just didn't want you expecting me," I said, when she released me from her hug.

Sarah frowned at me and walked over to where breakfast was waiting to be set out on the table. "There will be none of that, dear; you will just have to take this with you," she said, handing me a breakfast burrito.

"Wow, this is amazing, thank you!" I smiled, wrapping it up in a napkin and waving as I left the kitchen.

Stepping out the front door, I was shocked to see Jay's Jeep idling in the driveway. The passenger window rolled down, revealing Jay in the driver's seat. "Get in, you're gonna be late."

His words made me jump into action, and as soon as I hopped up into the car, we were off. I noticed that Jay was just in sweats and a T-shirt, which he never wore. He was always ready for anything to happen at any moment. Seeing him so relaxed was nice to see for once.

"Did you just wake up?" I asked, unable to keep my curiosity to myself.

"Yes."

Okay, strange. He's always up at five am to go running or work out. Seems like everyone had a late night last night. Then a thought struck me.

"By any chance, did you wake up just so you could take me to class?"

"Yes."

Seriously, I thought we'd gotten past the one-word-answer part of our friendship.

Wait, does he no longer want to be my friend because I slept with Brayden? No, that doesn't make sense, you don't wake up to take someone you're not friends with to class. Chill, you're making more out of this than you need to. Just be grateful; you probably would have gotten lost as it is on your own.

"Thank you," I said, and shoved my burrito in my mouth so I couldn't question him more.

Jay's gray eyes flicked to me then back to the road as we pulled into the parking lot. "You're welcome. Call me if you need a ride back."

Jumping out of the Jeep, I flashed Jay a grateful smile.

"Sure thing," I said, and shut the door, heading to class.

My first class went without a hitch, even if I struggled to keep my mind on the material that Professor Phillips was having me go over. I kept drifting back to all that had happened last night. Days like yesterday made me wish I could go back in time to when I was a simple girl from Wisconsin. Then my mind would bring up images of my night with Brayden, and I went back to thinking that I wouldn't change a thing about my life now.

Class finished early enough for me to get a chai latte before my psych class, which I was eternally grateful for. I didn't notice the looks everyone was giving me as I waited for my drink until someone knocked into me.

"Trash," someone said under a lame, fake cough as the girl continued on her way.

I looked around the coffee shop to see everyone glancing at me. Some snickered behind their hands, as I was totally clueless to what was happening. I grabbed my drink as soon as they called my name and headed for the door. That's when I noticed the bulletin board near the entrance. Pictures of my dorm room were plastered all over it, showing everyone what they had done. I was rooted to the spot at the horror of realizing the whole school knew and that they'd left these pictures here for me to see.

As my anger increased, power rose within me, burning through my veins. I wasn't even trying to hold it back. I was over being a doormat for these bitches. I was *sick* of it! As I pulled my power around me, I noticed it was stronger than it had been yesterday, and I could see my golden energy tinged with flickers of green. The Bond seemed to have added to my strength, and it made me grin.

With this much power, I could bring everyone to their knees. They would know how inferior they are and beg for mercy that I wasn't going to give them. I didn't start this fight, but I was going to end it in a way they would remember.

I let my power pool into the ground below my feet, and with a swipe of my hand, I collapsed the wall the bulletin board was hung on and watched it crash down into the fissure that I created on the floor. Another swipe of my hand, and I shut it so no one would ever see those photos again. Then, pulling on my own golden energy, I let it swirl around me and let out a piercing scream that shattered all the windows and glass in the place. This caused everyone else to scream and dive for cover. There was no way out since I was blocking the front door, and in their panic, they didn't think about a back door. Watching their tear-stained faces plead with me to let them live pleased me, but mercy wasn't what I was going to give them—

"*Lailah!*" Parker shouted.

Suddenly, the whole scene around me shattered, and Parker was standing in front of me shaking my shoulders. Panic was all I could see in his normally playful brown eyes.

CHAPTER 15

PARKER

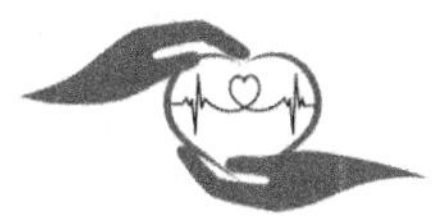

"**G**od damn it, woman, don't scare me like that," I said, resting my forehead against hers.

"What just happened?" Lailah hesitantly asked, her voice shaky with confusion as she looked around the quad.

"Come on, let's talk somewhere quieter," I said, putting my arm around her shoulders and guiding her away from the gawking onlookers. Once we were away from the majority of people, I pulled her to sit on a short wall bordering trees on the walkway. I didn't press for answers right away; I just held her to my side, giving her a moment while I texted Brayden.

PARKER:

Hey, something weird happened with Lailah and I think you need to be here to keep her grounded.

BRAYDEN:

What happened?!

PARKER:

I'm not too sure but she seems to be really freaked out by it. We're sitting by the tech lab building.

BRAYDEN:

Ditching class now, give me a minute and I'll be right there.

I took a deep, calming breath, knowing that freaking out wasn't going to help. Normally, I wasn't at the school this early since my classes were later in the day, but I had to do some work in the Tech lab before class started. Thank God I did, because if Lailah had been left alone much longer, she would have exploded like a nuke and taken out the whole damn school.

"Care to share what's going on in that brain of yours?" I asked.

My words made her jump a little, like she'd forgotten I was there. She looked up at me and reached out to touch my cheek with a slight frown on her face. I had to admit, it was kind of cute to see that wrinkle between her brows. I quirked a questioning brow at her as she continued to poke at me.

"I know I'm attractive, but let's try not to get too distracted," I teased, grinning at her.

"Sorry, I just needed to make sure this was really happening. Apparently, I'm imagining things," she murmured, not even blushing at my joke like normal.

I frowned. "What does that mean?"

"What was I doing when you found me?" Lailah asked, shifting so she could look at me better.

"Nothing. Standing in the middle of the quad as if in a trance, but you were giving off crazy power vibes. I was afraid you were going to explode if you didn't get that shit under control. I tried to talk to you, but you didn't hear me or even seem to see me. It wasn't until I shouted at you that it seemed to bring you back," I explained, my panic still fresh in my mind.

"Have you been into the cafe today?" she blurted out.

"Random segue, but no, I haven't."

"This is going to make me sound crazy, but can you go and

see if there are pictures of my dorm on the bulletin board by the door?"

"Seriously?" When she gave me a stern look, I raised both hands in surrender. "Okay, I'll be right back."

Leaving her to sit there alone was not what I wanted to do right now. She strangely seemed more fragile than I'd ever seen her. Whatever happened had really messed with her. As I made my way back to the cafe, I ran into Brayden.

"Where is she? Is everything okay?" Brayden demanded, searching for her when he didn't see her with me.

I grabbed his arm before he could brush past me. "Wait a sec, would you? Look, she asked me to go to the cafe and see if someone posted pictures of the shit they did to her room. I have no idea what it has to do with anything, but just come look with me. Having two people confirm will be better than just one."

Brayden looked at me, then back over in the direction of where Lailah was sitting. "I can feel the panic and chaos in her mind; she's terrified of something."

I envied Brayden having that connection to her. I knew I shouldn't be jealous of him. Yes, he was the first to bond with her, but eventually, we would all have to share. I clenched my jaw at the realization that the first time I thought about being truly committed to someone, she wouldn't just be mine.

"Let's go so we can hurry back. I don't want to leave her alone that long," I said, walking to the cafe and yanking the door open.

Brayden followed me in, and we both stopped in front of the bulletin board. Without saying anything, I pulled my phone out and took a picture of it, then headed back out.

"What the hell do you think is going on?" Brayden whispered to me as we approached Lailah.

"Fuck if I know, but we need to get this figured out sooner rather than later," I answered, back just as quietly.

Lailah was sitting right where I left her with her head in her hands, and I panicked at the thought she might be crying. *What the hell was this woman doing to me that I cared so much?*

"There are no pictures, Trouble," I said. She lifted her head and looked at me. "Here, I even took a picture so you could see for yourself that it's got all the same stupid crap on it that it always does."

Handing her my phone, I knew what she would see—the bulletin board covered in flyers and other news that students had left over the past few months. Brayden sat on one side of her, wrapping an arm around her waist as she handed back my phone. I sat down on her other side, taking her hand in mine, needing to feel connected to her.

"What's going on, Angel?" Brayden pressed, rubbing the small of her back comfortingly.

"Everything was normal. I went to class, and then when it was over, I left and headed to the cafe to get a chai. I didn't get a chance this morning since I overslept," Lailah started, and Brayden shifted uncomfortably.

We all knew why she had been up late last night. Serves him right to squirm; he had no idea what kind of hell it was to lay there and listen to her sexy moans coming from his room. Never in my life had I been so hard and turned on for a woman that wasn't even in the same room as me.

"When I got there, everyone was staring and whispering about me and calling me trash," Lailah continued, pulling me back to the present. "I grabbed my drink and bolted, but that's when I saw the pictures of what they did to my dorm plastered all over the board. I was so mad, and I let my power overwhelm me. With the addition of your power, Brayden, I was even stronger, and I was able to manipulate your powers, and I might have ripped open the ground under the wall holding the board and sent it crashing to Hell."

"You *what?*" Brayden sat back, shocked.

"Oh, that's not the end of it. I used my powers to shatter every window and piece of glass in the building and send everyone screaming for cover. I reveled in their fear of me and was going to kill them all before Parker pulled me out of whatever the hell I was in," Lailah murmured, tears starting to trail down her cheeks.

My hands clenched into fists at seeing her this distraught over a situation that didn't even really happen.

"Brayden, am I broken? Did I do something wrong to turn out like this? Are we sure that a demon hasn't possessed me and I just don't know it?" Lailah babbled, clutching at Brayden's arm.

"Angel, no, you're not broken," Brayden said, pulling her onto his lap so he could hold her close. "Parker, I'm going to take her back to the house. Could you give Hudson a heads up? I'll make sure Beth knows what's going on too."

Fucker, why do you get to be her knight in shining armor? What about me? I'm the one who was here first.

"Yeah, no problem, text me if you need anything. I only have one class left for the day," I said between gritted teeth.

"Come on, let's get you home," Brayden said, standing and setting her on her feet.

Watching them walk away hand in hand was its own brand of torture, but I knew I just needed to make it through one more class, and then I could get back to her.

Fuck, this class was pointless. Why did I need to study old books that no one reads anymore? I was going for a technology degree. What did Jane Eyre have to do with anything? I looked down at my watch, counting down the minutes until the class was over. Suffering through this was hard enough already, but to know that something was going on with Lailah made it even worse.

That girl deserved her nickname—she found trouble without even trying. Remembering, for the millionth time, the image of her dead eyes looking at me in the quad made me shiver. That crystal blue gaze was always filled with some emotion or another. It's what made it so fun to tease her. Cami used to be fun, but after fifteen years of me messing with her, she had finally learned to fight back. Cami was like my little sister, even though I was only three months older than her, but she was still half my size. She used to follow all of us around during the summer when we were forced to spend time together before training started.

Thanks to that little punk, I was able to run into Lailah—literally. I was worried that she was going to turn Lailah against being my friend, but it seemed to do the opposite and made me want to be friends with her regardless of whatever trash Cami was going to spout. Now knowing that *Trouble* was Synergy changed everything. I wanted to give into the need, the pull to be close to her. Everyone always saw me as the big flirt, the guy who always needed to be around people and a party. They weren't wrong, but Lailah was different.

"Okay, class, I expect to get your second draft in by the end of the week. This final paper counts for twenty percent of your grade, and some of you cannot afford to do poorly," Mrs. Blackwell announced.

I burst out of my chair and headed for the door.

"Mr. Jones, a word."

I groaned internally, knowing what she was going to talk to me about. I turned to see Mrs. Blackwell signaling for me to join her at her desk.

"Mr. Jones, it appears that I still don't have your first draft that you promised you would have for me by Monday. I can't keep giving you extra time. It's not fair to the other students. I don't care who your father is, you are on equal footing here in this classroom, do you understand me?"

"Yes, ma'am, I understand."

"If you get me a draft by this weekend, I will count it as your first and second draft, so it better be good. You need this paper to pass my class, as I'm sure you know."

Taking a deep breath, knowing she was right, I had no other

option but to do as she asked. "Thank you, I'll get it to you by this weekend."

"See that you do. You may go," Mrs. Blackwell said, waving me off as if she knew I was a lost cause.

Not wanting her to change her mind, I raced out of the room and shouldered my backpack. I jogged to the parking lot towards my truck—the weather was getting to the point it was too cold to ride my bike. I grinned at the vintage Chevy twelve-valve five-nine Cummins. It was lifted, dually, in cherry red, with stacks. My bike was amazing, and I loved the freedom it gave me, but this baby right here was my pride and joy. I got her out of a junkyard and had her all fixed up. Technology and an engine had a lot of the same feel to them. It was bits and pieces that fit together in just the right way to make the whole thing work. I didn't share much about my mechanical side, as it was something I did just for me.

Climbing up into the cab, I let her idle for a bit. You never wanted to rush a lady; it was better to get her all hot and ready before you demanded things from her. I checked my cell just to make sure Brayden hadn't texted me needing anything. There wasn't a message from him, but one from Hudson.

HUDSON:

Any update?

I grinned. Looks like Hudson might have actually found a girl that would get his head out of his research for once.

PARKER:

Heading back to the house now.

In all the years I'd known him, I'd never seen him date. I knew his parents split, and he took it really hard, but even knowing him as a kid, he was just so closed off from emotions. Hudson and I got along well, and in our group, that was saying something. If Lailah hadn't shown up in our lives, there would be no family meals at the dining room table. I couldn't even remember the last time we all played video games together before she arrived.

The bigger miracle was that Micah was spending time around people other than Brayden and actually trying not to piss everyone off the moment he opened his mouth. Thinking about him made me grip my steering wheel tighter as I made my way back home. That bastard thought he was so much better than everyone else. He never wanted to be a Blessed Warrior. He resented the fact that he was forced into it and took it out on all of us. Oh, I'd tried to play nice and win him over, but a man can only be told off so many times before he says fuck it. If he wasn't going to be part of the team, then fine. Who needs the prick anyways.

Just as I pulled into the garage, my phone buzzed, and I looked down to see Beth had sent out a group text.

BETH:

Meeting in the library in one hour. This is not negotiable.

Fuck. That isn't good.

Dropping out of the truck, I made my way up the stairs into the kitchen, hanging up my keys in the lock box by the door. I noticed Sarah wasn't in the kitchen, and neither was Garrett. Smiling to myself, I looked around, making sure the coast was clear before making my way to the fridge. Sarah always had stuff in here for us to eat whenever we got hungry, but she also hid whatever delicious dessert or baked item she made on the top shelf. I treated my body like a temple, but my sweet tooth was my downfall. I could eat a whole cake by myself if I was allowed to. Anything sweet was good, but if it was chocolate then it was game on!

"Parker Allen Jones, I know you're not thinking about taking that chocolate cream pie I made for dessert tonight," Sarah's stern voice called out from behind me.

Cringing, I turned and looked at her over my shoulder,

knowing I was not going to talk my way out of this. But one had to try, right?

"How could you think that of me?" I said, letting my face show my horror at the idea. "I was merely peckish and looking for a snack to tide me over till dinner. I was going to waste away from hunger. Would you deny me nourishment?"

I knew I wasn't fooling her, but the twinkle in her eyes and the smile she was fighting meant she wasn't *really* mad at me. I have gone many nights without dessert because I crossed her. Contrary to popular belief, I was a fast learner if the punishment was harsh enough.

"If that's the case, you're in luck. I just finished making the power bites that Jay likes, on the second shelf in there," Sarah offered, knowing I hated those overly healthy oatmeal balls of death.

"Yeah, great, that should hit the spot," I said, trying to keep the grimace off my face.

Sarah started laughing at me, shaking her head, knowing that she had won this round. "Goodness, the look on your face— you would think I was offering you balls of dirt!"

"It would be about the same," I muttered.

A timer went off on the oven, and Sarah grabbed her oven mitts and pulled out a tray of muffins. "It seems you're fortunate enough to be around when these came out. I was going to take these to the staff working in the offices below, but I suppose you can have one."

I hugged Sarah and gave her a quick peck on the cheek. "I knew you loved me."

"Now take your muffin and scat, I don't want to hear you were lurking in my kitchen while I was gone," Sarah said, smacking me with one of the oven mitts. I took the delicious-smelling chocolate muffin to go.

"What if I need milk?"

"Go, now, or I'm taking the muffin back," Sarah frowned. I had reached my limit with her.

I saluted her and hastily made my way upstairs before she could follow through on her threat. As I entered the common room that all our rooms centered around, I found Brayden sitting in his favorite chair sleeping, his head resting on his hand. I wanted so badly to play a prank on him, to get even for the fact he was bonded to her and I wasn't.

"Leave him alone," Jay said, surprising me, causing me to jump and almost drop my treasured muffin.

"What the fuck, man!" I hissed, trying not to yell at him.

Jay just gave me a side glance filled with warning and headed to his room, leaving the door open a crack. He never left his door open; he was all about security and the sanctity of his space. I don't think any of us had ever been in his room or seen the inside of it since he moved in two years ago. Deciding it would be best that I hid out in my room, I left Brayden to his nap and retreated until the meeting.

CHAPTER 16

LAILAH

I never fell asleep, just laid on my bed, rehashing what just happened. When I couldn't take it any longer, I slipped out of bed and wandered over to the closet. I knew Beth moved fast, and I shouldn't have been shocked that all of my clothes were hung, folded, and placed on shelves, clean and ready for me. I grabbed some comfy clothes and headed for the bathroom, needing a shower to rinse off the rest of this crazy day. Turning the water as hot as it could go, I stripped down and hopped in. It was then I noticed everything I had in my shower caddy was placed in here, ready for me to use.

Beth really doesn't want me going back to the dorm.

Choosing to let that go further down on the list of things to deal with, I indulged in a long shower. I did not want to go back out there and face the conversation we needed to have about my meltdown.

"Trouble, you okay?" Parker called out.

I whipped around to find him standing in my bathroom.

"What the hell, Parker!" I screeched, trying to cover myself with my hands.

"Fuck, sorry," Parker said, turning around. "I knocked a few times, and you didn't answer me, so I was worried you lost it again."

"As you can see, I'm fine. What are you still doing here while I'm in the shower naked?" I demanded.

"Beth wants to see us all in the library. She sent a text, but I'm guessing you didn't get it," Parker explained.

"Great, thanks, now get the fuck out of my bathroom."

"Alright, I'm going, I'm going," Parker said, but he paused at the door and turned to meet my gaze. "You should swear more, it's kind of hot."

Before I could show him just how much I could swear, he left and shut the door behind him. I liked Parker, and he was becoming one of my best friends, but I wasn't in the habit of letting friends see me naked. I wasn't sure what pissed me off more—that he was totally comfortable waltzing into my bathroom with me in the shower, or the way my body tingled knowing he had seen me.

These are not thoughts you have about people who are your friends! You just started something with Brayden; you slept together. Get your head right. Parker is a flirt and likes to get under your skin. Deal with the man you know you can count on first, then figure out how the rest of them fit in all this.

Shutting off the water, I toweled off and got dressed before I dealt with my hair. If I had any other unwanted guests, I wanted to have clothes on. I rushed to finish up in the bathroom and headed out to make my way to the library. It appeared that I was the last one to get the memo since everyone else was seated, waiting for me. Glancing around the room, looking for a seat, I hurried and slid in between Brayden and Hudson on the couch.

"Sorry, didn't see the text," I mumbled.

Beth just nodded to me and looked over everyone else gathered. "Alright, let's start this off with the matter of Brayden and Lailah bonding the other night."

I could feel my stomach sinking at her words. *Please don't tell me we're going to talk about us having sex in front of everyone.*

Sensing my discomfort, Brayden grabbed my hand and held it in his lap, stroking my knuckles with his thumb.

"Lailah, there are a few aspects to being Synergy that I haven't discussed with you yet. There was so much to cover once you discovered who you are that I didn't want to add this on until it was necessary. It seems that things have progressed faster than I anticipated," Beth said as she glanced down at our conjoined hands.

"Remember when I told you that Aiden Reyvick, our school founder, had a vision about Synergy? He wrote in two different journals about the enlightened conversation he had with the angel that came to talk to him. One we were able to read right away and gave us the limited information we have had up to this point. The other was protected by an angel's seal and was only able to be opened when Synergy came into power." Beth paused, looking at all of to see if we were following.

It struck me then that whatever she was going to tell us, the guys didn't know about either.

"What I held back from telling you was that Synergy was meant to bond with each of the elements. You control the ability to harness your own power, but additionally, you can take and give power to those you are bonded to. Let me make it clear that the Oath and the Bond are two different steps. The Oath is the first step in bonding yourself to each element. That oath is to be taken very seriously—you are giving your word in front of the angels themselves. From this new information, we gathered there was a warning that the Oath can be broken if the Blessed Warrior turns his back on Synergy to serve the darkness. Once the Oath is given, then it progresses to the Bond.

The *Bond* is the physical part. Where the *Oath* is magical. Once bonded, it is believed to be an unbreakable connection. We are all adult enough here that I don't think we need to go further into the details of that interaction. I will only ask this once because it is my duty as your caretaker here. Lailah, do we need to get you to a doctor?"

My face flamed, and all I wanted was to sink into the couch and never be seen again. "No, I have an implant already, there's no need."

"Moving on then," Beth said with a swift nod. "Once both steps are completed, your powers are combined, and it will be that way forever. There is no changing what has been done. As each Bond is formed, we will need to work with both parties on how to control the new power levels they will both have. Any questions?"

The way that Beth was talking about the bond made me think that I was missing something in all this. It was staring me right in the face, and I just wasn't seeing it. Seeing or feeling that I was struggling to understand, Brayden squeezed my hand, drawing my attention.

"What Beth is trying to explain is that you and I are connected to each other for life."

My jaw fell open at the shocking reality of his words. Now that I had bonded with Brayden, he was tied to me for life. *How could I have done this to him without knowing!?*

"Angel, listen, you might not have known what it meant to have bonded—but I did. I went into this knowing that accepting the Oath meant that you would be the only woman for me for the rest of my life. Before finding out that you were Synergy, I struggled with keeping my distance, because I knew that at any moment I might have to leave you. Not everyone agreed with Ryevick's assumptions that Synergy would be human. I always suspected it would be a woman. How else could the Bond have worked between all of us?"

I sat there, silent, as I searched his face and reached for our Bond to understand what he was feeling right now. Finding what I was looking for, he let his emotions free, drowning me in his affection and confidence that he made the right choice. He didn't feel trapped or upset that he was stuck with me. Quite the opposite—he was thrilled.

"Lailah, I know this is a lot to take in, and you and Brayden

I'm sure will need to have a more personal talk, but there is more," Beth hedged, breaking me out of my connection with Brayden.

"Oh good, there's more," I muttered.

Hudson chuckled.

"Nona, Mr. Phillips, and I have all been going over the new journal the last few weeks, and there is a matter that we have to discuss with all of you." This caused all the guys to sit up a little straighter, their attention trained on Beth. "Synergy was brought to us as the ultimate weapon, but this weapon can be used by either side. What we have learned is that Lailah is in danger until she has bonded with each of you. This would cut off any chance that the demons could come and take her from us."

"More Elementi propaganda bullshit," Micah bellowed, jumping to his feet.

"Shut the fuck up, Micah, no one cares what you think," Parker growled, flipping him the bird.

Before the room could erupt into a fight between the two of them, Hudson cut in. "It might help if you could explain that more. I'm not sure I understand. How could the demons have anything to do with a heavenly being?"

Both Micah and Parker paused, waiting to hear the answer.

"That's the thing. Lailah isn't a heavenly being, she's a human. The rule of free will still applies, even to her. If she decided to turn away from us and leave to join the demons, then that is her choice. By completing the Bond with all of you, it is her deciding to stay on our side. She will bless us with the chance to fight the darkness and bring peace back to our turbulent world."

This information was like a slap in the face. It made all of my strange nightmares and the hallucinations I had make more sense. "Wait, why did the demon that took over Mallory want to kill me if they could use me?"

"We believe that they wanted to take you from the world before you came into power, removing the chance you would side with us. If the threat is taken out before it's a true threat, then they are no longer in danger," Beth answered. "But, this second attack on you had more to it than just trying to draw you to the Dark Lord. When he poisoned you, it gave them a hook into your mind. Parker and Brayden explained what happened today, and I believe it was induced partly because some of the demon venom is still in your system."

That made sense in a strange, twisted way. The whole thing seemed so unlike me that it was comforting to know it wasn't just me going crazy, but the demons using my fear against me. What I still couldn't wrap my brain around was that if I wanted to live without fear of turning demonic, I would need to fully bond with all five of the men in this room. I looked at them, studying each for a moment.

Jay was someone I counted on to have my back and to always look after me. Parker was the guy who could always make me laugh and forced me to have fun and try new experiences. Micah—Micah's anger, all of a sudden, became clearer. Of course he resented me for who I was—who wanted to be forced into a life-long relationship with someone? If what Parker said was true, and he didn't even want to be a Blessed Warrior, then he would hate being bonded to me. Then there was Hudson, my nerd with a heart of gold. He helped me take a deep breath and look at things logically. There was always a solution if you just took the time to find it. But I wasn't sure any of them felt any kind of romantic feelings towards me.

Wait, when did anyone say that it had to be romantic? Maybe what happened between Brayden and I was just that, between the two of us. I didn't have to sleep with all of them, did I? Then I remembered the feeling of the Bond solidifying into something unbreakable when we'd had sex. All hope I had to reason my way out of this was gone like a balloon being popped.

"What do we do now?" I said, more to myself than to anyone in particular.

The room was silent, as if no one really had the answer. I

tried to fight against the urge to run and hide in my room, but this wasn't just about me anymore. I had five other people who this directly affected.

"First things first, you will be living here from now on. I can't allow you to be alone and not have one of the boys around you after what almost happened. Besides this strange happening, it seems that your power has leveled out somewhat since you bonded with Brayden. I think you will gain more control each time you do so. The boys will keep a closer eye on you, much like they were doing before your powers came to light," Beth said, breaking the tension. "When school starts after Christmas break, I will be changing your whole schedule. We need to get you in physical defense classes as well as demonology, elemental manipulation, and the like. I know you and Mr. Phillips have been going over the history that you don't already know, but we need to get you on the fast track."

"Okay, it looks like you already moved me in for the most part anyway. I'll just need to go back and collect the last of my things," I said, knowing that everything she was saying was wise.

"No need, we have everything here already. They are just cleaning the last of it before they bring the boxes to your room. Does anyone have any other questions? I wanted to make sure we are all on the same page." After a beat, when no one made a move, she clapped her hands together and sent us on our way. "Dinner will be ready shortly, so don't go wandering off too far. Oh, Lailah, could you stay a moment?"

Staying where I was seated, Beth waited for the guys to leave the room before she turned her attention back to me. "With everything going on, I didn't get to tell you that if you still want the kitchen tomorrow, you are more than welcome to it. Sarah did say that if she could be of any help to please ask."

I had all but forgotten that tomorrow was going to be Thanksgiving. "I have a list of ingredients that I need. Would she be able to tell me what I need to get if you don't have it already?"

"I am sure she would be happy to. If you want to email me the list, I will make sure she gets it. Don't worry about going to get things yourself. We are more than happy to provide what you need. You are feeding everyone, so it only makes sense," Beth said with a smile. "I, for one, am very excited to try all that comes with a Thanksgiving meal."

I returned her smile, feeling a bubble of excitement well up. Finally, something fun to look forward to after all the crazy that's been going on.

CHAPTER 17

LAILAH

"You really don't have to help if you want to take the night off. This was my crazy idea, after all," I told Sarah.

"Lailah, I know you don't know me very well, but trust me when I say I would love to help make this meal. Cooking is how I show love, and these boys have been eating my cooking for years. I might want to strangle them from time to time, but they are all good boys deep down," she assured me.

"Yeah, way deep down in the basement under piles of cement," Cami chimed in, tying on the ridiculous apron she got just for today.

I couldn't help but laugh when she showed me. It was neon pink and had *Sorry, your opinion wasn't in the recipe* written on it. Knowing my love of sassy t-shirts, she got me one as well. Mine was a pastel blue, and my saying was *All this . . . and can cook!*

"Why are you so amazing!" I said, wrapping Cami up in a hug.

After the crazy past two days, it was doing me good just to have time with Cami and not worry about school, boys, or being Synergy. Today was all about Thanksgiving and stuffing our faces with food. I let my teachers know that I was still sick and wouldn't be in class today and asked if they could email me anything I needed to know. I just wasn't up to dealing with it today.

"The turkey is in the roaster, freeing up both ovens for us to use on other things. What should we start with first?" Sarah said, looking over the different recipes I had laid out on the counter.

"Cami, why don't you wash, peel, and cut the potatoes for us to boil. Sarah, I'll put you in charge of green beans and stuffing for now while I work on the pies," I delegated, knowing that I was the only one who knew my mother's methods to make her pie crusts.

In true Cami style, she turned on some music, dancing and singing along while she peeled. We chatted and laughed as we worked, making it feel just like it would back home. Cami had already warned me that she wasn't going to be much help but for the chopping part of things. She could handle a knife just fine, but other than that, we were putting the food at risk. Sarah and I worked together as if we had been doing it forever, just like my mom and me.

"So are you going to spill the details about you and Brayden yet?" Cami asked as she started washing up some of our mess.

I grinned over at Cami. "I'm amazed it took you this long to ask me about it. I for sure thought you were going to corner me yesterday when you got done with classes."

"Trust me, I would have if a certain sister of mine hadn't told me to leave you alone for the day. Beth said you had some kind of mental breakdown?" Cami questioned.

"I wouldn't call it a mental breakdown," I said, kneading the dough for the rolls. "It's hard to explain, it was more like having a dream while awake. I felt like everything was really happening, but it wasn't. It scared the shit out of me, Cami." I shuddered at the lack of mercy I'd felt towards everyone in the cafe I was about to destroy.

"Do we know what caused it?" Sarah asked.

Even though Sarah was part of the Elementi, I still wasn't sure what her clearance was to know all the information Beth told us. "They have a few thoughts, but truthfully, more questions than answers at this point."

"Everything will work out in due time, dear," Sarah said, patting my arm reassuringly.

"And that's enough heavy, depressing topics, let's talk about something more fun, like you and Brayden," Cami said, bringing us back full circle.

"Let's just say that Brayden and I bonded on a spiritual and physical level the other night," I said, feeling my cheeks heat with my blush.

"Thank the *lord*. It's about damn time you both gave in to the epic amounts of sexual tension between the two of you," Cami crowed and did a little happy dance. "I won't ask you the dirty details, because I know you won't tell me, *but* I have to know one thing."

I stopped working on the rolls and turned to look at her when she didn't ask right away. Cami walked up to me and grabbed both my hands in hers and looked me dead in the eye. I was beginning to worry that this wasn't going to be a good question, the way she was acting. Cami only became serious when it was about my safety.

"Am. I. Going... to be your maid of honor?"

My mouth fell open at her question. "What? Why would you ask me that? How did this turn into Brayden and me getting married?"

At this point, Cami lost it, and peals of laughter flooded out of her. Tears started to seep out of her eyes as she continued to laugh, keeping hold of my hands as she slid to the floor, still carrying on.

"Cami," I groaned, still not following her crazy logic.

"The money I would pay to go back in time and get a picture of your face when I asked that. I don't think I have ever seen you more terrified in my life." Cami finally stood and used her apron to wipe her eyes. "You poor thing, you have no idea what you've done, do you?"

"Now what *does* that mean?" I demanded.

"I know Beth told you that th*e Bond* is forever, right?" I nodded when she paused for my answer. "Since you and Brayden have done both, you're practically married. Hell, you're more than married, you couldn't even get rid of the guy if you wanted. I mean, I guess you could kill him if you really needed to..." Cami said, getting lost in her thoughts until she turned back to me. "Okay, okay, take deep breaths, Lala. Thatta girl. Maybe you need to sit down."

Taking Cami's advice, I slid down the wall of the counter and sat right there on the floor, staring off into nothing while my mind finally caught up. Beth tried to explain this to me yesterday, but I was so overwhelmed with everything else we had to talk about that I didn't really dwell on things with Brayden.

"Holy shit," I finally said when something else clicked into place. "He knew exactly what he was agreeing to and still did it."

Cami squatted down in front of me and placed her hands on my knees, grounding me. "Yeah, I kinda figured you weren't really understanding things with how calm you've been. If it's any help, that boy has been head over heels for you since the moment you ran into each other at the fountain, he just didn't know it till after your lame coffee date."

"How could you possibly know that?" I asked, dumbfounded.

Cami grinned at me. "You forget, I've known these boys almost all my life. Brayden never makes the first move, aka giving you his number. He never has to wait for a girl to text or call him back. Lala, he had to remind you that you never did. The other reason is that Brayden doesn't do *girlfriends*. He has girls that he spends time with and takes on dates, but he is never *real* around them, and he definitely never talks about his brother with them. We don't even know the full story about that situation, but I bet my sparkly ass you do."

I let my head fall back against the wall as this all settled in. "What am I going to do now? Beth wants me to be fully bonded with the others sooner rather than later. That means I will be more than married to *five* guys?"

"Now the lucky bitch gets it," Cami said with a wink.

I laughed just like Cami hoped I would, then she jumped to her feet, hands on her hips. "What the hell do you think you're doing? This dinner isn't going to cook itself, now is it?"

She pulled me to my feet, and I took a deep breath, then let it out. "Right, let's get to it. We don't have tons of time before the boys are back and demanding to be fed."

Throwing myself into the meal, I shut out dealing with my personal life until I could talk to Brayden, and focused on right now. With Sarah's expert skills of figuring out how to stage what went into the oven, things went without a hitch. As we waited for the last few things to finish, my stomach growled with all the delicious-smelling food around. We decided to skip lunch, knowing we would be eating dinner much earlier than usual. I had Beth text all the guys, telling them they had to be home by three for something important.

We tried to make it look like Cami and I were hanging out in the kitchen while Sarah cooked and kept all the food hidden away in the warmers. Jay was the first one home, but he went right to his room, so we didn't need to worry about him. Hudson was next, but he had his head stuck in a book and headed for the library, mumbling about something I didn't understand. The next three were the ones I was worried about spoiling the surprise.

"What if we just tell them they can't come in from the garage? Then we don't have to worry about them seeing a thing," I suggested.

"No, that would never work. The moment we do something like that, they'll know," Sarah said, making a good point.

"When Micah gets here, I'll just piss him off so he doesn't even care to know what we're doing here," Cami volunteered.

"Then you can just drag Brayden out of here with the promise of a make-out session."

"Let's be honest, Parker is the one who will be the biggest challenge," Sarah said. "He has this ability to know when I don't want him to find something in the kitchen."

"Oh, I can play video games with him!" I smiled, knowing that would get him for sure.

"Not if you're getting hot and heavy with Brayden," Cami said, wagging her brows at me.

"Who's getting hot and heavy with Brayden?" Parker asked, leaning on the counter next to Cami.

"Fucking tits on my ass, Parker," Cami yelled, almost falling out of her chair.

"When did you get here?" I asked at the same time Cami was swearing.

Parker just propped his head on his hand like he was an innocent little cherub. "You guys seem to be plotting oh-so-carefully over here, you didn't even notice me walk in. I have to admit, it hurts a little right here," he said, pointing to his heart. "Care to fill me in on the juicy deets?"

"Parker, the nineties called, they want their slang back," Cami said, rolling her eyes.

"Burn," I added, unable to stop myself, causing Cami and I to burst out laughing.

"Mock me all you want, but the nineties was an epic era, and I refuse to let it die," Parker said, waving off Cami's diss.

Then an idea hit me, and I knew how to get Parker out of the kitchen for us to get this all finished. "Parker."

His gaze met mine with a questioning brow and a smirk. "Yes, Trouble?"

"If I promise to share my next fix of sugar cookies with you, will you leave the kitchen and not bother us until we call for you?" I asked, batting my lashes at him.

Parker paused, and I could see he was really thinking this over. I thought for sure he would go for it without hesitation.

"I will agree to that, if I'm the one to go with you into town to get them," Parker countered.

"Wait, are you turning this into a date?" Cami asked, amazed.

Parker shrugged his shoulders and grinned wider. "Guess it's up to you on how important it is that I leave the kitchen."

Shaking my head, I wasn't able to fight the smile that was plastered on my face. "Fine, I agree. Now go," I said, pointing, enforcing my words.

Looking way too pleased with himself, Parker pushed off the counter and left the kitchen without further argument.

"Seriously, I think he was the devil in a past life. He is way too good at making deals," Cami said, and I agreed with her.

"I would say that we're almost done here, we just need to carve the turkey and get the table set up," Sarah said, looking over the list once more.

"Cami and I can do that." I looked down at my phone to check the time. "We are running right on schedule."

Just as we were heading to the dining room, Micah and Brayden walked into the kitchen. We apparently didn't need to worry, because they were arguing about something to do with Micah's car.

"I am not getting it converted into burning oil from Chinese restaurants. It's a sports car, let it be a beautiful blight on your environment," Micah grumbled as he passed by.

"Think of all the fuel that car burns! What about getting it switched for ethanol then?" Brayden pressed, not being dissuaded, following Micah close on his heels up the stairs.

I laughed as I grabbed the tray of silverware while Cami got the plates. During a previous break, I'd decorated the table from the stash of things Sarah kept for special occasions. It was simple, but let's be real—it was more about the food than the fancy folded napkins. Finished with the table, we headed back in to find Garrett carving the turkey for us, and the smell made my mouth water. I stole a scrap and had to hold back a moan at how perfect it was.

"I'll grab Beth, and she can get everyone else down here," Cami said, bouncing excitedly.

Sarah came over to me and gave me a side hug as we looked over all the food ready to be taken out. "I'm not sure we made quite enough . . ."

"You're right, a twenty-pound turkey, three kinds of potatoes, two kinds of stuffing, three different vegetable options, and three pies is not nearly enough for ten people," I said, shaking my head.

"Don't forget the cranberry sauce when we have both homemade and straight out of the can," Sarah added.

"Who could possibly forget the cranberry sauce when our hostess was so adamant about it?" Cami said with a laugh.

The sound of the guys making their way into the dining room gave us our cue, and I hefted the large platter of turkey. I found the guys standing, staring at the table as if they weren't sure what to make of it.

"Pick a seat, guys, and get ready to experience your first American Thanksgiving," I said proudly, setting my platter in the middle of the table.

"Oh, hell yeah," Parker said, sitting down and tucking his napkin into the collar of his shirt, grinning at me.

Following his lead, everyone took a seat while we brought out the rest of the food. I could see the guys' eyes getting wider as we kept placing dish after dish on the table. Parker reached out to grab a roll, but Micah slapped his hand away. "Didn't your mother teach you any manners?"

Parker scowled and flipped him off but sat back in his chair, crossing his arms and waiting for us to take our seats.

"If you don't mind indulging me, it's tradition to go around the table and say one thing we're thankful for," I said, looking around the table. "I'll go first. I'm thankful for coming to this school and meeting all of you. I know that the past few weeks have been crazy, and I am truly grateful for you all sticking with me through it." Turning to Cami, I gave her an encouraging nod.

"I am thankful for my kick-ass best friend and for my girl-friend, Maggs, who couldn't make it today."

"I am thankful for my husband, health, and for all of you," Sarah said, smiling at all of us.

"Right, my turn," Garrett grumbled. "Guess I'm thankful for still being able to work and have a purpose at my age."

"I feel like I have so many things to be thankful for—the wards are stronger than ever, we found Synergy, and my family is working together again," Beth said, with a nod of her head.

"I am thankful for the student lab getting a grant for upgraded equipment that will make my work more efficient," Hudson said.

"Um, dude, I don't think that's how this is supposed to work," Parker whispered loudly next to him.

"Why not? It is something that I am extremely grateful for," Hudson defended his answer.

"Guys, it's fine," I said, not wanting to start a fight right now. "What about you, Parker?"

"Well, I'm happy you asked. I am very thankful for this kick-ass meal that I get to eat soon, but I'm also thankful for the person who came up with the idea. Life has been a hell of a lot more interesting since you showed up," Parker said, his grin in full force.

I blushed under his gaze at being called out in front of everyone.

"I, too, am thankful for Lailah," Brayden started off and paused to clear his throat. "If anyone in the world had to be Synergy, I am thankful it's you, because I'm not sure anyone else would have been so perfect for us all."

Now I could feel my face burst into flames as his heated gaze and swoon-worthy words hit me.

"And barf," Cami said, breaking the tension in the room.

"Moving on. You're up, Cranky Pants McGee. Think you have anything you can come up with to be grateful for?"

Micah scowled at her, gripping his knife like he wanted to throw it at her. Cami just blinked at him with wide-eyed innocence.

"I'm fucking grateful it's almost winter break, and I get three weeks of not having to deal with all your sorry asses," Micah managed from a clenched jaw.

"Encore! We demand an encore!" Cami said, standing and clapping her hands. "Look at that, you didn't even burst into flames or anything." Cami ducked as a roll went flying through the air at her.

"Micah, Cami, Sit down," Beth snapped from her spot at the head of the table.

Once they both sat and looked away from each other, I looked over at Jay. "Last but not least," I said, smiling at him.

"Thankful to be alive," Jay said, then grabbed the bowl of sweet potatoes in front of him and helped himself.

As if he broke the seal holding everyone in place, the guys dove into the food, piling their plates high. I smiled as I watched everyone enjoying the food that we had worked so hard to make. I took a small sample of everything; I knew better than to stuff myself on the first round. Besides, there was still dessert to come.

The rest of the meal went without any further incidents since everyone was distracted with the food in front of them. Easy talk filtered among the table, and I learned that Sarah and Garrett had two grown children that were not part of the Elementi. They both took a vow of silence and left to live their lives more normally. Because of this—and the fact that they are full-time here, looking after all of us—they didn't get to see them often. It made me sad to think of them not being able to see their grandchildren, but it gave me a window into another side of the Elementi. You were either all in or you were all out, no room for the in-between.

The boys all helped bring in the dishes, and we all tackled the major task of cleaning up. Cami had helped along the way, but there was still so much to deal with. Hudson washed the dishes while Brayden dried them. Parker and I were putting things back while Jay helped to pack away the leftovers. Micah, being the social butterfly he is, was clearing the table of all the decorations and putting out dishes for dessert. Many hands made quick work and gave us time to make room for dessert.

"Sarah, I have to say, you have outdone yourself on these pies," Parker said as he tried not to drool over them.

"I didn't make those. That would be Miss Lailah's work," Sarah said with a wink.

Parker came over to me and dropped on one knee, taking my hand. "Will you marry me right now?"

"What?! No, stop that, get off the kitchen floor," I said, pulling my hand out of his and taking a step back.

Parker pouted and stood back up. "Come on, where else am I going to find a girl who is smart, kind, sexy, puts up with me, cooks, *and* bakes? That is a perfect storm of a woman, and I know it."

As I looked at Parker, I couldn't tell if he was totally messing with me, or if he meant any of that. His chocolate-colored eyes seemed to glow with his feelings, but I still couldn't decipher what they were. I didn't want to be a notch on Parker's belt. He was too important to me for me to take the wrong step with our relationship—friends or otherwise.

"Parker, lay off, you're making her uncomfortable," Brayden said, walking up behind me and putting his hands on my hips.

Parker's eyes flicked to where Brayden's hands were, then back up to my face. I could almost see a flash of hurt in his gaze before it was gone. "Calm down, lover boy, I was just yanking her chain."

Turning, he grabbed two of the pies and made his way back to the dining room. I followed after him with my eyes, feeling like I might have misjudged the situation.

"Stop thinking so hard, you're going to give yourself a headache," Brayden whispered into my ear before he kissed my neck. "Come on, I can't wait to taste your pie."

"That's what she said," Cami called out as she walked by with the last pie.

Brayden groaned and grabbed my hand, pulling me after him.

CHAPTER 18
BRAYDEN

After we were all stuffed beyond reason with all the amazing food that Lailah, Sarah, and Cami made, everyone dispersed for the night. I grabbed Lailah's hand and took her to a sitting room that we never really used. It had a large sectional couch with a fireplace and a TV over the mantle. I flipped on the switch, turning the gas on and lighting the fire, which warmed the chilled room quickly. Lailah grabbed a blanket off the back of the couch, and we snuggled together under it.

"Thank you for sharing Thanksgiving with us," I said, kissing the top of her head.

She nestled in closer to me, tucking her head under my chin. "You're very welcome. It was also an apology for being such a bitch the past few weeks."

I chuckled at how apologetic she was. "Angel, I think I've known you long enough to know that isn't your normal. Don't beat yourself up about it."

"Who knows what my normal will be now? I could lash out at anyone or have a psychotic break in a dream and start hurting people who have wronged me."

At her words, I thought back to yesterday and how distressed she was. Lailah was a pure spirit, and to see herself capable of doing something like that, even in a hallucination, must've made her question everything.

"Lailah, you don't have to handle this all on your own. You have all of us to help you, no matter what happens. I have no doubt that you'll win this fight against the demons' tricks. You are filled with pure light, and it's much harder to cast a shadow where there is nowhere to hide," I said, running my hand up and down her back.

"I hope you're right, because if things change, I don't think anyone could stop me," Lailah muttered.

Seeing that she wasn't ready to believe me on this yet, I let the topic drop. We could come back to it later when wasn't not so fresh in her mind. "Hey, what do you think about coming home with me for Christmas? We get three weeks off, and I figured you could use the chance to get away from school."

"That actually sounds amazing," she said, sitting back to look me in the face. "I told my parents I wasn't going to have them fly me back for Christmas. It would be way too expensive. Instead, I'll go back the whole summer. Three months is better than three weeks."

I grinned at her. "I'll let my parents know, they're very excited to meet you."

"You've told your parents about me?" she asked, blushing.

"I have talked about you to them, yes, but when it came out that you are Synergy, all the important members of the Elementi were informed," I said. "It doesn't change the fact that they are wanting to meet my girlfriend."

Lailah frowned, and I tried to hide my surprise. Did she not think she was my girlfriend?

"There has to be a better word to describe what we are. I feel like girlfriend isn't a strong enough word for someone you're bonded to for life."

I laughed. "You had me worried for a moment. I thought you were going to tell me you didn't want to be my girlfriend."

"*No*, that's not what I meant at all," Lailah said, grasping my arm.

"Well, until you come up with a better word you want me to use, then I will just settle for calling you my girlfriend," I teased.

"Where does your family live?"

"In another country, but I want to keep it a surprise. I have a feeling you're going to love it." Excitement flooded through me from her as she thought about the possibilities.

I smiled and placed a gentle kiss on her lips, unable to hold myself back. When I pulled away, she chased after me; apparently, she wasn't interested in such a chaste kiss. She curled her fingers into my hair, and it sent a shiver down my spine.

This woman had no idea what she did to me. My body craved her, and the more I had her, the worse it got. The love and affection that she could bestow on someone were more magical than the powers we both held. Never had a woman made me feel so wanted, and not for the typical reasons. Most wanted the benefit of money, my family name, or the power we held in the Elementi. No, Lailah, saw me for who I was, never knowing that I was willing to give her anything she wanted.

Without breaking our kiss, I scooped her up and laid her down beside me on the couch so our bodies touched from head to toe. She moaned into my mouth, setting me on fire. I gripped her ass and pulled her even tighter to me, tossing a leg over her hip. Responding, she ground against me, making me growl at her in encouragement. Sliding my hands under her shirt, I slipped it over her head, exposing her creamy white skin.

I kissed down her neck as she wriggled in my arms, trying to pull my shirt off of me. Quickly, I let her go and yanked the fabric off so she could have the access she wanted. Her soft hand roved over my chest as if she were memorizing every part of me. My cock twitched, pressing painfully against my jeans, trapped, wanting her attention. Surprising me, she licked my nipple, and I groaned, one hand sliding into her hair to hold her to me. My other hand went to the fastener on her bra and flicked it open.

Rolling her under me, I slid the bra off her body and showed her breasts my appreciation, molding one with my hand while torturing her with my mouth on the other. I noticed the other night how much she enjoyed having her nipples played with, and I was more than happy to oblige. Shifting so I could get her jeans off, I undid the button but took my time slowly peeling them off of her. I wanted to enjoy her body and the delicious sounds she made when she got frustrated at me.

"Brayden, please don't tease me. I need you." She panted once I got her jeans and underwear off.

Shucking off my own jeans, I crawled up her body, placing kisses along the way until I reached her perfect lips. "My Angel wants for nothing."

I lowered my body, and she spread her legs for me to nestle against her core. Bucking her hips encouragingly, I reached between us and stroked her, feeling how wet she was for me. The ego boost you got from having a wanton woman begging you to take her was amazing, but when it was also the woman you loved, it was incomparable. I slid a finger in, then a second, and pumped them in and out a few times just to make sure she wasn't too tight.

Last time I thought I was going to bust a load before I got all the way in, she was so narrow. This time she gave under my touch faster, and I knew she was getting close. For a moment, I thought about tasting her before I entered her, but looking up and seeing the need in her eyes settled it. Lining up, I kissed her deeply as I slammed home, causing her to cry out. I trapped it with my kiss, not wanting her to feel ashamed of the noises she made in her enjoyment. To me, the sounds she made when she lost herself in passion were everything, but this moment I didn't want to share with anyone. She was mine for now, and I was going to take full advantage.

Pulling her legs around my waist, I pulled her up so she was sitting in my lap, and I leaned against the back of the couch. Thrusting into her, I clutched her to my body, holding her steady as I moved. She wrapped her arms around my shoulders and muffled her cries in my neck. Even though she wasn't as tight as the first time, it was still almost too much. Feeling myself edging on release, I tried to slow down, not wanting this to end. Lailah shared her opinion on this by setting her teeth to my neck. She didn't bite down hard, but it was a clear warning she didn't agree with what was going on.

Picking back up the pace, I could feel sweat beading on my skin as I kept the rhythm. Lailah tensed, letting me know she was close too, then she cried out, and her teeth latched on to me, sending me off the edge. I lost it, thrusting up into her as deep as she could take me and moaned my own release. Never had sex been this satisfying, making all others experiences pale in comparison. Lailah released her hold on my neck and rested her head there, panting. Neither of us moved, not wanting to break the closeness of this moment between us.

"Lailah, I know this is crazy to say, but I'm falling in love with you," I whispered into her ear.

Pulling back, she looked me in the eye, searching, trying to determine if what I was saying was true. She leaned in and kissed me, showing me with action how she felt.

"Please don't hate me, but I'm not ready to say those words to you yet," she answered, her lips grazing mine as she talked.

Kissing her quickly, unable to miss the opportunity, I answered, "I could never hate you, and it's fine. I'll wait however long it takes. I'm not going anywhere."

"Good, because I kind of like having you around," she said, grinning at me before her face seemed to fall into a more serious expression. "Is it weird for you knowing that I have to bond with the others to keep myself safe?"

I paused before I answered, searching her eyes and seeing that this had been something she'd been rolling around in her brain for a while. "The idea we all had to share Synergy is not new to me, we always knew that was going to happen. Does that change because you are human and a woman that I am falling head over heels for… yeah. Am I relishing the fact that I get you all to myself right now? Hell, yeah. On the other hand, knowing that bonding with them will keep you safe, how could I stand in the way of that?"

"So you don't like it," Lailah said with a slight wrinkle on her brow.

"Pretty sure that's not what I said," I chuckled. "I am fine with you bonding with the others. It will take some time to adjust for us all. Some will have an easier time than others, but I trust them, and we were all made for you. Each one of us was picked to be in the generation that would be your guardians and everything else that comes with the Bond."

"You make this sound so easy. I haven't even had a real relationship, and now I'm going to be bonded to five guys for the rest of my life? What if they change their mind and don't like me anymore or get tired of me?" Lailah said, snuggling deeper against my body.

"I can only speak for myself on this, but there is no way that I would ever change my mind. Lailah, you are everything that I've been looking for in a woman. I want to spend the rest of my life with you." I placed a gentle kiss on her forehead, letting it linger, needing her to believe my words and the feelings behind them.

This seemed to get her to relax again, and I could feel the anxiety bleeding away from our connection. "Would you be upset if I asked you to keep our relationship quiet around school? I'm afraid that the bitchy girls will lose their minds if they find out we really are dating."

"I can understand that, but when it's just us or around the guys, I'm not holding back," I said, knowing that it would be a struggle not to want to hold her and kiss her all the time.

Lailah lifted her face to me and smirked. "Deal."

Enjoying the intimacy a while longer, I hummed to myself as I stroked her bare skin.

LAILAH

"Why the fuck would we do that? I get to leave all you fuck heads for three weeks, and you want us to come back a week early? Hell no," Micah growled, stabbing his knife into the dining room table.

"Micah, no matter how upset you are, please do not take it out on the furniture," Beth chided, giving him a look that made him remove the knife.

"Just because your cunt of an aunt called to bitch at you today doesn't mean you get to act like more of an asshole," Parker taunted. "I was just thinking it would be fun for all of us to be together for New Year's, especially since it will be Lailah's first one in Europe."

"If Micah wants to stay behind at home, then let him. The rest of us have already agreed," Hudson said, settling the issue.

I looked around the dinner table, smiling at the interaction that was now becoming strangely normal. The past two weeks had flown by in a blur of studying, finishing papers, and projects for finals. I was thankful that no other strange happenings had occurred, and I was able to find a new normal living in The Manor. Jay was making sure that I was swimming laps and working out with him to help me adjust to the added power I now had from bonding with Brayden. It took me a few days to stop jumping at shadows, worried that the girls would be even more vicious against me because I'd moved in. Then I found out the school had taken action against those who did the prank, quieting them for now.

Tonight was the first dinner we'd had all together in a week, and I'd missed them. Even though one of them was with me all the time, our group hangouts didn't happen as often. It was strange—in one way, I felt like we were one big family, and our dynamic was growing stronger. Then other times, it seemed that there was no way some of them could get over themselves and get along.

"We have one day left to survive each other before we all go our separate ways for the holiday," I said, drawing everyone's attention. "What will you three be doing?"

Parker grinned with excitement in his eyes. "My dad loves Christmas and goes all out. We host parties, go caroling through the neighborhood, and eat a shit-ton of food. Oh yeah, and of course, there's the presents to open too. We compete to see who can give the best gift. I've won the past four years running."

"Okay, now I wish I was going to your place," I tease, giving Brayden a wink. "What about you, Hudson?"

"My parents are divorced, so my siblings and I will be doing Christmas Eve with one and Christmas day with the other. We don't really do a whole lot, but it will be nice to spend time with everyone," Hudson informed, and we all turned to Jay.

"We don't celebrate Christmas," Jay said, shocking me. "I'll be in Tokyo visiting my mom."

My ears perked up at this new information about his family. He said so very little about his mom that I jumped on any tidbit I could gather.

"Did you grow up in Japan?" I asked, hoping he would answer me.

"Yes," Jay said, flicking his eyes up to me. "Until I was thirteen."

I couldn't hold back my smile, pleased that he'd given me just a little more information about himself. Was it dumb that I felt moments like this were a victory of sorts, that each step in him opening up was like winning a new level?

"Remind me why can't we leave sooner? I'm done with my classes, and Brayden, you're done tomorrow morning," Micah asked.

"Lailah has a final later in the afternoon. I figured it would be better to leave Friday morning instead of rushing," Brayden answered for me.

"You have your own private plane. How is it rushing when it comes and goes when you tell it to?" Micah challenged.

"Just leave it. Twelve hours won't make that big of a difference," Brayden said, fixing Micah with a glare.

Micah's answer was to mutter something under his breath, shove his chair back, and storm out of the room. While I was glad that he wasn't going to pick a bigger fight, him running away didn't ever fix things. He was the only one that didn't do anything with me one-on-one. He was only around when it was a group setting or something Beth mandated he needed to be at. I secretly was hoping that in the next two weeks, we might be able to grow our friendship from someone he had to tolerate to maybe an actual friend.

"Oh, is Micah not having dessert? I made his favorite," Sarah said, holding a plate with what looked like a large tart on it.

"He needed to cool his head," Brayden said with a sigh.

"I see. Well, I'll just make sure to save him a slice," Sarah said, putting the dessert down and serving us each a slice.

"What is it?" I asked, curious to find out what Micah could consider a favorite.

"It's a dark chocolate truffle tart with sea salt," Sarah said, handing me a plate.

"Of course the bastard would only like bitter chocolate," Parker grumbled, but still took his slice.

"Brayden, you have your own plane?" I asked him to come back to that tidbit of information.

"Technically, it belongs to my dad's company, but when it's not in use, then we do that over flying commercial," Brayden explained.

I couldn't keep from jumping in my seat. I was going to fly on a private plane for the first time! "It's crazy. Sometimes I forget that you guys are from some of the biggest families in the eastern hemisphere. Then I find out you have a private plane."

"Trust me, it has more downsides than up," Hudson said.

"Yeah, but a private plane is one of them," Parker grinned, shoving Hudson with his shoulder. "Let Trouble be excited about the experience, would ya?"

Hudson looked back over at me and gave me a small smirk. "If you think a plane is cool, then you should see the yacht my dad has for his ocean research projects."

"What are the chances of him letting us have a party on it over the summer?" Parker asked, pouncing on the idea.

"Depends. Are you coming?" Hudson asked Parker with a raised eyebrow.

I felt my mouth fall open, then started to laugh. "Oh my God! Hudson just made a joke!"

The whole table broke out into laughter, and I wasn't sure if it was from Hudson's joke or if they were laughing at me.

"Yeah, yeah, laugh it up everyone. See if I get a super badass toy and share it with you all. Ungrateful assholes," Parker said, pouting.

"Lailah, are you going home for the summer?" Hudson inquired.

"Yeah, since it will be for three months, I decided that would be best," I said. "I could use the work at the diner for more spending money."

The guys all looked at each other as I shared this information, and I could tell they didn't love the idea. Yet none of them said anything about it and let it drop, moving on to other subjects.

As everyone dispersed throughout the house, I took the plate Sarah set aside for Micah and took it with me. I paused outside his bedroom door; I saw the light was on, but the room was quiet. I knocked and waited but didn't hear anyone moving around. I knocked again, louder, but still no response. I sighed and almost turned to walk away but changed my mind, squaring my shoulders. I grasped his door handle and pushed the door open.

I found Micah laying on his bed in just boxers and head-phones. His foot tapped to the music as he was lost in the song, eyes closed. Looking around his room, I was amazed. The walls were a dark slate gray with black and white photos of concerts and bands covering the walls. An electric guitar hung on the wall with an amp under it. His desk was covered in clothes, clearly unused. His room told me more about him that I had learned in the months I'd known him.

Unsure of what to do, I decided I'd already made the choice to leave the dessert in his room, so I entered. Walking over to his desk, I shoved aside some clothes and set the plate down. I was just going to walk out of the room, but I felt Micah's gaze on me. Glancing over at the bed, I saw his deep sapphire eyes trained on me. Frozen like a deer in the headlights, I wasn't sure what to do. Suddenly, this seemed like a horrible idea.

Slowly, he pulled his headphones off and settled them around his neck. "Who the fuck told you that you could come into my room?"

"Sarah said this was your favorite dessert, and I didn't want Parker to eat it all, so I brought you the last piece," I rambled. "I did knock, but you didn't answer, so I thought you might not be in here."

"Which gives you the right to come into my room?" Micah challenged.

My shoulders sagged in defeat. "I'm sorry, you're right, I shouldn't have come into your room without your permission."

Micah brushed his hands through his hair, which was loose and fell past his shoulders. I didn't think I had ever seen it down before. "Fuck, it's fine, just don't do it again."

I gave him a sharp nod and hurried out of the room.

"Lailah . . ."

Looking over my shoulder, I saw Micah standing by the desk. "Thank you. It is my favorite."

"You're welcome. Sleep well," I said, giving him a soft smile and closing the door behind me.

Thursday came and went. Cami and I spent most of the day together since I wouldn't see her for the next two weeks. She helped me pack for staying at Brayden's, which I was thankful for, not being a fashionista. Cami warned me that there might be fancy dinner parties and other posh events I hadn't even considered. Slowly, Cami was adding to my closet, trying to even out the trendy with my sassy saying shirts.

"Girl, what are you wearing tomorrow? This is a big deal, after all. You only get to meet your in-laws for the first time once," Cami said, hands on her hips, looking over the options we had laid out.

My stomach clenched at her words. For me, it was still hard to wrap my head around the fact Brayden and I were dating, let alone bonded for life. "You pick, I think I'm going to throw up."

Cami just rolled her eyes at me. "It wouldn't be so bad if you had told me that the only winter coat you had made you look like a damn green Michelin Man."

"That jacket will keep you warm in negative degree weather, I'll have you know," I said, defending myself. "How was I supposed to know I would need to worry about dinner parties?"

Cami grabbed my hand and dragged me out of my room and

down the stairs. We went past the library into the other side of the house that I really didn't go into. Stopping at a door, Cami knocked, and without waiting for an answer, she flung the door open.

"Cami, how many times do I have to tell you the purpose of knocking is to let the occupant answer you?" Beth said, looking up from her tablet, seated in an overstuffed wingback armchair.

"Lala needs a winter jacket for her trip to Brayden's. I know you have like fifty of them, and you're closer to her size than I am," Cami said, marching right into Beth's closet.

Shaking her head, Beth went back to reading as if this was a normal occurrence.

"I'm sorry, Beth, I keep telling her I have a winter coat and that I don't need to borrow another one," I said apologetically.

Beth looked up at me with a gentle smile. "It's quite alright, Cami isn't wrong. The Dolton family is a prominent family, and the chances of you going to a party are high. Brayden is the heir to the Dolton estate and will be expected to be there as well. You being his significant other means you will attend with him, so you'll need the jacket."

I gulped. "You make this sound like I'm dating royalty."

"In a way," Beth said, setting aside her tablet and giving me her full attention. "All of the boys are from the five most influential families on this side of the world. It is the purpose of the Elementi to be present where demons would most likely attack. We can gain access to almost anywhere with the connections we have from the five boys alone. Add in the network of thousands of other Elementi placed all over the world, and we are unstoppable."

Even with all the extra studying I'd done with Professor Phillips, I'd only seen the tip of the iceberg of the influence this society has.

"When you get back from holiday, we will get you more up to speed," Beth said as if reading my mind.

Cami popped back out of the closet with two jackets in her

hands, and both of them looked classier than anything I'd ever owned.

"What do you think, Gucci or Burberry?" Cami asked, holding them out for approval.

Beth didn't answer, she just looked at her sister for a moment.

"You're right, she needs both," Cami said, folding them over her arm and heading back out of the room.

Beth chuckled at whatever expression was on my face and waved me to chase after her little sister.

"Thank you, Beth," I said before leaving her room.

Back in my room, I took in the two large suitcases and my carry-on pack, all ready to go. "I don't think I have ever had this much luggage for a two-week trip before."

"Then you have been vacationing all wrong, Lala," Cami pointed out from where she was lounging on my bed, eating popcorn.

"I've only been on family vacations, and we are not the type to do anything crazy. Really, we were lucky to get one since my parents had the diner to run."

"What if I came out this summer and we went on a girls' trip?" Cami suggested.

I flopped on the bed next to her. "Really? Oh man, that would be amazing."

"Lovely. Because it was going to happen whether you liked it or not."

Grinning, I took the whole bowl of popcorn, dumped it on her head, and ran out of the room before she could retaliate.

CHAPTER 20

LAILAH

Stepping onto the plane, I felt like I was still sleeping, because this could only be a dream. Moments before, Beth had dropped us off at the small private airport, where they took our bags, leading us out onto the tarmac where the plane was. I'd envisioned something close to what I saw from watching *Criminal Minds*, but this was way nicer than that.

Boarding, I found myself in what looked like a living room with a geometric-patterned carpet and a black suede couch, throw pillows and all. Next was a set of captain's chairs with a small table between them. On the other side was a larger table and four chairs around it. Setting my stuff down, I went down the small hallway and found a bedroom with a bathroom adjacent.

"Holy shit," I muttered, taking it all in.

Brayden peeked his head in, grinning at the shocked look I must have had on my face. He walked over to me and took my face in his hands, placing a gentle kiss on my nose, then my lips. I grinned up at him and caught his lips, wrapping my arms around his waist.

"It's going to be nice having you all to myself these next

couple of weeks," he murmured against my lips. "You've been a hard lady to get alone."

Butterflies fluttered in my stomach as our energy wrapped around each other, making me sigh. It was almost like our powers missed interacting as much as we did. We agreed to keep things between us on campus limited so I could study at the library hidden in the Elementi's private section. If I was at the house, Parker always found some way to talk me into playing with him and getting distracted.

"Hate to break up the love fest, but they are ready to take off as soon as we're seated," Micah said from the doorway.

Micah, I was finding, was the biggest cock-block in existence. He always seemed to know when Brayden and I had found time alone, and suddenly he needed something. I glared at him as Brayden took my hand, and we walked up front to the couch, where he pulled me down next to him. Micah plopped down in one of the captain's chairs and immediately placed on his headphones.

"How long did you say the flight would be?" I asked, resting my head on Brayden's shoulder.

"Smooth flight, a little under two hours. It sure beats the ten-hour drive or the fourteen-hour train ride," Brayden said as he ran his hand up and down my back absently.

I loved that he was always doing little touches like that when we were at home. Other than my parents, physical touch wasn't something I had practice with. Brayden seemed to need it, and I was more than happy to oblige, having gotten a taste of how good it could feel. Most nights, I'd taken to sleeping in his room, and even though we didn't have sex, it was nice to be held. After the last experience in his room, it had made me paranoid of being heard again. We made up for it in the sitting room we had taken ownership over.

"Sorry to disturb you, Mr. Dolton, but can I get you or Ms. Mackenzie anything?" a strange male voice asked.

I opened my eyes and found that I'd drifted off to sleep and was now laying on Brayden's lap, curled up on the couch. A flight attendant was standing, poised ready to take care of any need we might have.

"I would love some coffee," Brayden said, then looked down at me. "Do we have the chai tea?"

"Yes, we made sure we had it stocked per your request, along with the sugar cookies," the attendant said as I sat up. "Would you like me to get those for you as well?"

"That would be great, thank you," Brayden said as I just blinked at him. Swiftly, the attendant went off to grab our requests.

"You made a special request to have chai tea and sugar cookies stocked on your dad's plane?" I said, shocked.

"Of course. I also had them make sure we had Micah's favorite energy drink and Cheetos, along with my favorite organic fair trade coffee. It's another perk of having your own plane. It has what you like," Brayden said, amused at my reaction.

I leaned over and kissed him. "Thank you, that was very sweet."

"Not as sweet as you," he countered.

"Barf. Barf, barf, barf. You're going to make me sick." Micah groaned, apparently having decided to include himself in our conversation.

"Fuck you, no one asked your opinion," Brayden shot back.

I looked over at him in surprise. He never talked to Micah that way, no matter how mean he was.

"Is this what I have to look forward to this whole trip, because if so, I need to invest in some barf bags. It's sickening to watch you both."

"You're just jealous," Brayden said, yanking me onto his lap and wrapping his arms around me. "I have her all to myself, and I plan to live it up before you lot join the party. Don't be too disappointed when she keeps coming back to me, ignoring you. It happens when they practically lose their virginity to you."

Micah's face darkened into a scowl. "How the fuck can you be so chill knowing that eventually you and four other people will be sticking their dicks in the same woman? I know I'm no saint, but that's just fucked up, and the fact that she is totally willing makes me disgusted."

Micah's words slapped me across the face as he verbalized my worst fears. If he was feeling that way, then did the other three think the same thing? Would I fail at the one purpose I had—to bring this group of warriors together—by splitting them further apart? The angels picked the wrong person. I wasn't going to be able to do this; I wasn't strong enough. Seeing this unfold around me sent me reeling; I just wanted to leave and hide somewhere, but I couldn't while trapped on this plane.

"Angel. Lailah, wake up," Brayden said, shaking me and pulling me up so I was facing him and straddling his legs. His worried eyes searched mine. "Lailah, take a deep breath, you need to calm down."

I tried to do as he said and noticed how fast my heart was racing and how ragged my breath was. Was I having another episode? I looked around and saw the cabin of the plane filled with a slight haze of golden power.

Oh my God, was I going to crash the plane if I didn't calm down?

Any calm I had was now blown away, and new panic crashed into me. I was too dangerous to have around; anything could set me off. What was even scarier was that I couldn't even tell what was real and what was a dream. Another set of arms grabbed me, and I was whirled around to face Micah. I couldn't look at him after hearing those words come out of his mouth, real or not. I was fairly certain he felt that way, even if it was a dream.

"Lailah, you need to get your shit under control before you destroy this fucking plane," Micah snapped, shaking me a little, forcing me to look into his eyes again.

He trapped me with his burning gaze, and this time, I clung

to it like a life preserver. Something moved behind me, but I couldn't lose focus. If I did, I would drown for sure.

"No, Brayden, gentle isn't going to work this time. We need her to snap out of it *now*," Micah said, his hold on my arms so tight I might bruise. "See if you can ground her. If we get the edge off, it might be just enough to steady her."

It was surreal to be trapped in my brain, unable to control what my body was doing, lost in the flow of power. Another pair of hands settled on my hips, and I could feel his energy surge into me, but it didn't fill me. Instead, his power seemed to be absorbing mine, but it wasn't working fast enough for me to fight through this power-induced panic.

"Micah, reach out and see if you can burn off some of the energy. My power isn't strong enough this high in the air," Brayden said, fear in his voice.

Micah faltered at this suggestion, fear and doubt creeping into his eyes. I was right—he didn't want there to be any chance he might bond with me. He was more willing to let the plane crash than to possibly end up with me bound to him for eternity.

"Micah, get your head out of your ass and do something," Brayden yelled, snapping Micah back to attention.

CHAPTER 21

MICAH

Panic surged through my body. I couldn't help her. My power was too volatile. I could hurt her. Nobody understood how much effort it took to keep my power in check, and now he wanted me to use it against Lailah!

Fear screamed at me through Lailah's eyes, which latched onto mine. Behind that fear, I saw hope that I might be able to help and save us. The plane rattled around us like we were in rough turbulence, but I knew it was Lailah's power trying to burst from the confinement of the small space. I had to do something, and trying to get her to snap out of it on her own wasn't working. I took a deep breath in, practicing the meditation that I'd been taught so long ago.

The need to close my eyes was strong, but I couldn't leave Lailah alone without an anchor. Inwardly, I traveled deep down into my center, finding the well of my power. I always thought of it in a metal box wrapped in chains and padlocks, keeping it at bay. Slowly, I started to unlock my power, and halfway through, it started to leak from the lid. Pausing, not wanting to let more out, I directed the wild flame upward and down through my arms into my hands.

I heard Lailah gasp when my energy lashed out at her,

flames licking up her arms. I could feel it devouring her excess energy, reveling in the ability to wreak havoc with my blessing. Lailah's body began to shake as she regained control, sweat breaking out on her forehead. My power coursed through her body, and I felt her strength and determination, but it was overwhelmed by fear and doubt. It was then that I realized that she and I might be more alike than I thought. Both of us feared our power and how dangerous it could be. She was just in the beginning stages of this, and it brought back memories of my own journey.

Refusing to revisit the past, I shook them away and refocused on what was happening right in front of me. Her eyes were clearer now, more in control. I don't know when she brought her hands up to grab my arms, but I could feel them bridging the connection. We were a perfect circuit as our energy flowed between us.

"Lailah, I need you to help me push my power out of your body." It was having way too much fun for it to listen to me alone calling it back. "Pull your power back from me. Make sure not to leave anything behind. I will do the same, but once you have your power back, I need it to flush out the rest of mine before we cut the connection."

What I wasn't telling her was that if her power accepted mine, then we would start the bonding sequence, and I was definitely not ready for that shit to happen. This whole experience showed me how not ready I was to be responsible to care for someone other than myself. If Brayden hadn't challenged me, I would have waited too long to use my powers. That was always a last resort, not considered until it was our only chance.

I grunted as Lailah thrust my power out of her body, taming it to her will with ease. Searching her for anything left behind, I slammed my power back into its box and locked it down tight. I pulled away from her, flopping back into my seat. Panting, my adrenaline still high, I let my head hang between my knees as I tried to slow my heart back down. When I felt as centered as I got, I looked up and found Lailah cradled in Brayden's arms, tears streaming down her face.

Brayden looked up at me and mouthed *thank you* before turning his attention back to Lailah. He knew what he'd asked of me, the risk I'd taken. It was proof that he was worthy of being her guardian, and I had a long way to go before I could even consider that. Leaning back into the chair, I pulled my headphones up and got lost in the music, the only thing that seemed to calm me down.

CHAPTER 22

LAILAH

It took the rest of the flight to calm me down. Brayden took me to the back bedroom and cuddled me close, playing with my hair and chatting about nothing in particular. I just listened to the sound of his voice and savored the feel of his body against mine. It kept me grounded to what was really happening.

"Up for talking about it?" Brayden asked, brushing my hair out of my face to place a kiss on my temple.

I wanted to pour my soul out to him, but I didn't even know where to start. "It always seems so real."

"The dream?" Brayden asked, continuing to comb through my hair.

"I never know when it starts, or how long I've been trapped in that strange reality until one of you pulls me out of it." Twisting, I turned to Brayden. I needed to see his face. "This time was much worse, but I think it's because I believed it so much more. That, or the demon taint on me is getting worse," I said, shivering at the thought.

Brayden's brows furrowed. "Explain that to me."

"When I was in the coffee shop, I knew it wasn't normal for me to want to hurt someone. I have always tried to avoid conflict in my life, and for me to attack first was just out of character." I paused, thinking back on this last episode. "This time it was more centered around you guys. I was more of a passenger watching you two fight."

"Wait, the two of us, as in Micah and myself?" Brayden asked, and I nodded. "Angel, Micah and I have been best friends since we were both twelve. We might argue, but we've gone way past the point of fighting each other. I know too many things that can hurt him, secrets I've kept. We don't fight."

"That was the first clue that something wasn't right. I've seen Micah fight with the others, but never as cruel as he was in my dream. It was almost like it was searching for what my biggest fear was and made him say it," I said, trying to explain.

"Fear is the greatest weapon demons have. They feed off of it, along with anger and deceit." Brayden cupped my cheek and let his thumb stroke against my skin, his eyes sad. "I wish we had found you sooner so you would be more prepared for this. It kills me that I wasn't able to do anything to help you. Thank God we had Micah here."

"Guess that's why they assigned five of you to deal with me, one wasn't going to be enough for all this crazy," I teased, giving him a small smile.

"Hmm, maybe Parker has been right this whole time. You are trouble," he murmured before his lips connected with mine in a slow kiss. He nuzzled into the side of my neck, whispering, "I'm glad you're okay."

Wrapping my arms around his shoulders, I held him close, needing the comfort as much as he did. "Me too."

A soft knock on the door had Brayden pulling away from me and moving off the bed to answer it.

"If we could have you back in your seats, we're about to land," the attendant said.

"Thank you, we'll be up shortly," Brayden said, then looked back at me with a grin, holding out his hand. "Ready to see where I live?"

Pushing aside all that had happened, I rolled out of bed and grasped his hand. I let him pull me to the other chairs near Micah.

When we sat down, Micah pulled off his headphones and met my gaze. "You doing okay?"

I blinked a few times before answering, startled that he would ask. "I'll manage. Thank you for whatever it is that you did. I still can't really tell what happened, but I know without your power, I might have killed us."

Micah searched my face for a moment, then looked down at his hands. "You're welcome."

I assumed that was the end of our conversation, so I turned to look out the window, but then he drew me back to him.

"Look, I know I'm an ass most of the time and not easy to be around, but if you need some tips on handling your powers, you can always ask. Fire is the strongest and most unruly of the elements for an Elementi Warrior to handle. After experiencing your power, I think it might even be stronger than mine, which is fucking crazy. If this is what you're like with only bonding to one of us, I can't even imagine. No one needs that much power," Micah said, starting to ramble. "What I mean is that I get it, fearing yourself and your powers. So, if you need help or someone to talk to, I'm around."

I struggled to keep a blank face at the shock hearing him talk. Micah was offering to help me of his own free will. Brayden squeezed my hand, but I didn't look at him, not wanting to jinx it.

"That means a lot, Micah," I said with a smile. "Thank you."

He flicked his eyes up at me guardedly. "Don't make a fucking deal about it, we're a team, right? We can't have you being a liability and getting us killed with your random episodes."

Ah, there was normal Micah. That didn't last long.

"Got it," I grinned, knowing it would irritate him. Brayden chuckled.

"Don't you even fucking start, Dolton," Micah challenged, pointing a finger at his best friend.

The landing was smooth, and we touched down without any other excitement. The flight staff didn't seem to act at all like the plane had almost crashed when they shook Brayden's hand as we disembarked. I still had no idea where it was that we landed. The airport sign was in another language, so that didn't give me much help. Brayden caught my hand, and we headed into the small building of the airport where they checked my passport and put a new stamp in it. On the page in bold letters was 'Republic of Austria, Graz.'

"Oh my God, we're in Austria," I said, doing a little hop of excitement. "I've always wanted to come to Austria, the art and history here is incredible. Just when I didn't think you could be more perfect, you live in Austria of all places."

Unable to contain myself, I bounced around, ready to hit the sights and savor what this amazing city had to offer. I was in one of the places in the world where the renaissance area was preserved for your viewing pleasure.

"Oh my God, I'm going to spend Christmas in Austria! Please tell me we can go to the Advent night markets!?"

Micah looked at me like I had lost my mind, and Brayden just had the biggest smile I had seen on his face in a while.

"Mr. Dolton, Mr. Lazonick, welcome home," a sharply dressed man said, bowing his head slightly to the boys before he turned to me. "Ms. Mackenzie, it is lovely to meet you. I'm Martin, valet to the Dolton household. If you would follow me, I'll take you to the house."

Wrapping my arm around Brayden's, I leaned in and whispered, "Your family has a butler?"

Brayden glanced down at me, smirking. "Martin is more than a butler to us, but yes, I guess his job would fall under that title."

Martin led us out to a beautiful white Mercedes SUV, opening the door for me to get in the back seat. Micah hopped in the front, and Brayden joined me in the back. The windows were so tinted it was hard to see the world around me, but it was much too cold to open the windows. Thankfully, I had two weeks to take in the sights.

The whole town was covered in a light dusting of snow, making it all seem so picturesque. Garland and other Christmas decorations were tastefully placed along the buildings, making it seem like a hallmark film. I felt like a little kid with my face plastered to the window, but I couldn't help myself. This was one of the top ten places I had always wanted to visit, and I was drinking it all in.

"Imagine my surprise when talking about places we both wanted to travel to, my hometown was listed," Brayden said, squeezing my leg, trying to draw my attention.

I leaned over and planted a dramatic kiss on Brayden's lips, making him laugh. "Thank you for keeping this a surprise."

"Seems like I might need to do them more often, seeing how happy you are," Brayden said, wrapping his arm around me.

"If they all are this amazing, be my guest. I love surprises."

In my mind, I was thinking Brayden would live in a mansion like the one in *The Sound of Music*. Instead, we drove down an alleyway to the back side of a historic four-story home in the middle of the city. It was whitewashed, with dark wooden shutters that had garland around them, and a single candle in each window. I saw traces of what must have been ivy growing on the house when the weather was warmer. Everything about it was charming and welcoming.

Micah led the way as we entered through the back door into the kitchen. It was like I had just stepped into a storybook. I half expected Cinderella to pop out from somewhere, it was so whimsical. Instead of Cinderella appearing in the kitchen, a young girl walked in, wearing some type of princess dress with her long, brown hair a wild mess. She looked up, surprised to see us in the kitchen, but once she recognized who it was, her face lit up.

"Bray-Bray!" she squealed, running and jumping into his arms, causing Brayden to drop the bag he was holding.

"Oof, Hope, look how big you've gotten," Brayden said, hugging the girl tightly. "Hey Hope, I have someone I would like you to meet."

"You do? I love making new friends," Hope said as he turned so she was facing me.

"Hope, I would like you to meet Lailah, my girlfriend. Lailah, this is Hope, the youngest of the Dolton gang," Brayden introduced before setting down the wiggling mess of purple tulle that came running over to me.

Without hesitation, Hope tossed herself at me next, not giving me much time to brace myself. She was young and small but could have easily knocked me over if I didn't get my balance. Hope wrapped her arms around my neck and snuggled in for a hug and a kiss on my cheek.

"I like you, you're really pretty," Hope announced before her face scrunched up all serious. "Will you play dress up with me? I feel like you would make a very pretty princess like me."

I giggled, unable to hold it in at the onslaught of pure emotion only kids can provide. "I would love to play dress up with you."

"Hope, no one wants to play stupid dress up with you," Kayley said, making an appearance in the kitchen, hands on her hips as she scowled at her sister. Then her gaze landed on Micah. "Hi, Micah."

Hope and I watched the interaction silently, and I noticed Kayley's cheeks start to pink as she talked to Micah.

"Kayley, are you getting sick? Your face is all red," Hope blurted out, breaking the silence that had filled the room.

Kayley glared at her sister and stormed out of the room, her face now red for an entirely different reason. I set Hope back down, and she took my hand, swinging it back and forth as she hummed a song I didn't recognize.

"Hope, why don't we go show Lailah where her room is?"

Brayden asked, grinning at me from ear to ear, his eyes shining with laughter.

Apparently, I had been adopted by Hope and wasn't going to shake the little princess anytime soon. "Sounds good to me."

The rest of the home was a mix of traditional carved wood accents and modern updates. The stairs were an ornate wooden spiral staircase that went up all four stories. We stopped on the third floor and walked down a narrow hallway that had doors on either side. Hope skipped her way down the hall until she threw open the third door on the left. Brayden rested his hand on my lower back, guiding me to follow her into the room.

It was magical. Even though the room was tiny, it had so much personality in it. The walls were painted a soft blue color, with white lace curtains bordering the one window. Walking over, I peeked out and found that the house next to Brayden's was shorter, so I got a view of the city. Turning, I took in the wrought iron bed frame that took up most of the room, but it had ornate designs in the headboard and the foot rail. The bedding was soft and inviting like the rest of the room. A small dresser with four drawers and a narrow closet completed my investigation of the room.

"What do you think?" Brayden asked, watching my reaction.

I smiled widely at him and walked over, wrapping my arms around his waist. "It's lovely."

"I know it's a little smaller than what you're used to, but in a city, living with this many people in a house doesn't leave much extra room," Brayden rambled, trying to justify himself.

Shutting him up, I placed a soft kiss on his lips. "Stop. I think it's utterly charming. Besides, my hope is that we will have so much to do that I will only be sleeping here."

"Come see my room!" Hope said, tugging on my coat.

"There you are," a young woman said, standing out in the hall, giving Hope a pointed look. "I told you not to bother them right away and let them unpack first."

Looking up at me, she smiled, and instantly, I knew she was

another one of Brayden's sisters. The fact they had the same hazel eyes helped, but the smile was a dead giveaway. "It is so nice to meet you, I'm Charlotte."

I gave her a small wave since I was still in Brayden's arms. "Lovely to meet you too, I'm Lailah."

"Charlie, I was going to show Lailah my room," Hope said with a stomp of her foot, crossing her arms.

Charlotte dropped her gaze at her little sister, her whole demeanor shifting into a woman I didn't want to mess with. "Hope Sophia Dolton, that is not how we act in this house. Lailah is going to be with us for a few days, and she will see your room. Now come here and let them settle in."

Hope didn't move, just stood her ground, glaring at her sister.

"One... two..." Charlotte started counting.

Before she made it to three, Hope dashed out of the room and down the hall without any further fuss.

"Do you have younger siblings?" Charlotte asked, looking back at me.

"One younger brother, but he was born an old man, far more interested in taking over the world one book at a time. Our biggest challenge was getting him to stop asking us to read the newspaper to him," I laughed, thinking of Kyle.

"Lucky," Charlotte said, heading off in the direction Hope had gone.

CHAPTER 23

LAILAH

Brayden left me to go unpack in his own room and let me settle in once Martin had brought up my suitcase and travel bag. There was just enough room in the closet for the few dresses and the winter coats that I had. Everything else went into the dresser. Thankfully, I had talked Cami out of making me pack even more than she already had. It seemed everyone on this floor shared one bathroom that was in the middle of the hall.

Wandering down the hall, I entered the bathroom with my toiletries and washed my face. There was something about traveling that always made me feel like I needed to wash up after. There was no shower, just a large claw-foot tub with a handheld shower attachment to the faucet. Shelves lined the wall, holding different colored towels and everyone else's bathroom items in baskets. I smiled as I found one with my name pinned to it, along with some cream towels. It seemed that Brayden's family had gone the extra mile to make sure I felt welcome.

After cleaning up, I went back to my room, flopped on the bed, and texted Cami.

LAILAH:

Made it to Brayden's. It's so cute and his sisters
are adorable, especially Hope.

CAMI:

Hope is the best! Glad you made it alright, make
sure to send me a lot of pictures!

LAILAH:

You got it! TTYL

Turning so I was looking out the window from my bed, I saw it had started to snow. Flurries danced in the wind, making it look so inviting. The soft dusting on the roofs in my line of sight seemed to add something magical to the world. I couldn't have been in a more picturesque place for Christmas.

My bedroom door crashed open, and Hope came running in and jumped on my bed excitedly. "Daddy's home! He never comes home so early in the day; he's even going to have dinner with us!"

"That is very exciting, I can't wait to meet your dad," I said, grabbing her before she rolled off the bed. "Is your mother going to be at dinner too?"

Hope paused and frowned at the mention of her mother. "I don't know, Mommy's sick, she keeps forgetting things and hurting herself by accident. Ms. Tabitha tells me that Mommy will get better if she keeps taking her medicine, but I tried it once, and it tastes gross."

"I'm sorry to hear your mom isn't feeling well. Who is Ms. Tabitha?" I asked. I already knew her mom wasn't doing well from what Kayley had told us.

Hope picked at some of the beads on her dress, pouting a little before she answered me. "Ms. Tabitha is our governess, but I don't like her, but I'm not allowed to say that, so don't tell Charlie that I told you."

"I promise, cross my heart," I said, making an X over my heart. "Why don't you like her?"

"She's scary, one time I caught her putting funny-smelling stuff in Mom's tea, and I asked her what it was. Ms. Tabitha told me it was medicine, but it didn't come out of a pill bottle like the other stuff Mommy takes. I tried to tell Daddy, but he just told me I was too little to understand," Hope said, jutting out her bottom lip.

Unsure of what to say, I poked Hope in the side gently, trying to get her attention. But instead, she fell over, letting out a peal of laughter. Grinning, I sat up and started to tickle her until she was crying and gasping for breath.

"What's going on here?" Brayden asked, leaning against the door frame, a soft smile on his face.

"Tickle war, but it seems that someone didn't put up much of a fight," I teased, freeing Hope to jump off the bed and run to hide behind Brayden.

"It was a sneak attack," Hope said, hands on her hips like some superhero.

Brayden chuckled, shaking his head. "Lucky for you that it's dinner time and father wants us all down in the dining room."

"Yeah," Hope whooped and tugged on Brayden's hand to get him moving. "Come on, we don't want to keep Daddy waiting."

Slipping off my bed, I followed behind as we made our way back to the first floor. The dining room was inviting, with a large wooden table that could easily seat twelve people. Place settings were out and candles already lit, waiting for us to be seated. Brayden pulled out a chair for me and helped push it back in. The rest of the family filtered in and took their seats, all of them looking excited, and I didn't think it was because of me.

Looking around the table, I noticed there was one sibling I hadn't met yet, Brayden's younger brother David. His chocolate hair was shaggy, much like a young Justin Bieber, and his eyes were a soft brown color. He had on a red and white soccer jersey that I would assume belonged to the Austrian soccer team. In a house full of girls, this young man was all boy. He must be thrilled to have Brayden and Micah back in the house.

Then an older gentleman walked in with a beautiful woman on his arm. The power couple that were Brayden's parents. His father was still in his suit from work, adding to his very orderly look. His dark brown hair was heavily salt and peppered, along with his neatly managed beard. His glasses had a wooden frame, which seemed to compliment his pale green eyes. His wife was stunning, even as she was letting her hair grow out to her now silvery-gray color. It was thick and full, cut in a very trendy just-past-the-chin bob. She was thin, almost too thin, her skin crinkled slightly as if it was lacking in nutrients. Her beautiful deep hazel eyes that leaned more towards the blue side seemed to be glassy, like she wasn't really there with us.

His father walked up to where I was sitting, so I rose, as did Brayden.

"Lailah, it is so lovely to meet you and to have you in our home," he said, smiling as he reached out to take my hand, then covered it with the other and gripped it tightly.

"Thank you so much for having me. It's very kind of you, Mr. Dolton," I said, returning his smile.

"Oh, now, none of that. You're family now that you and Brayden have bonded. Call me Oliver and my wife Adriana. Hopefully, one day, you will feel comfortable enough to call us Mom and Dad as well," Oliver said, his eyes misting over with emotion.

I slid my hand into Brayden's, feeling overwhelmed with emotion at how they welcomed me with open arms. "I would like that. Thank you, Oliver."

"Now let's get settled and eat the delicious meal that has been prepared for us," Oliver said, walking Adriana to her seat and getting her settled before taking his place at the head of the table.

Brayden's mother remained silent through the whole exchange and moved mechanically, as if she were just going through the motions. I could see why Kayley and Hope thought their mother was not well. Then, as she took a sip from her wine glass, it was like she snapped out of her fog and realized where she was.

"Oh, honey, you're home in time for dinner, what do we owe the occasion?" Adriana asked as she took the basket of rolls, helping herself and passing it along to Brayden.

"I wouldn't dream of missing meeting our son's girlfriend. It's the first time he's ever introduced us to someone special, isn't it, dear?" Oliver said, not even trying to address the fact she'd missed the whole introduction that happened right in front of her.

"Goodness me, how could that have slipped my mind," she said, peeking past Brayden, surprised to see me sitting there. "It's so lovely to have you in our home, sweetie. Brayden is one lucky man from what I hear." She grinned, winking at me before passing the platter of meat but not taking any.

"I have to say, I feel pretty lucky to have a guy like him. You raised your son to be a wonderful man," I said, resting my hand on Brayden's leg and leaning against him.

Adriana smiled widely at me. "Oh, now I really like her."

Oliver smiled and chuckled us as he dug into his food. Once everyone had filled their plates, we all dove in, not talking much. I watched, taking in the dynamic of the family, trying to get a feel for what normal was for them. Charlotte helped Hope by cutting up her food if she was having a tough time with it. I had the feeling that Charlotte was the real mom here, for the time being. David and Micah talked quietly about sports and other boy subjects, and a disgruntled Kayley poked at her food. My guess was that it had something to do with not sitting next to Micah, seeing as I was on his other side.

"Lailah, tell us about your family. Brayden hasn't been sharing much information with us," Adriana said, drawing me out of my musings.

"I'm the middle child. I have an older brother, Dylan, who is in school to be a lawyer. Apparently, getting an MBA wasn't enough for him, so he needs a second degree. Kyle is my little brother, he's a freshman in high school, taking all AP classes and smarter than all of us," I said, smiling to myself as I thought of my brothers. "My parents, Luke and Bonnie, own a diner, and it's the best place to eat in town."

"Isn't that lovely. Did your mother teach you her skills in the kitchen?" Adriana asked.

"That was something we all learned, whether we liked it or not. Each of us has spent the summers working there to make money; there were no handouts if there was a way to earn it," I said, remembering the early years washing dishes and busing tables. "I assume that will be what I spend my summer doing until Cami comes to visit."

"Camilla, how is that dear girl?" Adriana inquired, pushing Brayden out of her way when he leaned in to get more food.

"Cami is Cami, living life on the edge and pushing my boundaries to try new things," I laughed.

"Seems like she's bounced back from all that mess of last year. I thought we were going to lose her for good this time," Oliver interjected.

His statement caught me off guard. What had he meant by that? But he started up again before I could think on it too much.

"Enough of that talk. Brayden, what do you have planned for your time here? Can we still expect you at the shareholders' Christmas party next Saturday evening?" Oliver asked.

"Of course. I made sure Lailah knew about it so that we would come prepared," Brayden said, taking the chance to get another helping of potatoes.

"Very good. Micah, will you be attending? You are a shareholder, after all," Oliver queried.

I turned to look at Micah, my eyes wide in surprise. He, on the other hand, scowled down at his food, gripping his knife tightly.

"Is *she* going to be there?" Micah bit out.

"Not if you're going. No need to have both of you there," Oliver said, simply.

This information caused him to relax slightly, so I wasn't worried he would stab the table again. "Fine, I'll go, but if she does show up, I'm not to be held at fault for what happens."

Oliver grunted, nodding his head sharply. "That is fair."

I had so many questions, but I knew that this was not a subject I could ask about now. Who was this woman that Micah hated so much that he wouldn't share the same space as her?

The rest of the meal was uneventful and filled with trivia about Graz and Austria in general. Adriana and Oliver gave many suggestions on fun places to visit and museums to check out.

"I did come up with my own ideas, you know," Brayden grumbled.

"Oh honey, I'm sorry, are we butting in too much on this? Forgive your mother, it's hard to remember you're all grown up and have a wife already," Adriana said, patting Brayden's hand.

I froze and looked around the table to see if the others had caught what she said. It wasn't the fact that I wanted to keep how serious our relationship was; it was more that I didn't know what was common knowledge in their family. Did the younger ones know about the Elementi? What about the Blessed Warriors?

"Darling," Oliver said, his voice full of caution.

Adriana sucked in a breath and covered her mouth with her hand, her face awash with worry. Taking a moment, she cleared her throat and settled her hands back in her lap. "Right, well, it seems that I am getting tired. I think I'll turn in for the evening."

"Martin!" Oliver called.

Seconds later, the man himself was standing at the ready.

"Will you please escort Adriana to her room for the night?" Oliver requested.

Charlotte shot up from her seat, startling me. "I'll get her ready for bed."

"Charlotte, sit down. You are not her maid, you are her daughter. If she needs anything, she can call for Ms. Tabitha to help her," Oliver said, pointing for Charlotte to be seated.

"Dad," Charlotte started, but one look from her father had her shutting her mouth and sinking into her seat.

"The cook made us a lovely apple strudel, and I would hate for us not to appreciate the hard work that has gone into it," Oliver said, settling back in his seat.

"I love apple strudel. It's my favorite, just like you, Daddy!" Hope declared, causing us all to smile at how excited she was.

"My little princess has good taste," Oliver said, winking at her and making her giggle.

The strudel was amazing and everything that had been promised. Once done with the meal and bringing all the plates to the kitchen, I turned in for the night. Just as I was about to fall asleep, Brayden snuck into my room and cuddled up behind me, burrowing his face into the back of my neck.

"I hope I didn't offend you by giving you your own room. I didn't want to assume you would want to share one," Brayden murmured.

I smiled into the darkness of the room. "No, it's fine. I think if you had us sharing a room, it would have made me way too nervous. I don't know that we're quite there in our relationship just yet, and definitely not starting at your parents' house."

Brayden kissed my neck, pulling me even closer to him. "I'm excited for you to be here and with my family, but alone time with you is going to take some work."

"I'm sure we'll manage just fine for two weeks," I teased.

CHAPTER 24

LAILAH

There was no sleeping in when the house was as busy as the Dolton home was. Hope raced around the house with David as Charlotte tried—and failed—to keep them quiet. Kayley locked herself in the bathroom for what seemed like hours, so I had to find the one on the second floor to use. As I made my way back to my room to change and get ready for the day, I ran into Charlotte.

"I'm so sorry if they woke you up, we're a home full of early risers. Micah had to learn to wear earplugs growing up here if he wanted any peace," Charlotte said, brushing a strand of her long, wavy hair out of her face.

"Please don't worry about it, I am used to being up at the crack of dawn to go running, but since it's snowed, that has changed to swimming laps or working out in the gym," I said, resting my hand on her arm to reassure her.

Charlotte let out a huge breath as if she had been worried I would have been upset with her. "It would seem the snow is exactly what is getting everyone in a tizzy this morning. It snowed all night, and there's enough to go sledding. David and Hope are beside themselves with excitement, trying to convince Mom to let them go."

I turned to look out one of the front windows on the third floor, and sure enough, the world had turned white. Tracks in the snow showed where people had walked or driven through it so far this morning. The sun glinting off the pure whiteness made the world look like a picture.

"Sledding in this would be amazing. Do you think your mother will let them go if Brayden and I go with them?" I asked, looking at Charlotte over my shoulder.

Charlotte worried her lip as she thought. "She might, but sometimes the decisions she makes don't seem reasonable. After she lost Michael..."

"Yes, that makes sense," I said. Charlotte paused, giving me a questioning look. "Brayden told me about Michael, though it was more like he was forced into it when Kayley brought it up."

Charlotte rolled her eyes, shaking her head. "Of course Kayley needed to throw that in his face. Not like he doesn't have enough on his plate to deal with, she feels the need to add more."

"Siblings, right?" I said, giving her a light shove with my shoulder and a smirk. "Where is your mom? Let me go talk to her and see if I can get her to give us the go-ahead."

"Guess it can't hurt," Charlotte said, leading the way upstairs to the fourth floor.

The space up here was much more open and only had three doors along the hall. Charlotte walked to the first door and rapped on it, waiting a moment, then pushing the door open. I followed her inside and found a large study filled with shelves of books. There was also a large whiteboard taking up one whole wall that had math equations all over it. Sitting at a large vintage desk, Adriana sat flipping through pages of a book and scribbling notes down in a journal. Ink was covering her hands and had splattered on her white shirtsleeves.

"Mom," Charlotte said, heading over to the desk. "Mother."

Adriana acted as if she had no idea that we were even in the room, utterly focused on the work before her. Even with all my extra credit helping Hudson in his lab, I had no idea what she was working on. To me, it all looked like a foreign language or code to be deciphered.

"Charlotte, what are you doing in here? You know better than to bother your mother when she's like this," a woman said, walking in with a tray holding a tea set.

"Ms. Tabitha, I was just asking my mother if we could take everyone out sledding. She would never just let us leave without checking with her first," Charlotte said, looking like this woman had taken the wind out of her sails, head bowed, voice soft and unsure.

Ms. Tabitha was tall and willowy, with sharp facial features. If I had ever pictured a governess before, it would have been just like her. Gray hair pinned tightly back in a French twist, face bare of any makeup, and piercing dark brown eyes. Everything about this woman seemed rigid and cold. She set the tea down on the desk and poured a cup for Adriana, setting it next to the journal she was writing in. Without hesitation, Adriana paused in her work and took up the tea. Ms. Tabitha then handed her a small dish that had pills in it, and Adriana took them all in one gulp. Once done with that, she resumed her work, still not acknowledging anyone in the room.

As Ms. Tabitha picked up the tray and headed out of the room, she paused. "Since I was charged to look after all of you, then I will tell her I gave you permission to take them out. Go, enjoy time with your family. I know they aren't visiting for long, and getting outside will do the young ones good."

This woman was giving me whiplash. I couldn't decide if I liked her or not, she was full of contradictions. One moment she was upset to be here then she was sending us off for a nice day together. I decided to put a pin in that until I could get more information.

"Come on, before she changes her mind," Charlotte said, grabbing my hand and dragging me out of the room.

She led me down all the way to the kitchen, where everyone

was eating breakfast. Everyone but Micah—he must have been wearing his ear plugs. Brayden smiled at me over his cup of coffee, which I returned as I was handed a mug.

"Oh, I'm sorry, Martin, I don't drink coffee," I said, in reflex.

The older man just smiled patiently. "Then it is a good thing I handed you a cup of hot tea. We don't have any chai, but I hope this traditional Austrian Sacher blend is to your liking. They serve it only at the finest hotels in Vienna."

I took a tentative sip and then another, letting the flavor roll over my tongue. "It's wonderful, thank you. I might even need to get some so I can take it home with me."

"I am pleased that I was able to guess your taste; tea drinkers can be a fussy bunch. Speaking for myself, that is, being London-born and all," Martin said, ushering me to a seat next to Brayden. "Now, let's get you some breakfast. The cook is off on the weekends, but we all seem to make do with a simple fare."

Turns out their version of simple fare was far from simple. I was given a plate with a roll slathered in butter, a thick slice of ham, two soft boiled eggs, and a bowl of something called muesli, their version of cold oatmeal with fresh fruit and berries finished off with milk. Set on the table, there were also sweet pastries, croissants, and other small cakes with jam.

"Just for the record, this is not simple," I muttered as I navigated my way around all the food. Not being a breakfast person, this was overwhelming.

Charlotte sat on my other side and giggled. "Here in Austria, we believe that breakfast on the weekends is the main meal. It fortifies you for the day of fun ahead. Speaking of, we talked to Mom, and we are all going sledding!"

David jumped out of his chair, whooping, punching his fists into the air. Hope let out a screeching sound to show her excitement, wiggling in her seat and knocking over her glass of orange juice.

"Have fun, losers, I'm going to stay at the house and relax.

Besides, I wouldn't want to leave Micah all by himself," Kayley said, leaning back in her chair, sipping from her coffee mug.

"Why would you need to do that when I'm going with them?" Micah said, entering the kitchen and taking the proffered mug from Martin. "I promised David last night I would go if Mom said yes."

I tried not to gape as I took in this new side of Micah. One, he was being social and willing to participate in things, even making plans to do something fun. Then there was the fact he called Adriana *Mom*. I knew they had told me they would love it if I did that, but it was just strange to hear it come out of his mouth.

"Great, then I'm coming. I was only going to stay behind for you," Kayley said, doing a complete one-eighty.

"I thought you said sledding was stupid and who wants to spend time out in the cold getting wet snow down their backs?" David taunted.

"Shut up, no one asked you," Kayley said, slamming her mug down and storming out of the room.

Did she learn that from Micah?

"We should get ready, the sledding hill will only get busier the later it gets," Brayden said, sliding back his chair and taking his and Kayley's dishes to the sink.

"You really should stop doing things like that for her, she needs to learn responsibility," Charlotte said, frowning at Brayden.

At her words, Brayden looked sheepish, ducking his head from being called out. Shrugging his shoulders, he cleaned up after himself and headed out of the room. Hope dashed after him, yelling the whole way to her room how excited she was to go sledding. David finished his food and silently cleaned up and left the room. I couldn't put my finger on it, but there was something missing in him. Almost as if he felt like an outsider in his own home and was used to doing things alone.

"You forgot to put earplugs in last night, didn't you? Otherwise you wouldn't be up this early on break," Charlotte said, giving Micah a knowing look. "Or was there another reason to be awake?"

I saw the sideways glance in my direction, but I wasn't going to call her out on it. I was thoroughly intrigued by this new version of Micah.

"Like I said, I promised David I would go sledding with him. You and Lailah just beat me to asking Mom if we could go. The poor kid's a loner, and being in a house with all girls, home-schooling doesn't help. He needs time with guys, not sitting around watching you all do needlepoint or whatever the hell that old bat is teaching you."

Charlotte rolled her eyes and sighed. "It's not the middle ages, Micah. We don't learn needlepoint—until senior year, that is."

Micah tossed his cloth napkin at her, frowning before taking his dishes to the sink.

"It's refreshing to see someone give Micah a taste of his own medicine. Most of the time, people are too scared of him or too in love with him," I said, nudging Charlotte with my elbow.

Micah whirled and pointed a finger at me with a stern look on his face. "Don't get any wild ideas, woman."

Charlotte and I burst out laughing, causing him to storm out of the room.

Growing up in Wisconsin, it always snowed enough at least once that we could go sledding. To me, that meant going to a park that had a sledding hill and walking up and sledding down fifty times or so until your legs gave out. Sledding in Austria was on a whole other level. It took us an hour to drive to the mountain that we were going to be sledding down. That's right, a mountain.

"Okay, explain this to me one more time," I said, shifting to face Brayden better as he drove. "We take a bus up to the top of this mountain, rent a traditional wooden sled, then proceed to sled back down."

"You got it," Brayden said, nodding his head and grinning at me.

"It's the coolest thing about living here. You can get up to fifty kilometers on the straight-aways," David added. "This year, I'm old enough to have my own sled."

I quickly googled what that speed was in miles per hour and found it was thankfully only about thirty. Incredibly fast for sledding, but I was picturing Olympic luge sledding where they got up to eighty miles per hour.

"How do you even steer a sled?" I asked, feeling more panic set in.

Charlotte, who was sitting next to me, took my hand and gave it a squeeze. "They'll teach you how to do that. Lots of foreigners come to do this, so they will tell you everything you need to know. Although it is very simple—you just use your feet like rudders."

"Do they have helmets?" Everyone in the car laughed at me like it was the silliest question I could have asked.

Now I was grateful that I had still packed my un-fashionable winter jacket, because I was perfectly comfortable in the biting cold. I borrowed a hat and gloves from Charlotte, so I was set for this adventure. Brayden and I sat next to each other on the bus, Hope in my lap.

"I want to ride with Lailah." She pouted for the hundredth time.

"No, Hope, let her get one ride down before we saddle her with a passenger. You'll ride with me, and then we will see what Lailah thinks for the second run," Brayden answered, his tone leaving no room for argument.

"Wait, you're going to make me go down by myself?!" I was shocked. I had assumed Brayden and I would be sharing a sled.

"I'll share one with you, Lailah, for this first run," Charlotte piped up, turning to look back at us.

I sighed, letting my shoulders sag in relief. Cami was always pushing me into things like this, but she'd learned early on I needed a little hand-holding at first. "Thank you."

The bus dropped us off at a building that was half sled rental and half cafe serving hot drinks, wine, and beer. Brayden and Micah went to get our sleds while Charlotte and I hung back with David and Hope. The track that we would be sledding down was wide enough for a car to drive easily and wound its way down the mountain.

"How long is the track?" I questioned.

"Hmm, seven kilometers, so four and a half miles, give or take," Charlotte answered, following my gaze. "It starts out fairly gentle, then gets a little more exciting towards the end. The forest is the tricky part—more turns to avoid the trees."

"That is so not helping," I muttered.

We wandered over to a beginner's class that was going on so I could watch them explain the basics. Just as they finished up, the guys returned with the sleds and ski goggles. We shuffled into line with the others, letting groups go together, then waited for a gap to build before letting the next group go.

"I'll sit behind you, but I want you to be in the first seat so you can figure out the steering. I'll back you up if you need it," Charlotte said, getting settled on the sled as we all lined up in a staggered formation.

The starting attendants gave us a shove, setting the sled in motion. Brayden and David were in front of us, with Micah and Kayley behind us. I was grateful for the goggles, because the wind blowing past us as we gained speed would have been awful without them.

"Okay, our first turn is coming up; hover your right foot over the snow, and then dig your heel in as we get closer," Charlotte yelled in my ear.

I followed her instruction and put my heel down—too hard

—and almost spun us out of control, but she corrected us. Easing up on the pressure, I figured out the balance and eased us into the next curve. As we accelerated and I became more confident, the excitement finally reached me. We flew across the packed snow, weaving in and out of people who were going slower than us. Laughter started to bubble up, and I let out a whoop as we drifted perfectly around the turn, hardly slowing at all.

Micah and David were racing, tossing snow at each other like their own version of Mario Kart. Kayley was laying down on her stomach, trying to keep up with them and avoiding being hit by snow. One more curve, and we were in the forest area. The trees were dense, and if you wiped out, trying to avoid hitting one would be a miracle. For some reason as we zoomed past, I felt this lurking unease that there was something out in the woods and it wasn't anything good. I wanted to get Brayden or Micah's attention, but they were too distracted.

A loud crack sounded through the quiet forest, and a huge tree started to fall. I looked back to see that Brayden and Hope just made it past before it blocked the sled path. I dug my heels in, trying to slow us down so he could catch up to us and I could make sure he was okay. Then I noticed movement in the forest and knew what that gut feeling had been.

"*Demons,*" I screamed before grabbing Charlotte and bailing from the sled as one came hurtling towards us.

CHAPTER 25
BRAYDEN

Everything happened in a blur. Narrowly getting crushed by a falling tree, Lailah screaming, then demons flooding the path. I had never seen so many minor demons of various kinds swarming before. They poured out of the trees, some flying while others crawled. Hissing and screeching echoed around us. Hope clung to me, sobbing as a demon dive-bombed us, but I was able to roll us out of the way.

The chaos made it hard to see where everyone was. Balls of fire were being tossed in all directions, giving me a clue as to where Micah was. I picked Hope up and held her to my front, wrapping her legs around my waist and her arms around my neck.

"I need you to hold on to me as tight as you can. I need my arms free to keep us safe, can you do that for me?" I asked, trying to keep my voice calm. Not speaking, she whimpered into my neck, clinging as hard as she could.

"Brayden, over here," Lailah called, kicking a demon away from Charlotte, who was trying to beat a demon off with a stick.

Feeling my daggers form in my hands, I charged over to them, slashing and stabbing as I went, not stopping to see if I had killed them or not. Seeing a boulder off to the side, I used my power to pick it up and send it crashing into a group of demons trying to overwhelm the girls.

A demon latched onto my leg, trying to slash through the snow pants I had on. I tried to shake it off, but it only held on tighter and dug its claws in deeper. Needing backup, I looked around for Micah but couldn't find him anywhere. Then the demon was engulfed in flames, and a boot kicked it off my leg, sending it screaming into another demon.

"What the fucking hell is going on?" Micah demanded, whirling to slice off the head of a demon trying to tackle David. Micah and I, having grown up and trained with each other for years, moved seamlessly together. I handed Hope off to Kayley who was with David, and circled to keep the three of them in the middle, while Micah and I moved us towards Lailah and Charlotte.

"How the hell should I know what's going on?" I snapped when I caught a second to answer.

"The two of us can't keep this up, there are way too many of them and too many people we have to look out for," Micah said, giving me a hard look. "You need to do something drastic, and fast."

Before I could answer, Lailah sent out a pulse of power, blasting all the demons away from us. Quickly we gathered, panting and sweating from the effort of fighting in winter gear.

"Please tell me one of you has a plan," Lailah said, her worried eyes flicking between the two of us.

That's when the reality of the situation hit. Most of the people I loved were here with me and under attack. With only two of us that could defend and protect, the odds were not looking good. Micah was right. I needed to step up my game and think big.

"Brayden, can you make an avalanche?" Charlotte asked, pulling David close to her side, her body rigid with fear.

"It could work," Micah said, nodding his head, slashing away at encroaching demons with his swords.

"The fuck it could work. How do you plan on surviving that? I can't really control how it happens once it starts. We could get buried alive," I fumed, throwing one of my daggers at a flying demon.

"Better than what the demons would do to us," Micah countered.

"I can make us a shield to protect us from the avalanche," Lailah said, stabbing at a demon with her sai.

Micah and I both looked at each other in shock, then over to her. "How do you know you can make a shield? No one has done that before," Micah demanded

"Does it really fucking matter at this moment?" Lailah barked. "It's not like we have that many options. Trust me, I can keep us safe. I know I can do this."

Just when I didn't think things could get much worse, a second wave of demons flooded out of the trees. There was no more time to figure out a better plan. It was now or never.

"Okay, cover me while I figure this out," I yelled.

A wall of flames burst up around us, slowing down the demons' advance. "I can't hold this for long, so make it good, man," Micah said through gritted teeth.

Closing my eyes, I took a deep breath and sent my power into the mountain beneath my feet. I felt along the ridges that were farther from the ski resort, not wanting to endanger more people. Finally, I found a weaker section that I could shake loose and send the snow falling. Reaching deeper into my power, I pulled up as much as I could and sent it out to do my bidding.

The ground rumbled under our feet, and I could sense the shift on the air, but it wasn't enough. I was too far away to get the right punch I needed to break the ground loose. Then a hand slipped into mine, and golden power flooded my system, sending out a shockwave that hit the mountain right where we needed it. A loud *CRACK* reverberated through the air, then a muffled *WHUMPH* of the snow breaking off signaled the start of the avalanche. The ground bucked under our feet as the earth shifted against the oncoming wave of snow. When we saw it coming in the distance, it looked like a fast-moving wall of clouds that would be harmless.

I grabbed Kayley and David, hugging them close while Charlotte and Hope gathered around. Micah framed them in, opposite of me, trying to keep everyone close. I lifted my head in time to see Lailah throw her arms wide, facing down the avalanche like she could tame it with that look alone. Praying that the angels would give her the strength she needed, I watched as the first wave hit.

When the snow slammed into her shield, it shone like a golden dome surrounding us. Lailah took a step back but didn't falter as she held her own against the onslaught of snow. Having only seen this sort of disaster on TV, I was blown away by the power it had to take down the trees like they were nothing more than a blade of grass. Time seemed to still as we waited for the snow to settle, and I could see Lailah beginning to struggle. Stepping closer to her, I rested my hand on her shoulder just as Micah did the same. Our powers flowed into her, and the dome became awash with green and red, along with the gold.

The rumbling stopped, and the world became quiet. I could feel the earth had settled and everything was calm. Confident that the avalanche was over, I took a deep breath.

"How the hell are we going to get out of this damn snow?" Kayley grumbled. "Seems someone didn't think this all the way through before bringing a mountain down on us."

"Really, Kayley, now is not the time," Charlotte snapped, cutting our sister a look to shut the hell up.

"I should be able to melt a way out," Micah said, looking up at the snow above us.

"Try it. I'll hold the shield until you test it so we don't have a cave in. It will at least tell us how deep under we are," Lailah said, looking pale and exhausted.

Rubbing his hands together, Micah got them to heat up and placed them above his head against the barrier and the snow.

Seconds later, sunlight shone through, showing that we were buried under only a few feet of snow. Lailah slowly let the shield fall, and the snow tumbled in, but it was nothing we couldn't wade out of easily.

As we looked around, it was like a whole different world. The trees had snapped off, leaving branches and tree trunks poking up all around. Thankfully, there was no sign of any demons. Now I could relax and figure out our next step. We didn't need to wait too long before a search and rescue team on snowmobiles showed up to take stranded people back to the ski lodge.

CHAPTER 26

LAILAH

Drained from the amount of energy that I used to make the shield, I passed out the moment I leaned against the window of the car. Charlotte sat next to me with a sleeping Hope in her arms, who refused to be put in her own seat. Kayley and David sat silently in the back of the SUV. No one knew what to say about what just happened on the mountain. I had no idea what was known as common knowledge, but whatever it was didn't prepare them for what we experienced.

Micah drove back this time. Brayden was just as worn out as I was, having brought down a mountain around us. Before my eyes closed for the rest of the drive, I locked eyes with Micah in the rearview mirror. He gave me a nod and the hint of a smile that I took to say I had done good today.

My dreams were fitful and full of demons jumping out of the shadows to attack me. That had been the second time that I had been swarmed while out in a forest. *What did that tell us? Could we have done something differently? How did they find us? Did I lead them there with my tainted blood?* Question after question filled my mind with doubt. *Was I a danger to this family?*

"Lailah," Charlotte said, shaking me awake. "We're home."

Slowly, I sat up, my neck feeling stiff from being smashed up against the window the whole ride back. I rubbed the grit out of my eyes, trying to pull myself out of the haunting thoughts that I'd been trapped in. Solemnly, we all entered the kitchen, shedding our winter clothes and putting them in the mudroom. Charlotte took Hope and David upstairs to put them down to rest. Even though David hadn't said anything, you could just see the lost look in his eyes, unsure of what to do or say. Kayley went to the stove and put a kettle on to boil water.

I sat at the kitchen table, watching as Kayley pulled down five mugs, plopping a tea bag in each of them. As if on cue, Charlotte rejoined us as the kettle started to whistle. Once everyone had their mug and was seated, we all took a deep breath.

"We have to tell Father," Charlotte said, breaking the silence.

Brayden lifted his head to look at his sister, eyes tired and filled with sadness. He nodded. "We can't let him tell Mom. If she knows it will send her off the edge."

"Especially since Father won't let her go to a hospital after what happened with Michael. He would rather treat her at home than let her out of his sight," Charlotte agreed, gripping her mug tightly.

Kayley finally broke and slammed a fist against the table. "Who the hell is going to explain what the fuck happened back there?"

"Language," Charlotte snapped.

"Right, because that's something we need to worry about when there are goddamn demons running wild in the woods. Do I need to worry about them attacking us here at home?" Kayley snipped, rolling her eyes.

"The house is warded, no demon should be able to get in," Micah said, voice muffled from his head lying on his arm folded on the table.

Kayley shot up from the table, causing her chair to crash to the floor behind her. "What do you mean the house is warded? Are we witches or something? Is that what the Elementi are?"

Brayden let out a sigh and ran his hands through his hair.

"No, the Elementi are not witches. Far from it. We are the good guys fighting against the demons and keeping the world safe."

"Right, sure. The good guys, because causing an avalanche, manipulating fire, and making magical shields is totally normal stuff," Kayley said, crossing her arms. "You better have a fabulous explanation for all this."

Looking around the table, I could see that everyone was running out of steam to handle her torrent of questions.

"Do you know the story of how the Elementi was started?" I asked, surprising everyone.

"No... just that our family and many others have been a part of it for generations," Charlotte said, catching me off guard.

I glanced over at Brayden, who wouldn't meet my eyes. "So you have no idea who and what Brayden and Micah are?"

"What the hell does that mean?" Kayley demanded. "Up until today, I've never seen anything strange like that going on, and I grew up with both of them."

"The three of us are Blessed Elementi Warriors, gifted with elemental powers by the angels," I said, meeting Kayley's eyes, then Charlotte's.

Both of them looked at me like I had just told them they were adopted. Kayley took a moment to right her chair and then sank into it. Charlotte gulped down the rest of her tea as if that would calm her.

"I mean I knew about some things but... Explain what that means—please," Charlotte whispered.

I reached over and took her hand, giving it a squeeze until she looked at me. "I'm new to all of this too. I didn't learn who I was until about a month and a half ago. I understand how shocked and betrayed you must feel."

"How did you find out?" Kayley asked, making it sound almost like she was accusing me of something.

"When I was being attacked by a demon much worse than what we faced today. It was trying to kill me, and my powers saved me until the guys could kill the demon," I said, nodding at the boys to my right. "Parker, Jay, and Hudson are also like us."

"Speaking of them, I think we need to fill them in on what's going on. They could have something like this happen to them too," Brayden said, pulling out his phone.

I smiled at him, but the dark thoughts from earlier told me that I was the reason that we had been attacked. The further people were away from me, the better things would be for them. Now I had to take responsibility for putting them in danger and explain this whole crazy world that I was now a part of.

"Brayden, Micah, Parker, Jay, and Hudson are known as the Five Blessed Warriors who were gifted with elemental abilities. It is passed down the family line—any male could be the next blessed warrior. Brayden told me it was your uncle who was the last Earth Elementi Warrior," I said, starting with the basics. "The Elementi are a branch off of the Knights Templar and have been working to defeat the demons causing chaos in the world."

"If there are only five, then how do you fit in?" Charlotte asked.

"When the original Five Warriors were blessed, they were promised a power that would turn the tide in the battle. If they stayed true to the cause, then when they needed help the most, Synergy would be given to them. It was never known how Synergy would be presented. Some thought it might be a weapon or some other mystical object. Only one man thought that it might be another person. Turns out, he was right, because here I am," I said, waving my hands to present myself like I was Vanna White or something.

Kayley snorted. "Right, you expect me to believe that you are some magical woman who will save the world. I know I'm young, but I'm not stupid enough to believe in the bullshit."

"Really, then was I in a different avalanche protected by a force field that was made by her?" Micah said, lifting his head to give Kayley a blasé look. "No one has ever been able to do something like that before."

Kayley opened her mouth to argue but then shut it again and flopped back in her chair, glaring at me. "Whatever, it still doesn't explain why demons came out of the woodwork to attack us today."

Just as I was about to confess my thoughts on the situation, Brayden's phone started ringing. He answered it and put the phone on speaker.

"What the fuck to do you mean you were attacked by demons?! You've only been gone for a day! Is everyone okay? Trouble didn't get hurt, did she?!" Parker's frantic voice blasted from the speaker. "I will kick your ass if she gets hurt again."

I couldn't hold back my smile hearing how worried he was; it warmed my heart to know he cared so much. "I'm fine, Parker. I even learned a new trick."

"What kind of new trick?" Hudson asked, butting into the conversation.

"Seems like I can make a shield strong enough to withstand an avalanche," I said, and everyone on the other end of the line fell silent.

"Is that an estimation of its strength, or has that specific scenario been tested?" Hudson questioned, his voice unsure if he wanted to know the answer.

"If Brayden dropping a mountain's worth of snow on top of us counts as being tested, then yeah, I'll say that's a sure thing," Kayley interjected.

"We're coming to you," Jay said as the call was disconnected.

I looked from the phone to the guys, then back again. "Wait, you don't think he means right now, do you?"

"It's Jay," Micah pointed out. "My money's on seeing them at dinner tonight."

"Where will they all fit? We don't have enough rooms to house everyone here," Charlotte said, worrying her bottom lip.

"It's fine, there is an Elementi safe house here near the city they can use," Brayden said, rubbing his face with his hands. "Now I just have to tell Dad what's going on."

"How much trouble do you think you'll be in?" Kayley asked.

At first, I thought she was being passive aggressive with that statement, but looking at her, I could see the worry in her eyes and the way that she was picking at her nails. She was genuinely nervous about the reaction their father would have about this. Then I remembered Brayden telling me the story about how their mom locked Kayley in her room for weeks after she tried to run away. We could have died today—what extreme outburst would Adriana have when she learned this information?

"Only one way to find out," Brayden said, hitting the speed dial on his phone for his father.

I could hear it ringing, but there was no answer, and he went to voicemail. Brayden hung up and then texted his father to call him when he could about an urgent matter. Having done what he could, he set his phone aside and let his head fall into his hands, waiting for the world to drop around him.

I stood up and walked over to him and put my hands on his shoulders. Leaning down, I whispered into his ear, "Come on, why don't we lay down for a little while. You have to be as tired as I am. We will figure this out, but trying to do it while we're this exhausted won't help anyone."

He nodded, got up from his chair, and headed upstairs. I paused a moment and placed a hand on Micah's shoulder, causing him to jump slightly and look up at me. His deep blue eyes were guarded and vulnerable at the same time. As if he was waiting for me to say something but hoped I didn't.

"Thank you for trusting me, Micah," I said and kissed him on the cheek, letting it linger before following Brayden.

I could hear Kayley snarl something behind me, but I didn't care. It was obvious that she had a thing for Micah, but I also knew that he saw her as a sister and nothing more. Even though I was still coming to terms with bonding with all the guys, I knew they were mine. Micah needed time to build a friendship and trust me before it could ever be more. This trip was showing me there was so much more to learn about him as a person, and what I was seeing made me want to know more.

Checking my room first, I found Brayden sprawled out on his back across the bed, arm thrown over his eyes. Shutting the door, I crawled into the bed next to him and rolled to my side so I could watch him. I could feel the guilt of his supposed failure at keeping his family safe rolling off of him through our connection. Typically, he kept his side of our connection shut down, so I didn't read much from him, but right now, the door was tossed wide open.

"Brayden," I said, my throat tight with emotion, unable to tell if it was his or mine. Tears pricked at my eyes, causing them to burn as I shut them, refusing to let the tears fall.

Brayden rolled over and buried his face in my stomach, clutching me close to him. I wrapped my arms around his head and just curled around him, lending him what little strength I had to offer.

We must have fallen asleep like that, because the next thing I knew, a phone was ringing and Brayden stirred to answer it.

"Hey, Dad," Brayden said, sitting up to lean against the headboard. "Can you talk privately? It's Elementi-related." There was a pause, and then Brayden's eyes widened, and he gulped. "You're already on your way home? Yeah, everyone is fine. Okay, we'll talk more when you get here."

"That didn't sound good," I murmured, yawning and rubbing my eyes.

"It seems that the Elementi HQ here in Austria reached out to my father when they detected the abnormal demon activity and the avalanche. Combined with my phone call and the notice that the other guys requested to use the safe house, Dad put two and two together. He doesn't know the whole story yet, but that's why he's on his way home," Brayden explained as he absently played with my hair, looking out the window. "Lailah... I can't be responsible for causing another family member pain."

My chest ached with our combined guilt, and I couldn't look at him or I would start crying. "This time has nothing to do with you. I'm the reason they attacked us; it's me they are after, and your family was just a casualty to them. If anyone is to blame for this, it's me."

Brayden stilled beside me, then he tried to get me to look at him, but I wouldn't. I just hid my face in the covers. I didn't want to see the look of betrayal on his face for having me bring my trouble to his family. A loud bang of a door slamming caused both of us to scramble off the bed, guessing it would be Oliver.

Brayden took my hand and led me to the second floor, into a study that was clearly his father's. Charts of plant growth and ground levels were covering both the desk and the large corkboard behind the desk. Instead of books on shelves, there were various plants labeled with numbers. It was the sunniest room in the house, with extra windows added for the plants. Brayden pulled us down onto the leather loveseat, and Micah entered next and seated himself in the armchair near me, even moving it so it was closer. Almost like he wanted to make sure I knew he was on my side when things went down.

Oliver's thudding footsteps could be heard coming down the hall before the office door was tossed open, slamming against the wall. The calm, kind man I'd met last night was nowhere to be seen. His eyes flashed with anger, and a vein on his forehead pulsed as he tried to contain his fury. Kicking the door closed, he tossed his briefcase on the desk, followed by his coat, before he started pacing, not even able to sit down.

"Who wants to explain to me what the hell happened today," Oliver snarled.

"It was my fault—" Brayden started, but I slapped my hand over his mouth and stood.

Oliver stopped his pacing at the sudden actions, glaring between Brayden and me. "Well?"

"Mr. Dolton," I started, and he narrowed his eyes at me. "Oliver, what happened today was no one's fault but mine. I'm demon-tainted, and I believe that draws them to me. Because of who and what I am, it puts everyone around me in danger."

The shock of understanding bloomed over Oliver's face. "But you're Synergy, how can you be tainted by a demon?"

"I'm still human. They were able to remove almost all of it, but there is still a small amount left. Until I'm bonded to all five of the elements, I won't be free of it. As of right now, only Brayden and I are bonded."

Oliver blew out a sigh as he finally sat in the armchair, his anger abating. "Why haven't you just bonded with the others so this isn't an issue anymore?" he asked, looking between Micah and me.

Stunned at his question, I didn't know how to answer it right away and sank back onto the couch. Brayden grabbed my hand and gave me a soft smile before turning back to his dad.

"That's not how it works, Dad. Once you make the choice to bond, there is nothing that can break it. It's a lifelong commitment that comes with a connection that is deeper than anything I've ever known before. I can literally feel every emotion she feels, and it's the same for her," he said, trying to get his father to understand.

"Like in any relationship, you need to build trust before you even think about asking someone to marry you," Micah said, shocking me. "We've only known each other for a few months, and Lailah didn't even know who she was or anything about this world we grew up in. So on top of that, you want her to just jump into a relationship with five guys?"

"No, of course not. I didn't think that all the way through; please forgive me," Oliver said, running his hands through his hair. "I was informed that the other three are on their way here. Do we need to worry about them attacking so soon after this event?"

"Honestly, I have no idea. It's not normal for them to attack us the way they did. Who knows what their next move might be at this point," Brayden said, watching his dad with a worried crease on his brow.

Oliver leaned forward, resting his elbows on his knees, taking the three of us in. "We can't let your mother know about this. If she finds out, I don't know what she will do."

"Madam, please, you are not well! Come back to your room, I'm sure your husband will fill you in on what's happened," Ms. Tabitha's voice called from the hallway.

The one thing we had all hoped wouldn't happen did. Adriana burst through the door, her silver hair wild like she had been pulling at it. Her eyes were crazed, like an animal trapped in a cage trying to get out. When they landed on me, she let out an ear shattering screech and lunged at me. No one was able to move fast enough, and a resounding slap sounded as pain bloomed on my cheek.

"How *dare* you put my family in danger. Isn't one son enough to lose over this meaningless war?" Adriana fell to her knees in front of me, grabbing my shoulders. "Why would you need to take all my children? What have I done in my life to be so punished?" Adriana demanded, tears rolling down her cheeks as she shook me.

"Mom," Brayden yelled, standing and trying to get his mother to let me go. "This isn't Lailah's fault; you need to let her go."

"Enough," Oliver bellowed. "Unhand her, Adriana."

Hearing her husband's words, she melted to the ground, sobbing at my feet. Her whole body shook with the strength of her crying. "Please, please, keep them safe. I beg of you. Don't take them from me. They are all I have left that is pure in the world."

On instinct, I leaned over to comfort her, but that was the wrong move. The moment I touched her, she screamed, throwing herself away from me and crawling towards Oliver. "No. No, you can't be here. You have to leave, I won't have you in my house." She clung to her husband's legs and looked up at him, anger marring her face in a sudden transformation. "Oliver, make her leave. If you don't, then I will have to take matters into my own hands."

The pain in Oliver's face as he looked at his wife told me all I needed to know. I stood, not wanting to force him into the choice. "It's fine, I agree with her. It's not safe for your family if I stay here. I'll join the others where they are staying."

"I'll be going with her," Brayden said, standing at my back.

Micah stood as well but didn't say anything as we left the study to pack.

CHAPTER 27

LAILAH

The car ride to the Elementi safe house was silent, but the air was full of tension at the unspoken words. Martin drove us since we couldn't take a taxi to the location; it was also out of the main city and up in the mountains. I didn't get a chance to say goodbye to anyone in the house—we had to sneak out like some dirty secret. Knowing that I didn't want to push Adriana any further than we already had, I didn't argue. It's not like it would be the last time I see them or talk with them. Brayden had Charlotte's number, so I could at least text her and let her know what was going on. I hoped that David and Hope didn't get the wrong idea about us leaving, but Charlotte promised she would talk to them.

Martin turned off the main road and started on some winding track along the mountainside. The view was breathtaking and made me feel so small in the world compared to the impressive nature of the mountain range. After a few miles, we entered a plateau of sorts between two mountain peaks that had a helipad and a charming three-story wooden home. A helicopter was already sitting on the pad, its black metal shining in the sunlight reflected off the snow.

As we stopped in front of the house, the door was yanked

open, and Parker started waving at us from the porch like we wouldn't be able to spot him. His wide, welcoming grin made my heart melt, and I felt overwhelmed by how much I had missed him. It hadn't even been two days, but Parker was one of my best friends and always knew how to make me feel better. I hopped out of the car and ran right into his arms. He hugged me so tight, I thought I might crack.

"Trouble, I can't leave you alone for a minute, can I?" Parker chuckled.

I gave a laughing sob before I broke down, clutching his shirt in my hands as I cried. Parker didn't say anything; he just picked me up and carried me into the house and sank onto a sofa, holding me.

"What happened?" Hudson asked, a hard edge to his voice that I hadn't heard before.

"Mom freaked out and blamed Lailah for everything and kicked her out of the house," Brayden explained.

Parker just kept rubbing my back, letting me feel all of my emotions, not trying to fix it. Then I felt a trickle of his power caressing against mine, soothing the torrent of my emotions. Typically, being around Parker made me fearless, bold, and willing to try new things. Yet this time, it felt different; it was as if he was able to manipulate how I was feeling, like he was taking on some of my pain. I leaned back and looked Parker in the face. His warm brown eyes looked back at me with so many emotions, all of them full of comfort and understanding.

"What did you just do?" I asked, curious.

Parker shrugged his shoulders, and a pink flush crossed his cheeks. *Why was he embarrassed about what he had done?*

"I couldn't stand how much you were hurting, so I stole some of the pain from you. It's part of being Heart. It gives me the ability to give or take emotions from people, among other things," Parker explained, then his face fell to a frown. "You're not mad at me for using my powers on you, are you?"

I shook my head and leaned in, placing a gentle kiss on his lips. "No, not for something like this."

Sliding off his lap, I curled up next to him and wiped my face with the palm of my hand, trying to pull myself together. I looked around to see all the guys watching me cautiously from various places in the room.

"Man, I missed all you guys; everything goes to hell when we're not together," I said, with a forced smile.

My comment made everyone smile, relaxing the tension in the room. I had a sneaking suspicion that not many women broke down crying around them. They were going to have to get used to it, because I was definitely a crier when my emotions got too much.

"Do you want to talk, or would you rather go on a house tour?" Hudson asked, adjusting his glasses.

Glancing around, I took in the living room for the first time. It was beautiful, rustic, and homey, with a large stone fireplace as the center focus. The large sectional couch I was sitting on made a U shape around it, keeping everyone warm. A large stack of wood was packed into a square cutout for storage, filling the room with its earthy smell.

"I'd love to see the rest of the house," I said, extracting myself from Parker and the couch.

Hudson nodded and started down the hall but stopped and turned to me, holding out his hand. I grinned and grasped it, letting him pull me along. The next room we entered was an open kitchen and dining area with tons of windows showing a panoramic view of the mountains we were nestled between. The dining table was interesting; half was bench seating along the wall and the other half was chairs on the opposite side, and it looked like it could seat far more people than were here.

The kitchen was simple, with all the basic needs, and the fridge was even full of fresh ingredients. Tugging on my hand, Hudson drew me out onto the patio through a sliding glass door. The air was cold, but the breeze was gentle for being this high up. Sturdy wooden furniture was set out here for people to enjoy the view, and off to the right, I noticed a cutout in the floor.

"There's a hot tub here?" I gasped, looking up at Hudson.

He grinned, and his ice-blue eyes shimmered. "Yes, there is, and I believe they have some extra swimsuits too in one of the guest rooms."

"Yes. This is going to be epic," I whooped and did a little happy dance before we headed back in.

Hudson led me up a flight of stairs into an open concept floor with a wall of bunk beds. Looking closer, the beds were all full-size mattresses instead of the typical twin. One wall was a gigantic sliding glass door that led out to a short balcony and gave the room an open feeling. There was a large bathroom made for two or more people to use, easily. Heading up another set of stairs, we ended up in a master bedroom with its own fireplace and seating. The bed was large and welcoming, as was the rest of the room. Another patio door faced the view leading to a small outside sitting area.

"We didn't know that you were asked to leave, but figured there could be a chance you might sleep over, so we left this room for you and Brayden," Hudson said, leaning against the fireplace as I scoped out the bathroom.

Peeking out the door to look at him, I blinked. "Really?"

"Of course. It only makes sense since we might be working late, and it's an hour drive back to the city."

"That makes sense but wasn't what I was asking. I was more surprised that you're okay with Brayden and I sharing a room," I said, stepping back into the bedroom.

Hudson's eyebrows raised in surprise. "Why wouldn't I be?"

I dropped my gaze and fidgeted with my fingers, unsure of how to explain how I was feeling. Hudson was the one I seemed to turn to when I couldn't figure something out, but it was harder to talk about this when it involved him.

"Well—I—um," I stuttered, trying to figure out how to explain. I took a deep breath, then lifted my head to look Hudson in the eye. "It's hard for me to wrap my mind around being with all of you. In my soul, I know that it's how things are meant to be, but my brain isn't moving as fast."

"Hmm, so you're wondering how I can be totally fine with you and Brayden when I and the others want you as well," Hudson said, bluntly.

I gaped at him, stunned that he would just lay it all out on the table, so to speak. Not having the ability to speak just yet, I nodded my head in agreement. Hudson sat in one of the chairs by the fireplace and motioned for me to join him.

Oh God, he thinks I need to sit down for this.

Once seated, he crossed his leg and leaned back in the chair, watching me a moment. "I don't think that this would have worked if it wasn't with you. Tell me this—has it been hard since you met us all and became friends to spend time with us together and individually?"

I opened my mouth to answer, then took a moment to really think over his question. Had it been hard to juggle the five of them? In a strange way, it'd worked out that I found something that had become individualized for each of them. When we all spent time with each other, it had its up and downs, but it wasn't related in any way to me being around all of them.

"No, it's been the easiest friendships I've ever had," I answered, feeling something settle in me.

Hudson smiled. "Not many women can figure out how to equally share their time with so many men. You did it without even thinking about it. It might take me time to be comfortable seeing the others physically affectionate with you, but it's inevitable that all of us will be bonded to you, and that comes with the territory."

I laughed at how practical he sounded. "It's going to take me some time to come to terms with that as well. I've only ever dated one other person in my life, and that didn't end very well for me."

"Just remember we are all human, and no one is perfect, but all of us would rather die than let anything happen to you," Hudson said, getting to his feet, brushing a hand along my cheek. "What are the chances that we might talk you into cooking for us tonight? Sadly, most of us are not skilled in that area."

I chuckled and stood, wrapping my arm around Hudson's. "Come on, we don't want to let the others waste away from hunger. You guys made it out here fast."

"Fortunately, we were all packed ready to head out to our various locations," Hudson shared. "That, and the fact Jay has a helicopter to use whenever needed."

"Glad you guys were still at the house and hadn't left yet. Hopefully, we can get this figured out so you guys can be with your families for the holidays."

"One could argue that all of us together is being with family," Hudson said, shocking me.

There are a few people that I would have expected that to come from, he was just not one of them. Grinning, I tightened my grip on his arm. "I like the sound of that."

The kitchen was fully stocked with anything you would need to cook with and all the basic ingredients you could ask for. I whipped together some spaghetti, making the sauce from scratch since my mother never allowed us to use the premade stuff.

"Are you sure I can't help?" Brayden asked, hovering in the kitchen.

I stopped and turned to look at him, spoon raised so it was right in front of his face. "If you don't stop asking me that, I'm going to burn your portion. Now. Go!"

Brayden opened his mouth to argue once again that the over-cooked pasta paste wasn't his fault.

"Just let it go, man," Micah said, slapping Brayden on the back, grabbing two beers from the fridge.

Apparently, Beth never let them have alcohol at the house, but most of them drank on occasion. Brayden sighed, taking the beer from Micah and following after him into the living room. Never in my life did I think someone could be so bad at cooking that you could turn noodles into soggy goop. Parker offered as well, but I decided that for tonight I would just manage on my own. The others steered clear of the kitchen and watched a movie in the living room.

Taking a final taste of the sauce, I deemed it ready. "Dinner's ready."

Grabbing the salad and the bread, I set them on the table along with the dressings that I found in the fridge. When I turned back around, I found all the guys holding plates, practically drooling as they looked at the stove.

"Can you guys manage to dish things up yourself, or do I need to portion it out so everyone gets some?" I asked, hands on my hips.

They all looked at each other and nodded, so I waved them on. Grabbing the water pitcher, I filled the glasses as Jay walked over to me with a full plate. Setting it down, he pulled back a chair and pointed to it. Smirking, I set the pitcher on the table and took the seat he picked out for me. Jay had taken it upon himself to be my caretaker, making sure I didn't go hungry by making up my plate first. He also drove me to school every morning, so I was in class on time. Jay didn't need words to show that he cared; his actions spoke loud and clear. Once I was settled, he left to go get his own plate while the others settled around the table.

Parker moaned as he shoved more pasta into his mouth. "God, this is the best spaghetti I've ever eaten." He looked over at me with a glint in his eye. "Is it too soon to say that I'm glad you have to stay here with us, so we don't have to live off of Jay's cooking?"

"There is nothing wrong with my cooking. You get everything the body needs with each meal," Jay said, narrowing his eyes at Parker.

"Yeah but rice, chicken, and vegetables with no flavor for every meal is not nearly as enjoyable as this," Parker rebutted, waving his fork at Jay.

Jay looked down at his plate, then brought his eyes to meet mine. "He is correct on that; this meal is delicious and full of nutrition."

"Thank you, both of you," I said, feeling my cheeks heat at their words. Cooking like this is normal when your family does food for a living.

"Where do you guys want to start with this whole shitstorm?" Micah asked after eating a few mouthfuls.

Hudson set down his fork and wiped his mouth with his napkin before answering. "Why don't we start with the whole story. We only got bits and pieces from all different sources."

"There really isn't much to the story, we went sledding where we always go. Everything was normal until we got to the wooded part of the trail about halfway down. Then all hell broke loose—literally," Brayden said, finishing off the rest of his beer.

"You're forgetting the part where the demons blocked the trail by knocking down a tree. You know, the one that almost landed on you and Hope," I pointed out, not liking that he wasn't being very specific. If we were going to do something about this, they needed all the facts. "When we hit the forest, I could feel down in the pit of my stomach that something wasn't right. I thought it was just that I was scared of sledding, but then I saw the demons moving in the shadows like they had that night I was with you guys."

Hudson nodded his head, tapping away on his phone, making notes I assume. "Interesting. What makes you think the demons were responsible for the tree?"

"It was healthy, huge, and looked like something with claws hacked it down," Micah said.

I looked at him with a raised brow, impressed that he would notice something like that.

"What would be your best guess on how many attacked you? Our sensors said it was over a hundred, but that can't be right; never has that number attacked as a unified group," Hudson said, looking at some report on his tablet now laid on the table.

Parker pushed back his chair, walked to the living room, and returned with a laptop. Pushing his dish out of the way, he opened it and started typing away. "Okay, I'm hooked up with the Elementi HQ here and their number is, and I quote, 'an over-whelming amount.'"

"Overwhelming would be the right word for what we faced. It's the reason I had to create an avalanche," Brayden pointed out. "I wasn't even strong enough to do it alone, Lailah had to help give me a power boost."

The three that hadn't been there stopped and looked at me. "You gave a power boost and held a shield strong enough to hold back an avalanche?" Parker asked, jaw falling open. "This happened today, right? Why is she still awake?"

I looked at all of them, suddenly feeling very nervous. "Is that bad? Did I do something I shouldn't have?"

"Quite the opposite, actually. You've done something none of us could have. We are strong and have powers, but we also have limitations with how much power we can use. From the sound of it, you used far more than any of us. Even Micah couldn't have managed and stayed conscious," Hudson said, taking off his glasses to rub the bridge of his nose.

"I took a nap earlier," I offered.

Micah barked a laugh. "Your nap was only an hour before Dad made it back to the house, Lailah. Truthfully, I'm amazed that Brayden and I are still awake."

"You bring up a good point. I think we should call it a night and go over this tomorrow. The house is warded just like the school, so we are safe here. No need to rush with muddled thinking," Hudson said, collecting his plate and heading into the kitchen.

Now that bed was an option, a wave of tiredness hit me. After we woke up and everything went down with Brayden's parents, I'd been running off adrenaline. Now that I was safe and comfortable and had a full belly, nothing was holding back my fatigue. I picked up my plate and headed for the sink, but Parker blocked my way.

"Nope, not gonna happen, Trouble. You cooked, so we clean up. Only fair for the delectable meal you made," Parker said, taking my plate out of my hands. "Now, you march upstairs and get into bed, or I'm sending Jay to babysit."

"Fine, you win," I said, not having any fight left in my body.

Stumbling up the stairs, I made it to the bedroom Brayden and I were going to share. Then I remembered that I didn't bring up my suitcase, but there it was, sitting on the bench at the end of the bed. *Bless whoever did this for me.* Grabbing what I needed, I sped through my bathroom routine and had enough effort left to ditch my jeans and bra before curling up in bed. My body sunk into the mattress, and the pillow was just as welcoming, helping me to drift off into a dreamless sleep.

CHAPTER 28
MICAH

I watched Lailah head up for the night, and the mood in the kitchen changed. We all silently brooded as we cleaned up from dinner, each lost in our own thoughts.

Growing up without any siblings, I'd adopted the Dolton clan when they took me in. Knowing what it's like to lose family that you loved, I could connect with them. David and Hope were too young to really remember their oldest brother, but Charlotte always told them stories, keeping his memory alive. Today, I'd come close to losing every person in my life that I gave a shit about, and as much as I had been fighting it, Lailah was one of them. It also fueled my hatred of the demons that kept taking all that was good in the world from me.

I didn't know if it was fate or some angelic magic that kept pulling me to Lailah, but I was starting to get tired of fighting it. Seeing her step up and put her life on the line to protect all of us, and then taking responsibility with Oliver, hit me like a bullet straight to the heart. When I first met Lailah, I thought of her as weak because she never stood up for herself. What I didn't realize was that she might not defend herself, but she would do whatever it took to protect someone she cared about. The confidence she had in her eyes when she asked me to trust her gave me no other option than to do as she asked.

"How do you think she's really doing?" Parker asked, leaning against the counter and pulling me out of my thoughts.

"In what sense?" Hudson asked, putting away the plates.

"Seriously, Hudson?" Parker snapped. "I don't need to be bonded with her to know that this is taking a toll on her. The emotions that woman holds inside her are more intense than any of us could imagine."

Hudson paused and set down the glass he'd been about to put away and looked at Parker with a storm of anger in his eyes. "Do not lecture me on emotions. I might not be good at understanding them or expressing them to you all, but you have no idea the relationship that I have with Lailah. It is not lost on me that bringing her into our world has helped as much as it has hindered." Hudson paused to take a deep, shaky breath. "The reason I ask is because I wanted to know if you might have seen something I missed."

I smirked, seeing Parker put in his place by Hudson. It didn't happen often from the rational man, but when it did, he went for the kill.

"Fuck. Sorry, man, I didn't mean to jump on you like that. I just don't know how to help her, and we really have no leads on anything that would explain why this happened," Parker apologized, combing his fingers through his hair.

Not that I would ever admit it aloud, but I agreed with Parker. We didn't have much to go on, other than they were after Lailah. The attack was clearly planned, but our trip had been last minute. The only people who knew about it lived in the house, and they were all vetted by the Elementi before ever stepping foot in the house.

"We need to do better," Brayden said, deciding to come out of his shock at failing to be the white knight for once.

Walking over to a cabinet I'd discovered earlier that held the hard liquor, I pulled out a bottle of whiskey and shot glasses.

Plunking them down on the counter, I poured out five shots, took one for myself, and tossed it back. Parker and Jay grabbed theirs while Brayden and Hudson just looked like I'd grown a third eye.

"Take the shots, you babies. We aren't going to solve this tonight, and we could all use something to take the edge off," I said, gesturing to the two shots left.

Brayden rolled his eyes at me and drank the shot. Hudson glared at me, crossing his arms and looking at the small glass for a few moments before he huffed and knocked it back. He gasped and sputtered but managed to get the whole thing down and keep it down.

"Alright, so here are my thoughts," I said, pouring myself another shot. "Jay, we need you to work with Lailah on how to defend herself. She has the basics, but she needs more skills that are effective against demons. Parker, you need to catalog any demon movement in the area for the past few months. These demons didn't just show up overnight, and there were way too fucking many of them to go unnoticed."

Jay grunted, taking another shot while Parker just glowered at me. "Who died and let the asshole take charge?"

"You saying you don't want to keep Lailah safe?" I said, baiting him.

"Fucking dickhead, telling me what to do. I'll show you just how good I am at keeping Lailah safe. Fuckwit doesn't even know what's coming for him," Parker mumbled to himself as he poured his shot.

With a flick of my fingers, I lit his shot on fire just as he was going to take it. Yelping, he started blowing at it furiously, trying to put it out before it burned his lips.

"You fucking prick," Parker growled, taking a step towards me.

Jay held out an arm, stopping him from doing whatever he thought he might be able to do to me.

"Knock it off, you'll wake Lailah up. She wouldn't like us

fighting," Jay said, narrowing his eyes at the both of us. When neither of us instigated further, he relaxed slightly. "Micah is right, Parker. We need to know how the demons got here without us noticing. It's our job to notice."

"I'll work on it," Parker said, through clenched teeth.

Gulping one last shot, I felt it burn all the way down as I pushed away from the counter. "I'll work on giving her a crash course on demons since that was one of my strongest subjects in training."

"Because you are one," Parker jabbed, lamely.

Rolling my eyes, I headed for the stairs, hoping my slight buzz would knock me out and let me sleep dreamlessly tonight. The last thing I needed to do was wake everyone up with my memories, and I had a feeling that what happened today might bring on my nightmares again.

The first thing I noticed as I started to wake was how my body tingled with energy. Sparks of heat danced on my skin as I shifted against the solid form behind me. My breath started to come in shallow pants as the feeling built until it became too much, and I was engulfed. I let out a deep moan as I felt my orgasm being drawn out by skillful fingers.

"Good morning, Angel," Brayden whispered in my ear, causing me to shudder as my body still pulsed with arousal. "Sleep well?"

I turned to face him and grabbed his face, pulling him down to me, devouring him. That one orgasm had done nothing but make my body want him even more, and I wasn't going to be denied. Brayden was more than happy to follow my lead as I pulled him over me and yanked his shirt over his head so I could feel his skin. He managed to shimmy my shirt up and out of his way so he could lavish my breasts with attention. I arched under him, letting my body rub against his, needing friction against my bare skin. Working his way down, Brayden hooked his fingers on my underwear and slipped them down and off my legs to be lost in the room.

I let out a whimper as he massaged my legs and kissed my

inner thigh, avoiding the one place I was begging for him to pay attention too.

"Brayden, please," I cried as his fingers brushed across my center.

He just chuckled, peering up at me. "Please what, my Angel?"

Squirming, I frowned at him. "Don't play with me, Brayden. You started this, now it's your job to finish."

"Oh, trust me, this is not a job I plan to leave unfinished. I enjoy it far *too* much," he purred, right before he dragged his tongue through my center, causing me to cry out. "Now let go, and I'll take care of things from here. You need to relax."

As I was about to give my retort, Brayden latched onto my clit, biting it gently with his teeth. My body convulsed as another orgasm tore through me, but he wasn't done. Settling in further between my legs, Brayden slipped two fingers in and stroked along my channel, making me moan. My body was putty in his talented hands as I let my eyes close so I could enjoy the moment. I let everything wash away except the feel of him and what he was doing to my body.

His fingers teased the most sensitive spot inside as he swirled his tongue around my clit, working simultaneously to drive me crazy. I could feel another orgasm building as my breath became quicker, and the noises that came out of my mouth would make anyone jealous. Finally, Brayden seemed to decide to end the torture, speeding up his fingers and sucking sharply, tossing me into blissful oblivion. My body hummed with pleasure, tender to the touch, but fully sated and languid as I laid there feeling Brayden move to lay beside me. He kissed me tenderly, causing me to open my eyes and curl up against him, enjoying the closeness.

"I see you still enjoy watching," Brayden said, his voice rumbling through his chest against my ear.

Confused, I pulled my head away and looked up at him, brows creased.

"Anyone would have enjoyed seeing that," Jay's voice said from behind me.

Letting out a squeak, I yanked the covers up and turned to see Jay leaning against the doorway, arms crossed and heat in his eyes. My jaw fell slack as I looked back at Brayden.

"How long was he watching? Why didn't you say anything?" I demanded, scowling before giving Jay my attention. "Care to explain yourself?"

Jay pushed off from the door jamb and stalked over to me. This was a side of Jay that I'd never seen before; I felt like a rabbit about to be eaten by a wolf. It sent a shiver down my spine, but it wasn't with fear. I trusted Jay far too much to be scared of him. When he reached me, he leaned over, boxing me in with an arm on either side, never breaking eye contact.

"Why shouldn't I watch what will someday be mine?" Jay said before placing a ghost of a kiss on my lips. "Best get dressed, we have work to do."

With no other explanation, Jay left me stunned and Brayden laughing next to me, falling back against the bed.

"Angel, you should see your face."

I grabbed the pillow behind me and slammed it into his grinning face before I stormed off to take a shower. Brayden was hot on my heels, slipping under the water with me.

"Lailah, don't be mad. I'm sorry I didn't say anything, but I knew all he was going to do was watch," Brayden said, grabbing my shoulders, turning me to look at him.

"Wait, he's done this before?!" I demanded, gritting my teeth as the wave of anger hit me.

"No, I would have told you, I promise," Brayden said as if that would make this better. Seeing the scowl that I'm sure was on my face, he continued. "Some women like to be watched, and he is happy to oblige, but he doesn't do it with anyone but the four of us. That's the only reason we all know about it."

I slapped off his hold, grabbing the shampoo bottle and starting to wash my hair. I wasn't even sure why I was upset about what he was telling me. Surprisingly, I wasn't mad at all that he had watched Brayden and me, it was the realization he had done it with other women. I knew that none of them were virgins, and that didn't bother me either; what did piss me off was being told about them.

They were mine.

I paused at the force of that statement as I rinsed my hair. It was as if the switch had finally flipped, and I was getting it. My power knew they were all mine and loved to wrap itself around them when it had the chance, but I had been slow to accept it. This was the first time I'd thought about another woman getting close to one of them. Since we'd started hanging out, all of them had ignored the advances I'd seen other girls give them.

"Lailah, what's going on in that head of yours?" Brayden asked, taking a loofa and washing my back, kissing my shoulder.

"Just having a revelation is all."

"Care to share what it is?" Brayden asked.

I twisted to face him, placing my hands on his abs and kissing his chest. "That you're mine, and so are the others."

Brayden's face broke out into a wide grin, his eyes lighting up with excitement as he cupped my face. "Damn right, I am."

If I had any doubts about how Brayden felt when I walked into that shower, I didn't once I left it. Lovingly, he toweled me off, peppering me with kisses until I was sure that every inch of my skin had received attention from him.

"We better head down, I'm sure they're wondering what's taking us so long," I murmured, not wanting this moment to end.

"I'm fairly sure they have a good guess," Brayden said, giving me one last searing kiss before heading back into the bedroom.

Knowing it was just going to be the boys today, I dressed more comfortably and snagged one of the t-shirts I packed when Cami wasn't looking. This one seemed to fit how my day started off—*Ha, Ha, Wait What?* The house was cozy, but it was still winter in the mountains, so I pulled on thermal leggings and wool socks before skipping down the stairs.

Appearing in the kitchen, I found all the boys gathered around the table with some sort of technology in front of them. Parker had headphones on that looked suspiciously like the ones Micah always used. He was lost in a screen of data, a full plate of food next to him. Hudson was scrolling through a tablet, lying on the table with his coffee in the other hand. He looked up when I entered and gave me a soft smile. Micah was on his phone and appeared to be texting someone, his ever-present frown curving his lips. Jay, at the opposite end of the table from the boys, had maps and charts of the land laid out on the table with a laptop open. He kept reading, then going and marking spots on the large map over and over.

It seemed as though they weren't at all bothered by the fact Brayden and I had taken our time getting ready for the day. Jay gave no sign of the predator that I had experienced in the bedroom, for which I was thankful. I wasn't sure I could handle any more male attention than I had already, and I'd only been awake for a short time. I wandered over to the stove and saw there was food still left for me to pick from.

"Your plate is in the microwave," Jay said, not even glancing up from his task.

I couldn't help but grin at the fact he had set food aside for me. Opening the microwave, I found a plate with a huge omelet waiting for me. Glancing at the stove, I noticed the frying pan had scrambled eggs left, and that is what was also on Parker's plate.

Had he made this just for me?

Grabbing a fork, I sat at the counter since the table was overrun by their work. Cutting into the feast before me, I found it was stuffed full of vegetables and cheese. I, of course, preferred sweet to savory, but I wasn't going to say anything since it was made just for me.

"Fresh orange juice in the fridge if you want," Hudson said, looking over at me. "We don't have any tea, but I put in a request when we get the next grocery order."

"Might be some hot chocolate," Micah mumbled.

I perked up. "Really! That would be perfect. Do you remember where you saw it?"

"I don't fucking know. Go find it yourself, there's not that many cabinets to look in," Micah said, rolling his eyes at me.

All the boys paused and looked at him, and even Parker, who had taken off his headphones, frowned. Here I thought Micah and I had been making headway on becoming better friends after the experiences we shared. Guess the magic of the Dolton household was no longer working. Deciding to save the hot chocolate for later, I settled for orange juice instead.

The sliding glass door opened, and Brayden came in from the patio. "Just got off the phone with my dad, and it seems my mom has calmed down. He, of course, didn't take her to the hospital for a sedative, but they seemed to manage with what we had already at home from other breakdowns."

The chipper mood that I had been in faded instantly as I remembered his mother screaming at me yesterday. My fork clattered on the plate, and my shoulders slumped. Suddenly, I was no longer hungry. Brayden wrapped me in a hug from behind, hiding his face in the crook of my neck, holding me tightly.

"I don't care what you think; it's not your fault. My mom is not well, and anything could have set her off," Brayden said softly against my skin.

"That's not completely true. Like Parker said, I'm a magnet for trouble right now. This is better. I shouldn't be around people who don't know anything about demons, or it could get them hurt," I sighed.

Hugging me once more, Brayden let go and went to get himself something to eat. I turned in my chair, watching the boys work.

"What exactly are you guys doing?" I asked.

"We're trying to figure out how so many demons got here without anyone noticing. Parker is also looking into all the data that the Elementi here in Austria have gathered over the past year or so. The thing is, we are lacking information, so we're gathering every bit we can. Once we can put it all together, it will give a clearer picture of what we're dealing with," Hudson explained.

"Anything I can help with?" I ventured, feeling a little out of place.

"Finish your breakfast," Jay said, not even looking up from his work. "You and I are going to be sparring later."

Heaving another sigh, I turned back to my plate and did as he asked.

A few hours later, I found myself outside facing Jay, who was holding out two weapons that looked just like the ones my power created. I was bundled up in a jacket and snow boots, but the wind had died down and the sun was beating down on us from clear skies.

"These weapons are called sai. They are a defensive weapon but are handy in close-quarter fights. Today, all I want to do is get you familiar with holding them and maneuvering with them so you don't hurt yourself. These practice ones have no sharp points, so they are safe to work with," Jay explained as he adjusted my grip on them.

"They're a lot heavier than the ones I have," I commented as the cool metal rested against my skin.

"Our blessed weapons are not real; they are formed with our power and can only be used against demons. If I were to shoot a human with my bow, the arrow would just pass right through. Unless they were possessed, that is."

Knowing I couldn't hurt someone I shouldn't with these made me feel so much better. Jay showed me how to hold the weapon against my forearm safely and how to swing it around so I could use it to defend or attack.

"Now, do that motion fifty more times," Jay said, stepping back and watching me with a critical eye.

I could feel my brows dip in concentration as I did what he showed me again and again. I dropped each one at least ten times, making me thankful for my snow boots and that they weren't sharp. I would have lost a toe for sure.

"Stop trying to fight against the sai's natural balance. It was made to make this motion easy, so let it flow," Jay instructed as I once again dropped it.

My wrists started to burn with the strange movement, and the top of my arms ached from holding the heavy object. I could feel the muscle bunching up at the strange abuse it was getting. Yeah, Jay and I worked out my whole body when we did gym days, but this was not a muscle we focused on.

"Better. Now try and speed it up, alternate which one you flip forward. This needs to be something you can do in your sleep," Jay pushed, walking a circle around me.

I gritted my teeth and did as he asked, feeling as if my arms might fall off. Surprisingly, as I got more comfortable, my motions became more confident. I wasn't perfect, but I felt a change in understanding of what it should feel like when done right.

"Good, now let's do some blocking work. Remember your kickboxing classes—they will help you move, but what you need to focus on is keeping your sai flat to your forearm," Jay instructed, standing flush with my back as he showed me what he meant. "When you pull them back to your chest, make sure you keep them vertical so you don't stab yourself with the pointed yoke."

Even through my winter jacket, I could feel Jay's body heat against my back. Memories of what happened this morning flooded back and made me blush, forgetting everything we were working on. Jay nipped at my ear, making me yelp and jump in his arms, which were still holding mine. Having jerked my arms back, I was afraid that I was going to stab him in the gut with my weapons. I shouldn't have been so worried, though, because Jay swiftly moved out of the way, twirling me around so I was facing his chest.

"Do not lose focus, Lailah, it could endanger you or someone else. When you have your weapons in hand, you need to be prepared to defend or fight for your life," Jay chided, but I could see a glint of humor in his dark eyes.

I couldn't get over the change that was happening with Jay. He was becoming bolder with our interactions. He had always been opinionated in certain areas, always making sure I ate, driving me to school, and making sure that I was safe, but this was different. If I was being honest with myself, I didn't think I minded.

CHAPTER 30

JAY

I looked down at her, those crystal-blue eyes swimming with so many emotions. In some ways, I was as confused as she was about how I was acting towards her. Emotions had no place in battle or war, and right now we were always at war with the demons.

My father had told me that it was his duty to keep our family line going, so he married. I knew my parents cared for each other after being together for so long, but I wouldn't say they loved each other. Only honor demanded that they couldn't get a divorce. Mother lived in Japan because that is where her whole family lived; if she'd moved here to be with my father, she would have been alone. He had even taken me away from her when I was thirteen to start training with his men on our base of operations in Dubai. Long ago, I decided that I didn't want that for my life and never planned on getting married or having someone special."Not that I really mind waking up to find you in my bed, but what brings you to these parts?" I asked, running my fingers through his thick hair.

"Nope, too early, come back later with your questions," Micah said, his voice muffled from the pillow.

· · ·

Growing up as a soldier, I did as I was instructed to do and worked with the team that I was placed with. Father disapproved of the other four Elementi Warriors, but it was the one thing he didn't hold power to change. Now adding Lailah into the mix, the emotions that I felt for her were nothing I'd fathomed. I had read in many books how women could use tactics to distract men, but it had never worked on me. I wasn't swayed by a pretty face. At least I thought so—until this morning, when I walked in on Lailah and Brayden.

A man's needs were a distraction, so I slept with women to keep it from ruining my focus before a big job. I had also taken to watching, using it as sort of a desensitization tactic—that's what I told everyone, at least. It was my guilty pleasure to see a woman lost in passion, watching a man put the woman's needs first. Nothing would compare to seeing Lailah's angelic expression as Brayden brought her to climax. Being this close to her was suddenly more difficult, but I would never let my body dictate how I acted. I was a master of my choices.

"Why did you really watch this morning?" Lailah blurted out.

I was surprised it had taken her this long to bring it up. Women either loved it or thought it was some creepy fetish. Once again, Lailah didn't respond the way I thought she would. "I already told you why."

"Right, about that." Her porcelain skin glowed pink as she blushed.

I kept my expression blank, not wanting to influence what she was going to say. If she told me she didn't want me to do it again, I wouldn't. I would never make her feel unsafe around me.

"Brayden might have mentioned that you've done that before with some of the other guys."

Ah, I could see where this was going.

"Hudson and I talked yesterday about him being fine with Brayden and I sharing a room." I gave a small nod, seeing she was looking for confirmation from me as well. "He might have also mentioned that the rest of you want me, but I want to make sure that's true. I don't want anyone feeling forced into this just because some angel tells us that's how it should be."

I blinked, a little shocked this was what she wanted to ask. *Yet again, she never does things how I think she should.* "Are you asking me if I have feelings towards you?"

Her blush deepened. "Yes, I guess that is what I'm asking. I just don't want to read into what happened this morning if it's something you do with lots of other women."

I had to clench my jaw at the thought of watching someone other than Lailah again. After that sight, I don't think anyone else would measure up to her. "There are no other women."

"Oh, I see," she said, trailing off, unsure of what to do with that statement.

I tucked a finger under her chin and made her look up at me. "I don't need anyone else when I have you. Yes, Lailah, I do have feelings for you, and they started far before I found out that you were Synergy."

I gently placed a soft kiss on her forehead to make sure she understood me. I knew many times my words fell short of how I really felt about things.

She grinned up at me, her face shining with delight, causing me to relax right before I was knocked to the ground. Apparently, she had been paying attention in her kickboxing classes.

"You guys are leaving me here alone with Micah?" I asked, confused as they all pulled on their coats.

I had spent the last few days working with Jay on protecting myself, cooking for the boys, and helping catalog data. We had stumbled upon some interesting information about the project that Brayden's mom was working on. They wanted to go back to the house and see if they could find out any information. This then brought us to why I couldn't go—no one wanted to cause trouble with Adriana, least of all me.

"Way to make a guy feel special there, Cookie Monster," Micah drawled from where he was sprawled out on the couch.

I glared at him. "You're going to need to let that go, Micah. Yes, I did make a dozen sugar cookies and eat them all myself. No, I'm not sorry I didn't share, I made them—for me!"

"I wasn't the one that was all butt hurt about it, that was Parker. I'm just impressed you could eat that many," Micah said, swinging his legs around so he was now sitting up.

I turned to look at Parker, who was still pouting that I didn't share last night. "I promised that I would make more later, I just really needed a sugar rush after all the training that Jay has put me through."

At this, he perked up and grabbed my hands, his eyes glowing with excitement. "Does that mean there will be cookies when we get home?"

Rolling my eyes, I grinned. "If I survive the night with Mr. Killjoy, then yes, there will be cookies."

"Fuck yes!" Parker shouted with a fist pump. "Let's go, so we can get back already."

Parker, Jay, and Hudson headed out while Brayden hung back, walked up to me and wrapped his arms around me.

"We will probably end up being there for dinner, so don't wait on us. I'll make sure to say hi to Charlotte and Hope for you," Brayden said, kissing the tip of my nose.

"Thanks. I still feel bad that I couldn't say goodbye to them when we left. I know Charlotte and I text, but it's not the same as spending time with her in person," I sighed, wrapping my arms around his neck. "Be safe and text me when you guys are heading home."

Placing a searing kiss on his lips, I untangled myself from him and sent him on his way. I watched out the front door as they drove off until I couldn't see the taillights anymore. Heading back into the living room, I settled on the couch to see what Micah was watching.

"Seriously? You're a *Supernatural* fan? Don't you get enough of this in real life?" I laughed.

Micah just shrugged, flopping back on the couch. "You have a better idea of what to do in the middle of the afternoon on winter break? Because this is my ideal situation."

"How is this any different from what you do back at The Manor?" I teased.

Raising his head, he glared at me, pointing the remote. "Watch it, woman. There's no one to save you if you start a fight."

Shaking my head at him, I shoved off the couch. "I'm going to the kitchen for some snacks, you want anything?"

"Yeah, bring the Cheetos and some beer. I'm going to teach

you my favorite drinking game."

I looked at Micah, wide-eyed. "You want to play a drinking game at two in the afternoon?"

"Hell, yeah. Now that all the uptight members of our fucked-up little family are gone, it's time to get some real relaxing done. Something tells me that you need this too. Cami's not around to force you to have fun," Micah taunted.

I narrowed my eyes at Micah, unsure of if I trusted him enough to follow along with his idea. Going on this trip, I'd told myself that I wanted to get closer to Micah, and here he was, wanting to do something with me.

"Fine, but I'm getting us more snacks than just Cheetos," I mumbled as I headed into the kitchen.

Rummaging around the kitchen, I found popcorn, Micah's Cheetos, a large bag of M&M's, and then cut up some cheese to go with crackers. I grabbed two beers for us each, unsure of how this game was going to go down, having never played a drinking game before. I also made sure we had water too.

"Oh, we're going to need way more than two beers," Micah pointed out once I was back in the living room. "We're going to start at the very beginning, because I have a sneaking suspicion that you've never watched this show before."

"You're right, I haven't seen it, but I know what it is—someone would have to be living under a rock not to know who Sam and Dean are," I retorted before eating a handful of popcorn.

"Okay, here are the rules. You must drink every time the lights flicker, either of them talk about salt, get in or out of Dean's car, mention that Dad is missing, or a secondary character you just met is killed," Micah said, opening his beer and pushing play on the first episode.

Halfway through the first episode I knew that this was going to be the worst idea I had ever been talked into. Typically, I didn't watch any scary movies—they always made me upset.

Now I wondered if it was because of being Synergy that anything demonic made me uncomfortable on some level.

"Is any of this even real?" I asked after the first episode was over and I was almost done with my second beer.

Micah walked back in from the kitchen with more drinks, smirking as he looked at me. "Very little of it, but in some areas, they had the right idea. There are no vengeful spirits or ghosts; if the demons want something done, they will do it themselves. It's much more common for them to possess someone or to brainwash them. Their whole mission is to work in secret, not to draw attention to themselves."

"So what happened in the forest and on the sledding hill is really out of character," I mused, munching on Cheetos.

Micah landed back on the couch, closer to me this time, crossing over to reach the M&M's. "You could say that, but I think you being demon tainted and all might be making matters worse."

It had been almost a week since that last freak out on the plane. Micah had witnessed firsthand what it looked like when I lost control of my powers. I shivered at the memory and tried to focus more on the TV show, but I kept getting distracted by the thoughts running through my head.

"We found demonic runes outside the wards. What kind of demon would be able to do that?" I asked.

Micah paused the show and shifted to face me, an odd look on his face. "Depending on the symbol and what it meant, it could be a few different kinds. The small ones are what we call lesser demons, they are minions causing mischief. Let's say they needed to scare someone or get them to leave, lesser demons would be used to 'haunt' a place. The more someone fears something, the weaker it makes them against demons. Fear gives them more power, and the stronger you believe in something that scares you, the more it works in their favor."

"So like, if someone doesn't believe in ghosts and the supernatural, they would eventually frighten them into belief?" I asked.

"Close enough. The ones with wings are messengers, fairly self-explanatory. Then there are medium level demons, which are tricky because they're still weak enough that you don't notice them right away. They are the newly dead that are so evil they get turned into demons. We find them being used as scouts because they can be in the real world acting as real people for a short time. Ever wondered where the whole zombie thing came from? Yeah, it was them."

I scrunched up my face, grossed out at the thought of some-one's face melting off while I was talking to them. It would defi-nitely make me think of zombies.

"You're most familiar with one of the two higher level demons, the trackers. Once a mid-level has scouted out the perfect person, then this demon is sent out to bring them back to hell for a nice body takeover. People think it happens here on Earth, that they just inhabit the human, but we've discovered it's not true. See, the host can't have a soul if a demon is going to live in it. So, the soul gets a one-way trip to Hell, and the demon fills the void it leaves behind," Micah said, taking a long pull from his beer, his face shadowed in anger.

"Wow, that's a lot to unpack," I said, trying to break the tension that had settled between us at the talk of demons. "How many seasons are there of this show, anyway?"

"Twelve, I think," Micah said offhandedly.

I gasped, choking on my beer. "Twelve! I'm going to die if we have to drink through all of them."

Micah let out a surprised laugh at my reaction. "You're in luck, this game only works for the first two or three seasons."

"I'm not sure that's any better," I whined as he turned the show back on.

As we got further into the show, the more I became uncomfortable with what was happening. Something deep down in my gut was telling me something was wrong. The creatures in each episode looked more and more like ones that had attacked us. Others I'd never seen before but knew that they were demons who lurked in the dark. When it came to the episode where they went back to their old house where their mother died, I was curled up in a ball, hidden behind pillows. During a flashback of the scene, I saw a face appear in the flames. As I squinted to get a better look, the fire changed to a mixture of black and green.

The flames began to pour out of the TV like a mist taking over the forest. The room started to heat up as tongues of black fire spread around the room like wildfire, trapping me. I could feel my heart erratically beating as if it would burst out of my chest at any moment. Then, before my eyes, the sea of fire morphed into a shape that froze my body in terror.

It formed into a black exoskeletal humanoid creature, showing every bone that made up its form. The creature glowed with an aura of black flames, as if they were drawn to the creature like a black hole. The face was a hybrid of bat and human, sharp cheekbones and pointed ears. Where there should have been eyes in the sockets, there was only darkness so deep it pulled you in like an undertow. The top of its skull was shaped like a crown of black bone, flaring up with sharp points. There weren't any lips on its face, so silver razor-sharp teeth were in clear view. Its forked snake-like tongue flicked out towards me, brushing against my skin. I let out a squeak but couldn't pull away.

My reaction must have amused it, because it let out a husky laugh, sounding as if it had smoked way too many cigarettes in its life. A claw-like hand, tipped with long, black, deadly points, reached out to me. One sharp tip caressed my cheek, being careful not to scratch me. I tried to fight its pull, but as tipsy as I was, I didn't have the mental strength to free myself. The feeling of my mind being clouded swallowed me up. Desperately, I tried to fight against it, and pulling myself to the surface sent me into a hysterical panic. Trapped under his hold, the world around me froze, leaving me helpless with this demon standing in front of me.

"Synergy, we meet at last," it said with a deep, gravelly voice that made chills run down my spine.

Opening my mouth, I wanted to ask who he was, but no matter how hard I tried, I was so deep under his control my voice refused to work. A small exhale of air was all I managed as he stepped closer. I could feel the heat of the flames wrapped around him against my skin.

"Little Synergy, you know who I am," he chided, reading my thoughts. "You can feel it in your bones. After all, you hold a part of me inside you," he taunted, cupping my face with both his boney hands gripping tight enough I could feel each of his claws prick into my skin. If I moved, I would be dead. "My hold on you is stronger than you realize. These boys play at being warriors, but they are not worthy of the power you hold."

Visions of the boys fighting against a legion of demons floated up before my eyes. I saw them scream as they fell one by one, demons feasting on their flesh. Then I saw myself wrapped in a cloak of darkness, leading the horde as we scorched the Earth as we know it. The Dark Lord was right; the boys were nothing but fuck-ups unable to work together and do what was needed to be done. They had Synergy, the most powerful weapon in the world, but they kept me locked away, treating me like an inconvenience. The Dark Lord knew I was something to be used, shown off, and valued. With my help, I could give him everything he craved just as easily as I could crush him.

"Yes, my little Synergy, you are a goddess among these pitiful humans. Grow, become stronger, learn all you can from them; their time is limited. My plans are in motion, and when the time is right, I will send for you. Those loyal to me are growing and slipping in the cracks. The Elementi have become careless, little

Synergy," the Dark Lord said. "Follow what your heart really wants. I will show you what only true power can achieve."

Then he leaned in as if he was going to place a kiss on my forehead, but my golden energy exploded from me. The shockwave of power tossed the Dark Lord back, freeing me from his grasp on my mind. Understanding what had almost happened, I leaped to my feet, my whole body shaking with anger. My power heeded my call and burst out, battling with the Dark Lord's fire and keeping it at bay.

"You better stay the FUCK away from me!" I screamed, my golden power whirling around me like a cyclone as I stalked over to him. "I will never be your Synergy! Those boys may have a lot to learn, but I was made for them, not you. Together, we will defeat you and your demons. All you have done here is show me how I would rather kill myself than be used by you."

The Dark Lord just chuckled at me, and the sound of it was like nails on a chalkboard, setting me on edge. "The fire and vengeance in you burn so bright, even you cannot see how you are more like me than them. I did not put that scene in your head; no, that came from within you," he hissed, pointing a claw at me. "I will be back to ask you one final time, Little Synergy. If you throw my offer in my face again, you will not live to regret your choice, and neither will they."

Before I could offer my retort, in a swirl of flames, he vanished, but not before setting the room on fire and freeing it from its frozen state. I was trapped in the middle of the living room, surrounded on all sides by a raging fire. The walls of blue-purple flame flicked out at me as if it was teasing me before it killed me. I couldn't see anything through the blaze to know where Micah was. *Was he safe? Did the Dark Lord attack him as well?*

Cupping my hands around my mouth, I yelled as loud as I could. "*Micah.*"

I never knew that fire could be so noisy, but the crackling and popping sounds made it hard to hear if he was responding.

Sweat began to roll down my back as the heat began to climb, smoke swirling above my head along the ceiling of the room. There was no way out of this. I didn't have the feeling I had during the avalanche, the one that told me that my shield would work against this. Was demon fire different? I could feel tears streaming down my face as I came to the realization that I might not survive this. Apparently, the Dark Lord wasn't going to give me a second chance.

"*Lailah*, where are you?" Micah bellowed.

A cry escaped out of me as a glimmer of hope blossomed. Micah was alive.

"Over here. Near the hall to the kitchen," I yelled, hoping he could hear me.

I kept my eyes moving to catch any sign of movement, but then I noticed that the fire around me was changing color. It was no longer blue, but was slowly shifting into a bright red-orange color. Then, as if someone had pulled the plug on a drain, the fire around me flowed towards the direction I had heard Micah yelling. Tongues of flames wrapped around me, but this time, it was warm, welcoming, gentle and caressing. It reminded me of when Micah was burning off the excess power I had on the plane ride.

Lost in the wild swirling glow of the fire, I didn't notice when Micah was standing in front of me. His hair was loose and flowed around his head, his eyes wild with his power as he absorbed the flames. Shocked, I gasped and reached out to him, needing to make sure he was alright.

"Don't touch me. With this much wild power, I might hurt you," Micah said, his voice rough with his struggle.

Abruptly, my power surged up, showing me what I needed to do—how I could help him. He didn't need to fight this alone; I could help him just as he once helped me.

"I trust you," I whispered as I wrapped my arms around him, melding the two of us together.

A crack sounded, much like lightning hitting the ground

when it was too close to where you were. The ground rumbled at the impact of our combined energy. I let my power mingle with his, blending together seamlessly until it became a bright orange color. I could feel the damage that the demon fire had done to the house and the evil that permeated through the air.

"Lailah, what are you doing? You're making it worse. This much power is going to destroy the house and us along with it," Micah growled, fighting my hold on him.

Gripping him tighter, I nestled my face against his neck, right under his ear so he could hear me. "Micah, stop fighting your power like it's the enemy. Yes, fire can destroy and burn the world down around us, but fire is also pure. Your flames can purify what has been tainted, but you need to believe it can."

I felt him stiffen against my hold as he absorbed the words I was saying. Now that he wasn't fighting me, I pulled one hand back so I could place it on his heart. "Trust me once more, and I can show you another way."

He didn't need to use words to give me his answer. Slowly, he wrapped his arms around me and rested his head against my shoulder, surrendering to me. I wanted to weep with the joy I felt as our powers flowed through each other. Taking that pure emotion, I tossed our power out through the house, burning away any evidence of the Dark Lord's presence. That which was destroyed and broken was brought back and revived. Once it was done with that, it continued on and flowed out into the yard and down the mountain, purifying any trace of demon activity. This land was now sacred and blessed; no evil could survive while we were both here to keep it maintained.

"How are you doing this?" Micah murmured.

"Not me, us. This is the power of Synergy; this is the power of an Elementi Warrior. Too long have you hidden from what your calling is. We will purify the world and send the Dark Lord running; he will not survive us," I said, feeling that same angelic power overtake me, talking through me.

I pulled him away from me so I could look him in the eye. We were now surrounded in that pure white light, making Micah fall to his knees. I knew what was coming next, but I didn't know what his answer would be.

"Micah, Knight blessed with Fire's power, Warrior for the angels. I find you true of heart and mind, upholding the agreement given to your ancestors. Do you accept the eternal bond to protect the people of this world, and vow to cherish the vessel that holds the gift of Synergy, who has been placed in your protection?" I intoned with that angelic voice.

"No," Micah answered, raising his head to look at me.

My heart clenched, making it hard to breathe. I knew he might reject the oath. He'd been up-front about his feelings on the matter, but hearing it hurt far more than I thought it would.

"I am not worthy yet to accept the oath," Micah continued. "This vessel deserves more than I am able to give at this moment, but I hope someday that I will be able to accept this bond. I will promise to protect her, to become the man and warrior that is worth the gift of Synergy."

Tears slid down my cheek as his words struck me with his honesty. "Your request is an honorable one, blessed Knight, and will be accepted."

With that, the light was gone, and my body was released from its hold, causing me to crumble. Micah was there in a second, wrapping me up in his arms and placing a desperate kiss to my lips. I moaned at the contact, feeling the fire behind it, causing me to thread my fingers into his hair and hold him to me. Nipping at my lip, I opened for him and let him rule over our connection. Micah was an inferno burning me up from the inside out. All too soon, he pulled away and gently brushed my hair out of my face as he gave me a searching look.

"What the actual fuck just happened?" Micah demanded.

I couldn't fight back the grin. No matter what happened, Micah would always be Micah. "I got a visit from the Dark Lord."

Micah jerked his head back as if I'd slapped him. His eyes were wide and filled with panic as he started to pat me down, trying to make sure I was still in one piece. I reached up and grabbed his face and forced him to look at me, needing his full attention.

"He didn't hurt me. This time, at least. He wants me to choose him over you guys," I explained. Micah growled, his grip on my arms so tight it made me flinch. "Surprisingly, that is not what we should be worried about at the moment. He told me that his plans were in the works, and I needed to grow and learn all I could. To become powerful."

"We need to call the others, they need to know this," Micah snapped, helping me to my feet as he pulled out his cell.

"No," I said, grabbing his hands and stopping him from texting. "Let them be. Nothing will change between now and when they come back."

I looked him in the eye and waited for him to agree. "We can work on this together, and when they get back, we'll have more to go off of. I learned more from that interaction than I think that bastard realizes."

Micah smirked at me as he relaxed, dropping his hands. "Parker was actually right about something; it is sexy hearing you swear when you're mad."

"Asshole." I chuckled, smacking his arm as I walked into the kitchen.

Moving about, I pulled what I needed out of the cabinets and fridge to make cookies. I needed something to keep my mind busy to keep from freaking out while we talked. Micah was here, and I was safe, having purified the house. As long as I didn't leave this place for too long, I wouldn't have any trouble with demons.

"What did the Dark Lord tell you exactly?" Micah asked, sitting down at the counter with one of the boys' laptops.

As I scooped out the flour, I went over the interaction again. "Some of it was spoken, but much of what I figured out is from when he was messing with my brain. He wanted me to believe that you guys were failures and would never be able to win against him or value what I have to offer. The only way that he can get my power to work for him is if I choose to help willingly. There is something about Synergy that can't be forced."

Micah nodded his head as he got up and poured himself a finger of whiskey. "At least we have that going for us."

"The important part of what he told me is that his plan is in motion."

Micah rolled his eyes at me. "That doesn't tell us shit, babe."

I paused a moment from measuring out ingredients to look at him. Had he just referred to me as *babe?*

"Don't make a big deal about it or I'll come up with a nickname you'll hate," Micah grumbled into his drink.

I set down the mixing bowl, rested my hip on the counter, and gave him a look with a raised eyebrow. "What if I hate that one?"

"Well, then, Cookie Monster it is," Micah said with a wicked grin, seeming positive I would hate it.

I shrugged my shoulders as I turned to grab the milk out of the fridge. "Works for me."

CHAPTER 32
LAILAH

The boys didn't return before I went to bed, but I woke up with an arm wrapped around my waist, making me smile. Rolling over, I opened my mouth to wake Brayden up but found Micah's sleeping face instead. I paused, giving my brain a moment to catch up to the fact that someone new was sleeping in my bed. The scowl that was on his face ninety percent of the time was gone, and he even had the hint of a smile on his lips. Gently, I took a finger and brushed his chocolate locks out of his face to get a better look.

He'd always been handsome to me, but after what we had been through this past week, I saw deeper than face value. The man he kept trying to hide from the world was far more attractive to me than his outward appearance, as wonderful as it was. At my touch, he began to stir, so I rested my head on my arm and just studied him while I could. All too soon, his eyes fluttered open, and in the soft morning light, the sapphire color of them was breathtaking.

"Good morning," I whispered, not wanting to break the moment.

He grunted, shifted to pull me closer to him, and buried his head further into the pillow.

"Not that I really mind waking up to find you in my bed, but what brings you to these parts?" I asked, running my fingers through his thick hair.

"Nope, too early, come back later with your questions," Micah said, his voice muffled from the pillow.

I giggled and relaxed into the bed, enjoying the moment. A few minutes later, Brayden walked into the room with a wide smile on his face as he saw us together and walked over to me, placing a gentle kiss on my lips. "Good morning, Angel."

"Hi," I said, rolling over to give him another peck on the lips. "You guys made it back late last night. Have too much fun without us?"

"I could say the same about you," Brayden said, his smile shifting into a scowl. "Don't think we didn't notice the purification rites you did around the property. What happened, and why didn't you call me?"

I snuggled farther into the bed to get away from the wave of disappointment and hurt that Brayden was sending me through our connection. I knew he might be irritated that I didn't tell him right away what happened last night, but I didn't want to cause any more problems when he was with his family. Once he knew, he would have left and come back to the house, and there was no reason he needed to do that. Micah and I had managed just fine on our own.

I had maneuvered myself so I was hidden by the blanket and back shrouded by Micah's body. Feeling Micah shift, I was caught completely by surprise when he planted his foot in the middle of my back and shoved me out of bed. I landed on the floor with a thud and a yelp, while Brayden smirked down at me.

Micah's face appeared over me from the bed, his scowl in full form. "Don't you dare use me to hide from your problems. I was the one who said we needed to call them; *you* told me not to."

Gaping at Micah, I sat up, irritation bursting through me. "You agreed that we had it handled! There was nothing they could have done once we fixed everything the Dark Lord had burned."

"*What?*" Brayden barked, drawing both our attention to him. "Get dressed *now*," he said, turning on his heel and leaving the room.

"Oooh, someone's in trouble with Daddy Brayden," Micah chuckled.

I scrunched up my face. "Don't ever call him that again —ew."

Picking myself up off the floor as Micah laughed at me, I grabbed my clothes and headed for the bathroom to get ready. After scrubbing my face, I looked in the mirror and studied my reflection. *Was it really that wrong of me not to tell him right away? It wasn't like I hadn't planned on sharing, I just wanted to do it when they got home. They were the ones who got back so late.*

Making my way to the kitchen, I found them all standing around the counter, arms crossed and frowning. Parker even seemed upset with me as he held one of the cookies I'd made last night for him. I needed tea if we were going to start the day like this. Ignoring them, I bustled around until I had a steaming mug of chai made. I sat at the kitchen table and turned the chair to my jury.

"Okay, I'm ready; let me have it." I sighed.

I could see Brayden fighting to keep control, his jaw clenched and eyes narrowed at me. Micah just looked bored as he sat at the counter, sipping his coffee and watching the other four. Jay, of course, was the hardest one to read, but there was a slight downturn to his lips that spoke volumes.

Hudson, as always, took the high road and stepped forward to break the silence. "Having been newly introduced to our world, I'm not sure you understand the implications of what it means that the Dark Lord showed up here yesterday."

I knew Hudson wasn't trying to make me sound stupid, but having them all turn on me like this was getting my feathers ruffled. "Oh? So you've met him before?"

Hudson's brows furrowed at my remark. "No, no one has seen the Dark Lord since Aiden Ryevick's time."

"Then let me just tell you that he certainly leaves an impression on you," I snapped.

"Apparently, he gives you nightmares too," Micah added. "I could only get you to calm down by holding your hand—that's how I ended up in your bed, FYI."

"Let's back up and start with what happened after we left," Hudson said, sitting down at the table with me and motioning for the others to do the same.

I huffed and took a sip of my tea before I got into it. "Micah and I watched some TV, drank, and ate snacks. Then out of nowhere, the Dark Lord popped out of the TV and started to brainwash me into turning to the dark side. It was almost as if he was planting ideas and thoughts in my head. Just when he was about to place some crazy hex on me, my power freaked out and blasted him across the room. Then I got pissed and started yelling at him, so he threatened me and lit the room on fire." I paused a moment to take a deep breath. "Micah managed to turn the demon fire into normal fire and control it. We combined our powers together and apparently purified the whole mountain. I didn't even know that was a thing."

"Wait, the Dark Lord tried to burn down the house?" Parker interrupted. "How come there's no sign of that even happening?"

"It would seem that when you fix things that a demon ruined, it brings it back to its original state or better. We managed to fix any problem that was caused by a demon anywhere on this mountain," I answered, grinning because it really was kind of a cool trick.

"Why haven't we been able to do that before?" Parker demanded, looking at Hudson.

Hudson removed his glasses and rubbed the bridge of his nose, ignoring Parker before he looked at me. "I can see that you have no idea how close you came to dying or even being turned into a demon-possessed puppet, Lailah. This is not something you should have kept from us; we deserve to know if anything this important happens. We are a team, and that means we have to do this *together*."

"You guys are acting like I wasn't going to tell you at all. If you guys gave me a minute to explain myself without jumping down my throat, I would have shared what else we figured out last night," I grumbled, slouching in my chair.

They all looked at me expectantly.

"Oh, now you're ready to listen?" I asked, raising a brow at them. "Fine, while you guys were working on stuff at Brayden's house, Micah and I looked into things ourselves. We took all the data that you guys gathered and added in the information that the Dark Lord slipped up and gave me. Mainly, the point where he said the Elementi are not as impenetrable as we think."

Hudson froze and then looked at Brayden over his shoulder.

"Care to share with me what you guys found? Because I have a feeling that it might be tied to what we know," I said, resting my chin on my hand.

Brayden came to sit on the other side of me, and I turned my focus on him. "Remember that Charlotte told us that Mom was working on a new project? Well, Hudson was able to sneak into her office and get a good look at what it was."

"And..." I encouraged when he stopped talking.

"It's a new drug that helps make the brain more open to suggestion," Hudson answered.

"Wait, what?" I said, jerking back from both of them. "I was going to tell you guys that Ms. Tabitha was the spy in your house. Now it makes sense why they need her to be there, though."

"Back up, what do you mean Ms. Tabitha is a spy? For who?" Brayden said, grabbing my arm.

"The Dark Lord told me that his plans were set in motion and that the Elementi were not as powerful as they thought.

What he didn't know is that he let the thought slip that someone was in place in one of the families," I said.

"That still doesn't add up to it being Ms. Tabitha. She was checked out by the Elementi and has been with our family for two years now," Brayden challenged, his eyes wide with fear.

"Think about it. When did your mom start to lose it? I know your brother's death was the trigger, but your mom—from what everyone has told me—seemed to be able to manage her mental illness with medication. Now she is totally losing it. That, and when we asked to go sledding, your mom was so involved in her work that she didn't even notice that Charlotte and I were in the room. Ms. Tabitha told us to go have fun, and she would make sure your mom knew where we went," I said and watched the understanding light in his eyes.

"Ms. Tabitha must have also been the one to tell Mom what happened. I couldn't figure out who would have told her or why. None of us would have, and she also could have sent the demons after us while we were there," Brayden said, finally connecting the dots.

I grabbed his hand that was still gripping my arm tightly. "I think Kayley has been right this whole time. Ms. Tabitha must be spiking her tea. Do we even know if she was really taken to see a doctor? Ms. Tabitha did that as well, then came back with all these new holistic meds for your mother to take. What if she's using your mom to create this drug? She'd need your mom for the science behind it, but someone else would have to make it. Who is helping her?"

The tension in the room rose as I looked around the table. Everyone was looking at Hudson with varying looks of apprehension and fear.

"My dad is the other person working with her," Hudson whispered.

My jaw dropped. "Holy shit."

"Yeah, that's one way to put it," Parker agreed, nodding his head. "So, what do we do now?"

I sat back and looked at the guys around me. This was it; this was why I was finally brought into the world. The Dark Lord was gearing up for something, and we were the only ones that could stop it. Now, we just needed to figure out the game and the end goal of this whole thing.

"We do what we were created to do. Kick the Dark Lord's ass and make him wish he never left Hell to begin with," I said, holding each of their gazes. "We have to find out the big picture, and fast. Hudson, can you reach out to your dad and find out what he can tell us about this project?"

"Of course," Hudson said, nodding his head. "I can't imagine why he would be doing this project so secretly. Unless he wants to hide it from my mother for some reason."

"Only way to know is to ask," Jay pointed out.

"True, or we could do something more fun," Parker said, wagging his brows.

Micah groaned. "Please don't tell me we're going to be taking any ideas from this idiot."

"Can we at least hear him out before shooting down his plan?" I said, shooting Micah a look that he just rolled his eyes at.

"That big party for your dad's company is tomorrow, right? Why don't we just confront the evil governess right in the middle of an Elementi party?" Parker suggested, bouncing with his excitement.

"Because, dumbass, there will be normal businessmen and women there that have no idea about the Elementi. If we expose demons into the world like that, how well do you think that will go over?" Micah said, smacking Parker upside the head.

Parker growled at him, walked over to me, picked me up, and placed me on his lap.

"Are you using me as a human shield against Micah?" I asked, trying not to laugh.

"Yeah, some man that makes you. What makes you think that will stop me from hitting you?" Micah challenged.

Parker just wrapped his arms around my stomach and hid his face in the back of my neck. "Maybe it was just the excuse I needed to get some snuggles from Trouble. I haven't been able to spend much time with her since we got here. If Jay isn't sparring with her, then she's working on stuff or cooking. I just needed some cuddles is all."

I burst into laughter. It was probably one of the most adorable things anyone has ever said to me. "Works for me."

"Whatever," Micah grumbled, giving Parker a dirty look. "I still think your idea is shit."

"It might not be," Jay said, causing us all to look at him in surprise. "I agree we can't confront her in front of everyone, but what if we got her alone and did it then? It would keep it away from the family and in an area we can choose for the best advantage."

I grinned at him and gave him a wink. "This is why they pay you the big bucks, Jay."

"Trouble, hand me my laptop," Parker said, his lips brushing my ear and sending shivers down my spine.

Flipping it open and keeping me on his lap, I watched as his fingers flew over the keyboard. I hadn't a clue what he was doing, but I was impressed nonetheless. Moments later, a blueprint was pulled up on the screen, and when I saw the name on the top of it, I gasped.

"Did you just find the blueprints for the hotel they're having the party at?" I asked, amazed.

"Sure did. Now we can have the master of war look it over and see where our confrontation would best be held," Parker said, smugly.

"Hold on, are we really doing this asinine plan?" Micah cut in, throwing out an arm to stop Jay from grabbing the computer.

"We need information, and we can't let her stay in our house," Brayden said with a shrug.

"Logically, it has its risks, but if it goes well, then we will get our hands on a valuable asset," Hudson agreed.

"We all know it was my idea, so I'm in," Parker grinned.

They all turned to Jay expectantly. "I want to look over things, and if I feel it can be done with no casualties, then yes, I think we should move forward."

"Hey, isn't anyone going to ask me what I think?" I snapped.

Micah looked at me and set his head on his hand. "Cookie Monster, your answer is going to be to take the bitch out so we can keep the kids and family safe, no matter the danger to yourself."

Opening and closing my mouth a few times, I didn't have a comeback for that because he was right. So instead, I just leaned back into Parker and huffed, taking a swig of my now cold tea, causing the table to burst out in laughter.

"Now that we all agree, let the planning begin," Hudson said, clapping his hands.

CHAPTER 33

LAILAH

We spent the whole day Friday planning for what was going to happen Saturday. It was amazing to see the guys working side by side, each of them using their strengths. This didn't mean that fights didn't break out every hour or so between them, but we all managed to figure out a plan that we all agreed to. Needing a break from all the testosterone, I went upstairs and called Cami.

"*Lala*, babe, I've missed you so much. Can we please never go a week without seeing each other ever again?" Cami yelled through the phone.

I laughed. I missed her more than I realized. "Girl, you have no idea how much I could use you right now. Have they filled you in on what's been going on here?"

"No, I'm just your personal guardian who was made to stay home for this winter break because you were supposed to be safe at the home of one of the top Elementi families. Of course, I know. I'm more hurt by the fact that you haven't bothered to tell me jack shit about what's been happening. You survived an avalanche; don't you think that's a story your best friend in the whole wide world would *love* to hear?" Cami ranted.

I had to pull the phone away from my ear as she kept getting louder and louder the more upset she got. "You're right, I'm sorry. I should have kept you in the loop myself. I just got over-whelmed trying to manage all the disasters as they come."

"Humph," Cami pouted. "I suppose that is a legit reason, but I'm still not happy with you."

"Would you still help me pick out an outfit for the dinner party tomorrow?" I asked, knowing her answer.

"Tits on my ass, that's right. Of course I'll help you. Hold on, give me a sec. I'm going to turn this into a video chat," Cami said.

I cradled the phone in my hand, and her face popped up on the screen.

"Cami... did you seriously dye your hair neon green?" I asked, my eyes wide, taking it all in.

"Hell yeah, I did! Do you like it? I've been wanting to do this for a while. Maggs did it for me," Cami said with a proud grin on her face.

Shaking my head, I smiled. "It looks amazing. You're one of the only people I know that could pull that off."

"Now I match my car," Cami said, rolling on her bed laughing.

I didn't realize how much I had needed this, just to spend time talking and goofing off with my best friend.

"Okay, so remind me what dresses I made you pack," Cami said, sobering up to the task at hand. "Where is it being held?"

"The Hotel Das Weitzer," I said, looking at the invitation that Brayden had given me. "It says black-tie event."

"Oh, my baby girl's going to knock 'em dead! Now there is only one dress that you packed that will fit this event, and it's the one at the very bottom in the black garment bag. I'm guessing you're one of those people who don't unpack their suit-case if you haven't noticed it yet. Lucky for you, it doesn't wrinkle."

"I don't see the point in pulling everything out of my suit-case when I'm only going to be here for a short time," I muttered.

"Two weeks isn't a short time. Lala, I don't know about you sometimes," Cami laughed. "Now go save your dress and hang it up so it can breathe before you have to wear it."

Setting down the phone, I rummaged through the suitcase and pulled out the garment bag. Unzipping it, I pulled the dress out and examined it. Hanging before me was a stunning matte black dress that would hit me at the knee but had a mesh over-skirt that fell in a hi-low fashion. I hooked it on the back of the bathroom door and grabbed my phone.

"Cami! Where did this dress come from?" I demanded.

Cami was now sitting next to Maggs, who waved at me. "It's one of mine. Cami said you might need something with flair, so I donated to the cause."

I sighed and relaxed a little. "Oh, thank God, I thought Cami went shopping behind my back again. Somehow things keep showing up in my closet that I've never seen before."

Cami frowned as Maggs punched her playfully in the arm. "Baby, you can't keep treating Lailah like she is your dress-up doll."

"Thank you, Maggs," I chirped.

"Not cool, you guys; I can't have both of you ganging up on me. Lala, for the record, you're the one who told me that you wanted to start updating your wardrobe but hated shopping. I happen to have impeccable fashion sense and love shopping. Really, you should be thanking me for all the hard work I've done."

I rolled my eyes and pulled my hair up into a messy bun, having set my phone against the window in the room. "I'm going to try this dress on and make sure that it fits. Maggs is curvier than I am."

"Actually, that's why I picked that dress. It flares out at the waist, so it gives you more va-va-voom," Maggs said, leaning closer to the phone and giving me a wink.

"Don't flirt with my best friend!" Cami said, playfully yanking her back and starting to tickle her.

I grabbed the dress and changed in the bathroom, not wanting to start any fights between the lovers. It was nice to see Cami so carefree and real with Maggs; I hadn't seen her do that with many people. Quickly, I slipped the dress on and zipped it up as far as I could before walking back out to look at the long mirror hung on the wall.

The dress fit perfectly, and it was a higher neck that fit around the edge of my shoulders, showing off some skin but still keeping me covered. Like Maggs said, the dress puffed out slightly at the waist, giving the illusion of having hips that I'd never had before. I twirled and was happy to see the back went to the floor but didn't drag too much.

"Lailah, you look amazing," Maggs said as Cami let out a wolf call.

My face shone, and I had a wide grin on my lips as I turned back to them. "This is awesome, thanks Maggs. Cami, what would I do without you looking after me? Now, what am I going to do with my hair?"

The three of us spent over an hour chatting and deciding the last of the details for what I was going to do for tomorrow. I promised to take pictures so they could see the final outcome, and with that, we ended the call. I'd already removed the dress and hid it in the closet, so I lounged on the bed in sweats and enjoyed the quiet. I should have known it was too good to be true when seconds later, Parker ran into the room and jumped on the bed. He quickly crawled across and pulled me in front of him like I could hide him from sight.

"Where the fuck did that cocknugget run off to?" Micah snarled from the room below. "*Parker.*"

I peered at him over my shoulder. "What did you do now?"

"What makes you think I did anything, Trouble?" Parker drawled as he traced a finger down my arm, trying to distract me.

I slapped his hand away and narrowed my eyes. "You better tell me so I can make a judgment if I should protect you or not."

Parker's eyes widened. "You wouldn't?"

I opened my mouth to yell for Micah, but Parker stopped me by crashing his lips into mine. I froze as he wrapped a hand around the back of my head to keep me still. His full lips were as soft and playful as I thought they might be. As he pulled my lower lip into his mouth and let his teeth hold it there for a second, I groaned and opened to him. Rolling me over on my back, he caged me in his body, hovering over mine as he kissed me like we had all the time in the world. Nothing was going to rush him. I knew that he was known as a flirt and had far more experience than I did, but I never thought I would enjoy his skill quite so much.

I arched under him, wanting to feel him everywhere, wanting him to give the rest of my body the same attention he was paying my lips. Slowly, he drew back and peppered my face with soft kisses. I giggled and looked up into his face, his eyes glowing with heat that I had put there. I let my hands wander up his muscular arms and across his back till they met at his neck. Gently, I tugged at him so I could kiss him easier, but he resisted, playing with me.

"Now, what were you saying?" he asked, giving me a toothy grin.

"Micah, he's in here," I yelled.

The shock on Parker's face was priceless.

"Traitor," he gasped as he flung himself off the bed and ran to the balcony, tossing the door open and turning to look at me. "I'm so going to punish you for that, Trouble."

I just rolled over on my stomach and kicked my legs. "If you live long enough after Micah catches up to you."

He barked out a laugh as he leapt out the door just as Micah zoomed into the room.

"That sneaky bastard. When I find him, I'm going to wring his neck," Micah bellowed.

As I looked at him, something seemed to be off. His skin was tinged orange, like he had applied too much self-tanner, and it was blotchy.

"What happened to you?" I dared to ask.

Micah whipped around as if seeing me for the first time. "The fucktard put orange dye in my conditioner, and when I washed it out, it colored my skin. Asshole is gonna die when I get my hands on him."

Biting my lip, I tried to hold my laughter in because if he heard me, I was going to get killed right alongside Parker.

"Lucky for you, I know a few tricks to get color off your skin. I once tried self-tanner and turned myself into an oompa-loompa, so I needed to get it off," I said, sliding off the bed.

I grabbed his hand and dragged him after me down into the kitchen. Gathering the things I needed, I mixed them together in a large bowl, making a scrub out of lemon juice, baking soda, and sugar. Then I handed it to him and smiled at his confused look.

"Now you're going to take another shower, or even a bath, and scrub, scrub, scrub until you're back to your natural color. Feel free to use my shower if you're worried about other things being messed with," I said.

Micah looked down at the bowl then back up at me. "This will work?"

"It better, because I'm not going to show up with you to a fancy party looking like that. My date better look his best," I said, winking.

Before I lost my nerve, I walked into the living room and sat down on the couch. *OMG. Did I just outright flirt with Micah? What has gotten into me? Since I've been here, I've had Jay walk in on Brayden and me, made out with Micah and then Parker a day later. This is so unlike me! What if I took what Micah said the other day too literally? He did say he didn't want to be bonded to me, yet he did say one day he hoped to. That doesn't make him interested in being your date! Brayden is my date; he is the one I am bonded to. I mean, if you want to get real technical about it, I'll be bonded to all of them at some point.*

"Angel, if you think any harder, your head is going to explode," Brayden said as he sat next to me, wrapping his arm around me and pulling me against his chest. "You're not even blocking your freak out from me. What happened?"

I felt my cheeks heat. How could I tell him what I was freaking out about?

Brayden gently gripped my chin and forced me to look up at him. The love and trust in them gave me the courage to be honest.

"I kissed both Micah and Parker, and then there is the whole thing with Jay," I said, flicking my eyes away from him, feeling too overwhelmed. "When everything went down with the Dark Lord, Micah got asked if he would accept the Oath. He said no, he wasn't ready."

Brayden released my chin, cuddled me against his chest, and rested his head on top of mine and just held me. I felt his natural calm sink into me, showing me just how much this had been building up inside of me. This wasn't something I could talk about with Cami, it needed to be worked out by the six of us.

"I think we need to have a family meeting," I murmured.

"I think that's a good idea. It might also be a good thing for you and Micah to have a conversation one-on-one," Brayden said, kissing the top of my head. "He is opening up to you and finally learning to deal with the others. I know it doesn't seem like it, but he's never been one to play by anyone else's rules."

"Hmm, I hadn't noticed that. He's always so easygoing." I snorted. "Not sure he and Parker are getting any better."

Brayden laughed. "Angel, before, Parker would have never tried to prank him. If this had happened before you entered the picture, I'm not sure any of us could have stopped him from killing Parker. Now Parker is just getting his own revenge. This prank was retaliation from something that happened earlier in the week."

"Sure sounds like improvement when you put it like that," I said, snuggling in deeper against Brayden.

Sensing that I was done talking for now, he grabbed the remote and put on a movie.

CHAPTER 34

BRAYDEN

"I still think there are too many ways this plan can go sideways, man," Micah said as he got ready for the event tonight.

We'd all decided to get ready in the second-floor bedroom and leave the master for Lailah to use without us underfoot. The morning had been spent going over the plan, and everyone's part they were to play. I had called Charlotte to make sure that none of them were coming, so it would just be our parents. I wouldn't do this if they were at the party.

"Yet none of us had a better idea," I said, trying to get my damn bowtie figured out.

"The last thing we should be doing is poking holes in the Dark Lord's plans while Lailah is still vulnerable," Micah grumbled.

I paused and looked over at him. Not many people would see it, but Micah had been my best friend since I was twelve, and he was head over heels for Lailah. "She told me about you not accepting the Oath."

He froze and slowly raised his head to look at me from where he was tying his shoes. He licked his lips and brushed off imaginary lint from his pants before saying anything. "I couldn't. God,

I wanted to, but I knew I wasn't ready to make that commitment to her. Look at all the fucked-up things that have happened since you two bonded."

I raised a brow. "Micah, her getting demon poison in her system is what set all this in motion. It had nothing to do with us bonding. I wasn't even there with her when it happened."

Micah shot to his feet and got up in my face. "That right there is the problem! You left her to be looked after by the others when they aren't fully committed to this or her."

"What?" I scoffed. "So are you saying I shouldn't have left her with you the other day?"

"Damn straight. The fucking *Dark Lord* showed up. What good is one man who isn't even bonded with her going to do against that? She could have been killed, but my sorry ass was frozen, suspended in time until it was too late. It's only a miracle he didn't want her dead this time," Micah snapped.

I rested my hands on his shoulders and gripped them tightly so he had to look at me. "It wouldn't have mattered if it had been me or one of the others. None of us would have had a chance. Each of us keep being selfish and taking on the role of being the weak link when it's all of us. We are all failing her. Everyone keeps telling her that we're a team, and we need to work together if we want to beat this son of a bitch, but we don't even follow our own advice."

Micah sagged in my hold as my words hit home.

"Did you know she's feeling guilty that she kissed you and Parker? Lailah is so afraid of causing more of a divide in our group that she is pulling away from everyone, even me. Part of that is my fault—I shouldn't have assumed that she would be okay with Jay watching, but I will own that. At least they had a conversation about it, and he could share how he feels about her. What about you? Ever stop to think how she would respond to you saying no, then making out with her?" I took a deep breath, realizing how worked up I was getting. This wasn't helping anyone.

"You're right," Micah breathed. "I need to explain that I turned it down because I do care about her, not because I don't want her."

"Let's deal with this first, then we can all sit down and deal with family matters," I said, clapping him on the back.

Pulling on my tux jacket, I met the rest of the guys in the living room, all dressed and ready to go. Everyone looked a little nervous—well, except for Jay, but this is what he did all the time. Then I heard the telltale sound of heels clicking on the wooden floor, signaling Lailah's arrival. When she entered the room, everyone rose to their feet and took in the splendor that was our girl.

Lailah's golden curls were piled up on her head, but a few pieces escaped and brushed against her collar bone. Simple diamonds glinted in her ears, and I couldn't ever remember her wearing earrings before. The black dress hugged her body in all the right places, showing off her curves. I especially loved that the dress showed off her legs, perfectly toned from all the running that she does. Her black heels set off the whole outfit as they glinted in the light with black rhinestones. Never had I seen a more beautiful woman, and she was mine—well, ours—to cherish and love.

"Angel, you look stunning," I said, walking up to her, taking her hand, and kissing the back of it, not trusting myself to taste her lips.

The blush that crept up her cheeks just added to her look, and I couldn't hold back my grin as I saw the guys behind me stunned.

CHAPTER 35

LAILAH

Seeing the boys in their tuxedos took my breath away, and my body heated up at the same time. My instinct was to keep them all home, because I didn't want any other woman seeing them—they were *mine*. The possessiveness caught me off guard, but I swallowed and gave them each a brilliant smile after Brayden stepped to my side, tucking my arm through his.

"Who knew you guys pulled off the James Bond look so well? It's almost a crime to take you to a party where you'll put everyone to shame," I said, deciding to really share what I was thinking.

Parker's grin got wider, if that was even possible, and he sauntered up to me. "Is our little Trouble going to get jealous tonight?"

"Of course not, because you wouldn't do anything that would make me need to be jealous, right?" I teased, deciding to play along.

Parker laughed and kissed my forehead before stepping back from me.

Hudson walked up to me, and a soft blush graced his cheeks

as he took me in. "Lailah, you are truly radiant. I am honored to accompany you to this party with the others."

A finger trailed along my shoulders making me shiver as lips brushed against my ear. "Look what you do to us with a pretty dress and a simple blush," Jay whispered.

Micah let out a loud groan, walked up to me, grabbed my hand, and yanked me after him. "What is this, prom? Come on guys, we have bigger things to deal with."

I really shouldn't have been shocked by how Micah acted; the moment things got emotional, he bailed. Out front was the limo Brayden's dad had sent for us to ride into the party. The driver held open the door, and we climbed in and shifted to the far end so the others could sit.

Once settled, Micah leaned over, and I could feel his lips brush against my ear as he spoke. "You always look beautiful, but tonight you outdid yourself."

The butterflies that fluttered in my stomach at his words made me giddy. Micah would always be Micah, but seeing the glimpses of this softer side of him made me crave it, wanting more.

"Looks like you managed to get all the orange dye off your skin," I teased, not wanting him to know how much his words affected me.

Micah grunted. "My date told me she wouldn't go with me unless I got rid of it. Selfish request, don't you think? Who doesn't want a sun-kissed-looking date?"

I let out a bark of laughter. "God, she sounds awful. Why are you going out with her? I would have just ditched her and done my own thing."

"See, the thing is, I don't think that she really knows how much she means to me. Figured I would take this chance to be able to show her," Micah whispered and placed a soft kiss on my cheek.

My body froze as the meaning of his words hit me. *Was Micah trying to tell me that he wanted this to be a date? What about rejecting the Oath?* I turned to look at him, and my eyes widened as I took in his face. He had a gentle smile on his lips, and I could see his affection towards me in his gaze. Never had I seen him so vulnerable before, and it thrilled and terrified me at the same time.

"What are you whispering about over there?" Parker called from the other side of the limo.

Micah's soft expression instantly changed to one of irritation, and his normal scowl was back on his face. "Isn't the point of talking quietly that no one else hears what you're saying?"

"Yeah, but that always makes me want to know what they are saying more," Parker grinned.

"Idiot," Micah mumbled.

Parker leaned forward, cupping his ear. "I'm sorry, what was that?"

Just as Micah opened his mouth to share, I butted in. "Will there be any dancing at this gathering, or is it more of an eat fancy food and talk shindig?"

"It's been a few years since I've gone, but typically it's pretty formal with stuffy rich people that like to rub elbows with my parents," Brayden said, his head tilted back with his eyes closed.

"That doesn't mean that we can't start some dancing, maybe they just need someone to take the lead!" Parker said, wagging his eyebrows. "If there's music, dancing can always happen."

"This isn't some frat party, Parker," Micah grumbled. "Can you really dance, or is the bump and grind all you got?"

"Oh, because you know how to dance there, flame boy?" Parker said, baiting Micah.

Micah leaned forward, his elbows resting on his knees. "I was classically trained when I was younger. My parents found it was a valuable skill and helped with learning control."

Parker busted out laughing and almost fell out of his seat at the force of his laughter. "Oh God, I could just picture little Micah learning to ballroom dance."

Micah lunged out of his seat to tackle Parker, but I grabbed his arm.

"Enough, Parker!" I snapped. "This is not the time or the place to be picking a fight. We are going to a party, yes, but let's remember *why* we are at this event. Now knock it off before we leave you both in the limo."

Both boys stopped and looked at me, a little shocked. Parker picked himself back up and slid into his seat without another word. Micah settled back and turned to look out the window, resting his hand on his fist. The mood in the limo definitely dimmed, but I didn't really care; we needed to act like a team, even if we weren't.

The rest of the ride was quiet as we all turned to our own thoughts. I ran through the plan again, trying to look at it from all angles. I just didn't know enough to figure out what I might have missed. This was my first battle with a demon, and I had little else to go on other than faith and trust in myself and the boys. As we pulled up to the hotel, everyone seemed to come back to life as we exited the limo. I made to get up so I could exit, but Micah stopped me, grabbing my hand.

"Would you really have left us in the limo?" Micah questioned.

I leveled him with a look. "Without hesitation. We can't afford any more unknowns in this."

Much to my surprise, he grinned at me and pecked me on the lips. "That's my girl."

Flushed, I maneuvered my way out of the limo to where Brayden was waiting for me. He smiled at me and wrapped an arm around my waist as we headed into the hotel.

The Hotel Das Weitzer was beautiful, set right in the older section of Graz and overlooked the Mur river. The inside was very rustic-chic, decorated beautifully for the holiday seeing as it was only a few days before Christmas. A hotel staff member walked up to us, and Brayden spoke to them in fluent German before being led in the direction of the party. I gazed at the beautiful architecture of the hotel until we came to the ballroom filled with people dressed to the nines.

I gasped at the sight; it seemed like something out of a Christmas Hallmark movie. The ballroom had light wooden floors that shone in the light of a large glass chandelier. Fresh evergreen garland was draped along the ceiling, making the room smell wonderful. Beautifully decorated Christmas trees were set up around the room, adding to the festiveness. Cocktail tables were scattered throughout, with people standing by them chatting. Smartly dressed servers filtered through the crowd with food and drinks of various kinds.

"Holy crap, I wasn't expecting this," I whispered to Brayden. "This is so out of my league."

Brayden looked down at me and gave me a squeeze before he took my hand to lead me into the room. "Trust me, you'll be great; everyone will love you."

Taking a deep breath, I plastered a smile on my face and followed his lead. The other boys were at my back, lending me their support by sticking close. Brayden led us to the back of the room where some couches were set up, and I spotted Adriana and Oliver with a few gentlemen and another couple.

"Shit," Brayden said under his breath. He stopped and looked at me with worry showing in his eyes. "I totally forgot that this might happen."

"What?" I hissed, fear building in my chest at what he might be telling me.

"Parker, what on earth are you doing here?" a woman said, standing up, joy lighting up her face in a familiar way.

"I hope you don't mind meeting everyone's parents tonight," Brayden said with a sheepish smile.

My shoulders sagged in relief that it wasn't something demon related, but then his words hit home, and I jerked my head over to the people sitting with his parents. "Oh God, that's them, isn't it?"

"Yes, all but Hudson's mom. His parents can't be in the same room together," Brayden said in a hushed voice.

"Mom! I didn't know you guys were going to be here," Parker said, catching his mother up in a big hug that seemed to engulf her small body.

Parker's mother is where he got his looks from, but his height and build were all his dad. His mother had red hair as well, but hers was a deeper red whereas Parker's was more orange-red. Her warm brown eyes matched her son's, along with the smile that was lighting up the room.

"Well, son, it's nice to see you taking an interest in the business side of things," Parker's father said, giving him a side hug and slapping him on the back, rather hard by the sound of it.

Parker's dad was just as tall but bulkier than Parker. I could tell back in the day he had a more fit physique like his son, but age caught up to him and made him a little softer. His brown hair was graying at the hairline, but it was still thick and healthy. His hazel eyes were filled with humor, and smile lines were prevalent around them.

"When half my friends were going to be here, I figured why not. Oh, and I couldn't pass up seeing Lailah all dolled up. Speaking of..." Parker turned and beckoned me over with a hand.

Brayden gave my hand a squeeze before he let go with a little shove on my lower back. Once I was close enough, Parker snaked an arm around my waist and yanked me in front of him. "Mom, Pop, I would like you to meet Lailah!"

"Oh, isn't she lovely," Parker's mom said, cupping the sides of my face and giving me Parker's signature grin.

"It's lovely to meet you, Mr. and Mrs. Jones," I said, trying not to show my surprise at how touchy-feely they were.

"Oh Lord, please call me Dolly, Mrs. Jones sounds so old," Dolly tittered, waving a hand at me.

Before I could say anything, Parker's dad swept me up in a bone-crushing hug, picking me up off my feet. "We are so happy to finally meet you, Lailah," he said and set me down, resting his hands on my shoulders. "Please call me Tobias or Pop, whatever you're more comfortable with. We're family, after all."

I laughed, unable to hold it back with the amount of happy energy that I was surrounded by. I could now see why Parker was the way he was and could only imagine what it must be like at family gatherings.

"When you said you had something important to take care of, you could have just said you wanted to spend the holidays with Lailah," Dolly said, giving Parker a wink. "We would never get in the way of your budding family, or someone special in your life."

I blushed furiously at how casually they were talking about how I was going to be with more than just her son. Apparently, they were very open-minded people; I just wasn't sure that the others would be as understanding.

"Do you mind if I steal her?" Hudson said, coming up behind me.

"Of course not, son. As much as we would like to hog her attention, she has more than one family to meet," Tobias said in his booming voice.

If I could crawl under a rock, I would. The whole room heard what he said. Praying that not everyone here understood English, I slipped my arm around Hudson's, and he led me away.

"Don't worry, none of our families will judge you. To be honest, they're thrilled to be the parents of the boys who matched with Synergy," Hudson said encouragingly.

I looked up and gave him a small smile. "Thanks. I just was caught off guard. I totally wasn't expecting this tonight."

"With everything going on, I think it slipped all our minds. I was supposed to be with my mother first, so it didn't even dawn on me that Father would be here," Hudson said as we approached a stoic-looking gentleman.

His father was tall and lean, much like Hudson. His hair was dark silver with white sprinkled through and was impeccably styled. His beard was whiter, trimmed close and well maintained. Hudson had the same piercing blue eyes that were full of intelligence. This man was a professional through and through, everything perfectly in order.

"Father, allow me to introduce Lailah Mackenzie, the sixth member to our team," Hudson said once we reached his father.

"Pleasure to meet you, Lailah. I'm Chadwick Lacy," he greeted, holding out his hand to me.

A little thrown off by the drastic difference between the two families, I left him holding his hand out for a few seconds. Quickly, I gripped his hand and gave it a simple shake before he released it, and he tucked it away in his pocket.

"Hudson tells me you're from America. It must be quite the change to be here in Europe," Chadwick said, taking a sip of his drink.

Suddenly nervous, I cleared my throat before answering. "Yes, it was quite a big difference, but thankfully, I have Hudson and the others to help me out."

"I'm glad to hear that my son has been someone you can lean on. He tends to get so lost in his studies that he forgets there are other things in the world. My hope is that with you now around, he will get to experience more of what life has to offer," Chadwick said, surprising me by giving me a wink and a slight upturn of his mouth.

Smiling back at him, I nodded my head. His father was more of a surprise than I thought he would be. "I've already made him go to his first college party—there may even have been some dancing involved."

"My, my, you work quickly. Well, I won't keep you; I'm sure there are a few more people who would like to meet you. Until we chat again," Chadwick said with a slight bow of his head before he wandered off into the crowd.

Hudson let out a low whistle. "Wow, he must have really liked you. I've never seen him talk that much to a person he's just met before."

I gaped at Hudson. "That was a lot of talking? He could give Jay a run for his money."

We both laughed, and we headed back to where the guys were talking with Brayden's parents. I was a little nervous to see Adriana again, unsure of how she would react to seeing me. Brayden seemed to think that it would be fine, that she was just having a bad day when she threw me out. And if what we believed was true, then most of her mental illness was caused by the demon.

"Lailah! Oh, it's so good to see you again," Adriana said, a genuine smile on her face as she reached out to grasp my hand. "I am so sorry about how I acted before; from what Oliver tells me, I was just awful to you."

I faltered a little. *Did she not remember what she said or did? Should I bring it up or just leave it alone?*

"No hard feelings, I would be upset too if something ever happened to my family. Moms can't help but be protective," I said, choosing to follow her lead.

"I do hope all of you will be at the house for Christmas! It would be so lovely to have all six of you," Adriana pleaded, clutching my hands in hers.

I looked around at the boys to see what they thought, and they just nodded in agreement. "Looks like we're doing Christmas together then."

"Hey, Dad, is Ms. Tabitha around? I have something I wanted to ask her," Brayden said, reminding me that I had all but forgotten why we were here.

"She was joining us later once she got the little ones down for the night. Martin is a good man, but he's too easily persuaded to let them stay up too late," Oliver explained.

I glanced over at Brayden, and through our look, we both seemed a little uneasy at the fact she wasn't already here.

"Jalen," a man barked, startling Adriana and me, causing us both to jump.

I turned to see an older Asian man wearing a black and white traditional Japanese yukata. His face was stern with dark-brown eyes holding no warmth. His slate-gray hair was brushed straight back, neatly in order.

"What are you doing here? You are supposed to be with your mother. That is the only reason that you had the time off," he snapped, his accent heavy.

Jay's father was almost half his height, but that in no way made this man any less intimidating. The dominant air that was coming off him in waves set me on edge. I didn't appreciate how he was treating Jay either, and the only reason I wasn't saying anything was the slight shake of the head he gave me.

When Jay responded, he did so in Japanese, and whatever he said about made his father turn purple. His father, in a voice low enough not to cause a scene, ripped into Jay, his knuckles white as he gripped his polished wooden cane. Jay just stood there and took the tongue-lashing with a stoic face, but I could tell he had tuned out by how vacant his eyes were. Once his father had said his piece, he gave a huff and rounded on me.

"I know who and what you are," he snarled. "Let's hope that you are more worthy of the gift bestowed upon you than these other useless so-called Knights."

Astounded at his words, I just stood there, unable to think of a thing to say in our defense.

"Let it also be known that I forbid my son to ever bond with you. Just because you are blessed by the angels does not make you worthy of my son. His wife will be chosen for him as was mine, to bestow honor on our family," Jay's father said with a smack of his cane on the wood floor.

Having nothing more to say, the man stormed out of the room. Getting over my shock, I walked over to Jay and grabbed his hand in both of mine, letting my thumb gently caress the back of his hand. I leaned my head on his arm and didn't say a word to him, just let him feel my support. Nothing his father said changed my view of Jay. He had more than proven to me that he was nothing like his father.

"I'm sorry he said those things to you," Jay said in a low voice for only me to hear. "He has never thought the Elementi Warriors were any match against his military."

"Don't worry about me, I don't care what he thinks. Your opinion and the other four's matter to me, not some short-sighted man," I said, letting my irritation leak through.

I looked up when I felt his body shake slightly, worried I had upset him with my words. What I wasn't expecting to see was the grin on his face and the humor in his eyes. "I think you are one of the first people to ever call my father short before. Although, I would advise you not to do that to his face."

My spirits lifted knowing that I was able to put that smile on his face. I chuckled, leaning into him further as we looked out over the party. It had been far more interesting that I'd thought, not knowing anyone but the boys and Brayden's parents.

"Who the *fuck* let you into this party," Micah bellowed.

Looks like it's about to get even better.

CHAPTER 36

LAILAH

Peering around Jay, I saw Micah toe-to-toe with a short, rotund woman. She was dressed in a skintight black dress that did not flatter her shape, and was dripping with gems. Her dark auburn hair was pinned up, and her face was covered in gaudy dark makeup.

Was this the woman that Micah didn't want to share the same room with? Seeing how he was looking at her, I no longer thought he had ever hated me. The look of disgust that he was giving this woman would have curdled milk in seconds.

"Don't you talk to me like that, you ungrateful brat. You're lucky that anyone in our family took you under their wing. Do you know how much I have done for you?" she shouted back.

Micah scoffed at her and motioned to her outfit. "Looks like I've been the one taking care of you. How much have you spent out of my trust, you stupid cow? This is more than the contract you signed would afford you as the CEO of my family's business and estates."

"How dare you!" the woman screeched and raised a hand to slap Micah.

Now I'd had enough. No one was allowed to hit my boys. Without even thinking, I sent out a burst of power that knocked her away from Micah and on her ass as I marched over to them.

"Madam Lazonick," a man cried out, rushing over to help her get to her feet.

"Get off me," she grumbled, shaking the man off once she was upright and brushed herself off.

I had now reached Micah's side and stood proudly next to him.

"Do you have any idea who I am, you little bitch?" she growled, sparing me with her gaze.

I gave her a smile that was more teeth than would be friendly. "I don't give a fuck who you are, I won't let you talk to him or me like that. If you don't watch your mouth, I'll do it again."

"I am Micah's legal guardian, and the person who is entrusted with looking over all of his family assets until he is twenty-one. If he wants anything left to inherit, I would suggest you watch yourself, you little chit."

I laughed, unable to take this woman seriously. "It just so happens that I have a brother who is a lawyer, and I know the laws are different here in Europe, but I have a feeling that what you're doing is considered illegal. It might even count as fraud, which in most places would get you put in jail. So, I would take a step back and tone down the threats before you end up behind bars."

As I talked, I could feel my power twining its way around her, making her feel the weight of my threat. It would seem that our weapons may not inflict any damage to humans, but our power was another story. I didn't want to truly hurt this woman, but fearing what might happen was acceptable when it came to protecting my people, my family.

"Who. Are. You?" she gasped.

I leaned forward so I could whisper in her ear, letting the word fall from my lips. "Synergy."

Hearing her gasp, I held her in place with my power so she

couldn't pull back. "Just so we are perfectly clear, Micah is *mine*, so when you fuck with him, you fuck with me. You might be his family, but you're not mine."

Putting a smile on my face, I stepped back and freed her from my power and wrapped my arm around Micah's waist. Hesitantly, he put his arm around my shoulder, but when I put my hand on his chest, he held me tighter.

"If you don't mind, we have a Christmas party to enjoy, and you are not welcome here," Micah spoke, his voice hard, leaving no room for question.

Yet that didn't seem to stop his aunt. "You don't have the authority to do that."

"Then I'll say it. You are not welcome here, Muriel. I made it clear that you were not to show up at this gathering. Micah is the shareholder in this company, not you. Now leave before I have you escorted out," Oliver said, coming to stand with Micah, resting a hand on his shoulder.

Muriel huffed and thought about saying something, but just grabbed a glass of champagne and chugged it before waving to her attendant. "Don't think this is settled, Micah. You still have three years until you can take over." Turning on her heel, she made her way out of the ballroom, shoving people out of her way as she went.

"Can't imagine why I've never heard you talk about her," I drawled, looking at Micah.

"Everyone has that family member you not so secretly wish you could kill," Micah muttered.

Oliver chuckled, waving over a server that had a tray full of drinks. He handed us each one. "I think we all need one after dealing with that."

I wasn't sure what it was, but the short tumbler was half full of amber liquid. I took a sip, and the spice of the drink hit me first, then the smooth liquor caressed my tongue. Not having had much liquor before, I had no clue what I was drinking, but it was delicious.

"What is this?" I asked, taking another sip.

"Spiced brandy. Old family recipe that we only have made during the holidays," Oliver explained. "I wouldn't drink it too quickly—it sneaks up on you."

"Good to know." I smiled as he wandered back to Adriana.

Micah set his drink down on a table next to us and placed his hands on my hips, turning me to face him. "What did you say to her? I've never seen her look so scared before."

I gave him a soft smile and shrugged my shoulders. "Nothing really, just told her I didn't like how she was treating you."

Micah frowned at me, not believing me at all.

"Shouldn't you be proud that I stood up for myself?" I teased, poking him in the chest.

"I would be, if you were really standing up for yourself, but you weren't. You were defending me," Micah griped.

I searched his eyes, trying to see if I could figure out what about that had upset him. "Micah. I don't think *you* really know how I feel about you. I've claimed you as one of my people, and I will do anything for people that are close to me. It's the five of you and Cami; you guys have become my family out here. When someone does something to you, it's like them doing it to me."

Micah's eyes filled with so many emotions, I couldn't pick them all out. "Why would you do that? Getting close to people only gives them more power to hurt you along the way."

I smiled softly at him, knowing what he was getting at. "Those that are worth being part of my family may let me down or hurt me, but the difference is, they wouldn't have done it intentionally. They will also do whatever it takes to earn back my trust."

"How can you know that?" Micah asked, his grip on my hips getting tighter.

I shrugged my shoulders. "I have faith in them. Trust is not given or earned lightly, but all of you have never given me a reason not to put my trust in you. Eventually, you will see this too, but I'm not in a rush. I'll wait till you're ready."

I hadn't at all known I felt that way until the words came out of my mouth, but now that they had, I knew it was the absolute truth. Cami and these men of mine completed me, and I was going to show them that we were better together, rather than butting heads and arguing.

Out of the corner of my eye, I saw Brayden making his way over to us with a determined look on his face.

"Looks like it's showtime," I whispered, placing a kiss on Micah's cheek as he let me go.

As Brayden reached us, I felt fear slam into me from our connection. "What's wrong? What happened?"

"She brought Charlotte with her," Brayden said through clenched teeth.

"Fuck," Micah growled.

I looked around the room, and my eyes landed on Parker's mom. "I have an idea. All of your families are very close, right?"

Brayden's brows creased as he looked at me. "Yeah, I guess it's been a while since they have all gotten together."

"That's even better. I'll be right back," I said, rushing off towards Dolly.

Dolly smiled at me when I reached her, but then the smile faded and her face became more serious. "What's happened, darling?"

"I need you to do something for me and not ask any questions, because I don't have the time to answer them," I said quickly in a hushed voice.

Dolly just nodded, the look of a protective mother shining in her eyes. "I need you to find Charlotte Dolton and keep her away from her governess that brought her to the party."

"Done," Dolly said, and she was off like a shot.

That had been way easier than I expected that to be.

Seeing Hudson and Jay, I signaled them to follow me, noting Parker was already with the other two. Once all together, I explained what I did.

"That was brilliant, Trouble! There is no way that shifty

governess will suspect anything odd when an old family friend wants to catch up. I think it's been years since they've seen each other, lots to talk about," Parker said proudly.

"Now we have to set the rest of the plan in motion," Hudson said, pulling out his phone and passing it around. We all had one more look at the blueprints so we knew where to go.

I held a hand out in the middle of our circle and quirked an eyebrow at the others. Parker grinned and plopped his hand on mine, followed by the others, until it was just Micah. He rolled his eyes and set his on the top of the pile. I gave a sharp nod, and we broke, no cheer needed. I just wanted them all to acknowledge that we were all in this together.

Scanning the room, I found the exit that I needed to take and slipped out into the hall. I pulled the black zip ties out of my pockets and zip-tied the doors shut. I did the same for the two others before I made my way out into the garden, where we would have the confrontation. We needed to make sure none of the party guests accidentally made their way out here and got hurt in the crossfire. We didn't expect Ms. Tabitha to go down easy.

On silent feet, I felt Jay come up behind me. I would have never known if my power hadn't been out and swirling around me. It was ready for a fight, having gotten a taste of it with Muriel. Neither one of us spoke as we waited, tension high in the air around us. This was going to be our first stand as Elementi Warriors united with Synergy. A declaration of war.

"Brayden, I understand you are upset that your girlfriend got kicked out of the house, but we have to consider what is best for your mother. She is not well, and I fear that the next thing to set her off will do permanent damage," Ms. Tabitha said, her voice the only sound in the silent night.

"You're someone she will listen to. If you explain that what happened had nothing to do with Lailah, she would believe it," Brayden pleaded as they walked into the garden.

Ms. Tabitha stopped and turned to Brayden with a gentle

hand on his arm. "She is my boss and someone I care about. Using my position like that wouldn't be right. This is a family matter and should be handled as such."

Taking a deep breath, I steadied myself before I called out. "You're right, this is a family matter we need to talk about."

Ms. Tabitha stiffened ever so slightly as she turned her head to look at me. Unmasked hatred and anger were alight in her eyes upon seeing me. "What would you know about this family? I have been with them for almost two years. Looking after them, nurturing the little ones, and protecting their ailing mother."

I unfurled my power even more, letting it fill the garden, and when it reached her, she flinched. No normal human would have been able to feel my energy in such an open space.

"Ms. Tabitha, I believe you are nurturing the whole family, but I also think it's for your own agenda," I said, proud that my voice was strong and even as I approached her. "I got the pleasure of meeting your real boss the other day. He seemed to think that I might be useful to him, so I was surprised that he would send such an attack on us on the sledding trail."

Ms. Tabitha paled, and her eyes flicked around, searching for a way out. As I had been talking, the boys made a circle around us, and each of them had their blessed weapons in hand. If she tried to escape, then she would be met with force.

"I had trouble placing you, because I know you're not a demon. You aren't like the other greater demons I have interacted with that hide in the shell of a human, but you're also not a mid-level either. You have been around for two years, and most known cases say that your body can only survive a few months before it begins to deteriorate. So... what are you, Ms. Tabitha?" I mused, watching for any signal she would attack or flee.

"I am a true follower of the Dark Lord!" she snarled.

At this admission, her appearance began to change. Her eyes bled completely black, and her skin turned sallower and grayer. Black veins appeared on her skin, crawling up her throat and around her eyes. She looked like what you'd think a dark witch would look like. Her gray hair was released from its bun and floated around her, adding to her creepy look.

"For years, I have trained in the Dark Lord's ways. I was blessed with his seal, granting me access to his demonic powers." Ms. Tabitha said, showing us a symbol on the back of her hand. "While the world was waiting for you to be born, our Dark Lord and master was creating an army. We of the Dark Army cannot be traced like demons, and our ability to infiltrate the Elementi is unparalleled." Her voice boomed around us, aided by her magic.

Holy shit. This is not at all what I thought was going to happen.

"What are you going to do now, Synergy?" Ms. Tabitha sneered. "If you think you can simply kill me, then I should warn you that I tied my life force to his mother. Not only do I control her mind, but her life as well!" she said, starting to cackle.

My eyes shot over to Brayden. Nothing we'd prepared for would deal with a situation like this.

"Oh, does that change your mind on killing me? Look at you, so pathetic worrying about the death of one woman when she created the tool that the Dark Lord needed to gain more followers to his cause. The Elementi's time is up, and the Dark Army will rule the world. You can't stop us. The wheels have already been set in motion," she taunted.

My heart skipped a beat as understanding hit. "What did you do?! We know what Adriana was making, but she hadn't even developed an actual serum yet."

Tabitha looked at me with her emotionless black eyes and gave me an exaggerated frown. "Oh, you poor thing. You think we care for playing by the rules? Who needs that when all it takes is the right cocktail and some demon venom in the guise of a miracle drug? The rich and powerful don't want to wait; they will do anything, pay anything, for a cure to whatever ails them. Even if it hasn't been tested or approved. Besides, if one of the top pharmaceutical companies in the world produced it, who's to challenge it?"

"NO! My father would never allow something like that to happen," Hudson barked, taking a step forward.

"Silly boy, what do you know? You hardly even speak to your family since your parents divorced. You hide away and hope that it was all a lie," Tabitha said, baring her teeth at Hudson.

His face was stricken as her verbal attack struck a nerve. I could see the truth of her words in his eyes and the pain that was flooding them.

Oh, she did not just fuck with my family!

Trusting my gut and my powers, I lashed out at Tabitha, pulling strength from all the boys. I blended all of our powers together into a ball, then thrust it at her. It glowed bright white as it slammed Tabitha, but it was blocked by a shield of bright green flames. The attack enraged Tabitha, and she spoke words I didn't understand, a flaming green sword appearing in her hands. I felt my power manifest my own weapons.

The battle had begun.

CHAPTER 37

LAILAH

I knew that the boys had been training together since they were sixteen, but seeing them move as one unit was impressive. Micah darted in with his twin swords, blocking Tabitha from attacking me. Jay's arrow, propelled by the wind, hit home deep in her back, causing her to let out a scream that chilled my bones. Tabitha let out a shot of demon fire in Jay's direction, but Hudson blocked it with a shield of water. When the fire hit, steam billowed out, making it hard for us all to see.

"Is that all you have, little knights? I thought you would be tougher," Tabitha cackled.

Thankfully, I was able to see everyone's energy like a haze around them. Tabitha glowed in that neon-green fire and black void, so it wasn't hard to keep track of her. Parker swept in with his long-bladed staff, aiming for her legs. Tabitha blocked the attack but wasn't prepared for Hudson to appear on the other side, shooting her right in the head twice. She stumbled and fell to her knees, black blood seeping out of her hairline, but she shook it off and sent out a burst of green flame in all directions, pushing us back.

"We aren't strong enough!" Hudson yelled as he dodged

another attack. He wasn't fast enough and got nicked by her sword on the leg and let out a grunt of pain.

Parker lunged, his blade slicing deep into her arm, causing her to drop her sword and open herself up for Jay to land another arrow right into her heart. To my shock and horror, she yanked out the arrow and started chanting. The ground began to tremble, and the air became thin as she continued.

"What the fuck is this woman made out of?" Micah said, making his way over to me.

"Pure evil, if I had to take a guess," I muttered, my mind racing to find a solution.

Somehow, there had to be a way to kill this creature and make sure we didn't kill Brayden's mom. If it was even true that they were tied together—no one said demons were the honest type.

Not giving up, the boys bombarded Tabitha with everything they could think of, but nothing made it through the shield her power made. As the oppressive dark energy kept building, it sent me crashing to my knees. I clutched my heart, knowing that the pain I was feeling stemmed from the demon taint. The dark power she gathered called to it, almost as if it was going to pull it right out of me.

"Make it *stop*," I screamed, feeling blood in my mouth and something running down my face from my eyes.

"Fucking hell," Parker said, stumbling his way over to me. "Hang in there, Trouble, we'll figure this out."

My eyes were blurred red from all the blood as I knelt there, shaking. I wrapped my arms around myself, trying not to shatter. *How is this happening to me? I'm Synergy, the power that can turn the tide in the fight between good and evil! What a disappointment I am. Maybe they were right all along: I am the weak link, and I will get everyone killed. I should just give up and let them take me. It would be better than letting them harm anyone else.*

"Yes, Little Synergy, come to me. You need my help. I will

teach you what it means to have true power," the Dark Lord's harsh voice whispered through my ears.

I let out a sob as my mind and heart battled over what choice to make. Just when I felt like the pain was just too much, I felt a hand on my shoulder that burned like a hot coal. Then another that was cool and soothing, like a cold drink on a hot day. A soft breeze swirled around me, giving me the chance to breathe. Someone grasped my face and brushed away the bloody tears, sending me a burst of strength. The pain in my heart eased slightly, and I felt life flood my senses. Then someone took my hand, and the love that flowed through that connection, along with the calming steadfast reassurance, grounded me. I knew where I belonged, and it was with these men. Together, we were unbeatable.

Slowly, painstakingly, I gave *them* power this time instead of taking it. I let my power flow freely into them, flooding their system with my golden light. It melded with theirs, and each one burned brighter and hotter than before. When they'd taken as much as they could handle, I pulled back the connection but didn't close the door.

"Blast the bitch back to Hell, boys," I declared, my voice hoarse but strong.

They each released me as I wiped furiously at my eyes, trying to clear them. I needed to see what was going to happen next. My sight was still blurry as I watched in amazement. Each of the boys now were adorned with armor and upgraded weapons that glowed with holy light. I shifted, trying to stand by myself, and that is when I noticed that I had glowing armor too. Instead of my two sai, I had a short sword and large, round shield in my grip. I used the shield as leverage to heave myself to my feet. There was no way I was going to end this battle on my knees.

Tabitha, bloody and broken, hissed at all of us as the demon energy she had gathered swirled around her in a dark mist that was easily seen in the light we shed. "You might kill me, but you won't defeat the Dark Lord so easily. He is more powerful than you can imagine, and he gains more power every day."

Realization of what she was going to do sent my body into motion. "She's going to sacrifice herself!"

"Not if I stop her first," Jay growled as he nocked an arrow, locking onto his target. The arrow flew true and hit her right between the eyes, and holy light burst out, making her gasp and crumple to the ground.

"Duck!" I screamed as I hoisted up my shield, jumping to stand in front of them.

The blast of demon energy burst out, and a shockwave of sound followed like a bomb exploding. Digging my feet into the ground, I held off the blast from hitting us, but I could feel my feet slipping. Then my guys were right behind me, supporting me, keeping me strong and upright against this attack. When the demonic energy had dissipated, we noticed we'd attracted a small crowd of people. All the boys' parents were there—even Jay's father, hands clasped on his cane casually. I scanned the group, and my eyes landed on Oliver holding Adriana in his arms.

"Did we win?" Parker asked, breaking the silence as our armor and weapons faded away.

I'm not sure if it was the shock or the overwhelming relief I felt, but I burst out laughing. Eventually, the others joined in as we all huddled together in one big, laughing hug. We had done it! Had we almost died? Maybe, but we won in the end, and that is all that matters.

Finally, we broke apart, still chuckling, but Brayden reached out for me, holding my face in one hand and caressing my cheek with his thumb. "Angel, are you alright?"

"Honestly, I don't even know how to answer that. I'm in desperate need of a shower and a stiff drink," I said, leaning into his hand.

"I think we can arrange that," he murmured, placing a kiss on my forehead.

"Damn, Trouble, you look like you were trying out for the part of Carrie," Parker said, wrapping an arm around my shoulders and leading me towards the group of parents.

"I look that good, huh?" I teased, giving him a half-hearted smile.

"Nothing some sugar cookies and sleep couldn't fix," he said, smiling.

I groaned, leaning more into him. "God, that sounds amazing right now, but somehow I have a feeling that sleep is going to have to wait."

"Yeah, I figured that too. Parents are going to want a debriefing," he muttered, kissing my temple.

"Parents," I gasped and pulled out of his arms, moving as quickly as I could over to Oliver. "Is she okay? Please tell me she's still alive."

Oliver looked at me, his green eyes full of questions as he looked from me to his wife. "She is alive but unconscious. We were on our way to take her to a hospital because she was seizing when we stumbled upon... whatever just happened."

I blew out the breath I had been holding. "Thank God she's alive! If you give us someplace to clean up, I promise we will answer any and all questions you have."

"This is going to be some explanation, by the looks of it," Tobias said, shaking his head at me.

"You have no idea," I mumbled.

An hour later, I found myself in a hotel room, freshly showered and wearing sweatpants and a t-shirt that were both too large. We had to make do with what the hotel could provide for us from the gift shop in the lobby. They had nicer options to pick from, but I was looking to be warm and clean. I passed through the master bedroom into the living room of the penthouse suite we'd been placed in. There sat all the fathers waiting for us to get cleaned up—Dolly was keeping an eye on Adriana.

Oliver and Tobias had ditched their jackets and bowties, sitting more relaxed. Chadwick still looked put together, but his hair was mussed from him combing his fingers through it. Jay's father, whose name I still didn't know, sat in the armchair, back ramrod straight, hands perched on his cane, eyes closed. The moment I stepped into the room, he opened them and held my gaze for a second before closing them once again.

"Here, I brought up a bottle of the Dolton's family brandy for us to drink," Oliver said, handing me a glass.

"Thanks."

I settled in the middle of the long couch, curling my legs under me and taking a long drink out of the glass. The liquor warmed my belly and chased away the last of the chill from the battle. Hudson was the first of the boys to finish up and came to sit next to me. Then Brayden, Jay, and Micah followed, getting settled around me until Parker joined us last. He decided to sit on the ground, leaning against my legs and resting his head on my thigh. Unable to hold myself back, I combed my fingers through his damp hair, setting me more at ease.

"Where do we even start?" Tobias asked, giving us all a critical look.

When none of the boys spoke up, I decided to take the lead. "Let's start with what you don't know."

"How did all the boys end up here? That was not what we had been told would be happening over winter break," Jay's father demanded.

I took another sip of my drink, needing to center myself before dealing with this man. I reminded myself that he was Jay's father and would be in my life for a very long time.

"A week ago, Brayden, Micah, and I went with the other Dolton kids sledding. While going down the sledding trail, we were attacked by a horde of demons. We decided to reach out to the others to make sure they weren't also in danger." I paused and met his cool gaze. "They decided on their own to come here to help us figure out what was going on. I did not ask that of them."

"Parker, why didn't you tell us that is why you came here? We wouldn't have stopped you from dealing with Elementi business! We know that is part of being a parent to an Elementi Warrior," Tobias asked, disappointment written all over his face.

"We came just to make sure Lailah was okay, there was no way we could guess it would turn into something like this. Plus, there are other things you don't know about the situation that I couldn't tell you," Parker explained.

Tobias's frown deepened. "The Elementi do not keep secrets."

"It's not a secret when it's not your information to give. Certain things have happened that involved Lailah, and I didn't have her permission to share her private matters with others," Parker explained.

My heart warmed that he would be so considerate not to share all the things that had happened since I came into power. I knew the Elementi prided themselves on being open and honest —no locked doors, as Beth would say.

"What Parker didn't tell you is that I'm demon tainted. I was out patrolling and got attacked, and even though I was healed and cleansed, I still have some demon venom lingering. It has caused some side effects, and the Dark Lord is trying to use it as leverage to get me to join him," I started, not wanting to cause any trouble between the boys and their families.

"What?!" Jay's father spluttered, shooting to his feet. In his anger, he shifted to speaking Japanese, but you really didn't need a translator to tell that he was unhappy.

"Makoto, English, please," Chadwick chided the older man. "Now sit down and let the dear girl explain herself."

I was beginning to like Hudson's father more and more. Once everyone was settled back down, I continued.

"I understand that this may not be what you want to hear

from the mythical *Synergy* you've been waiting for. What you have to understand is that I am still HUMAN. That means I will make mistakes, unforeseen things will happen, and I might lose my way. On the other hand, I have five other people to encourage me and help me walk this path. Synergy isn't meant to be just a weapon, it's not an object or power that can single-handedly wipe out the demon race," I announced and watched as they shifted, unable to meet my eyes. "As you saw tonight, I am a conduit. I can pull their power into myself and use it, or I can pour myself into them, boosting their ability."

"The Elementi need to adjust their thinking when it comes to Synergy. Lailah is not an angelic holy being, she is human, and that is what makes her perfect," Hudson said, taking my hand and giving it a squeeze. "It was only because the Dark Lord came to her that we figured out about Tabitha. None of us had any idea. That was all Lailah and Micah."

Oliver leaned forward, rested his elbows on his knees, and rolled his glass between his hands. "How did we miss that? We had her vetted, and she passed all the tests that we threw at her."

"They are called the Dark Army," Jay said. "Humans that are blessed with demonic abilities when the Dark Lord gives them his seal."

Oliver nodded, draining the last of his drink before pouring more. "So the rumors are true? He has an army?" Oliver glanced over at Makoto. "Why didn't you tell us? You and Jay have been investigating this for months."

Makoto looked at Oliver out of the side of his eye and tipped up his chin slightly. "We did not have any definitive evidence. Each time we raided a camp, they'd abandoned the place, and there wasn't much left behind for us to gather intel from."

"Tabitha informed us that she was not the only one in the Elementi. In fact, she specifically said there was one or more in your company, Chadwick," I said, redirecting the conversation and getting to the heart of the matter we needed to talk about.

"Oliver, what do you know about the secret project Adriana was working on?"

"She didn't tell me much when I asked her. She always made some excuse that I wouldn't understand. I knew that she was working with Chadwick, but I didn't want to go behind her back to ask," Oliver said, his face looking more haggard. "I should have paid more attention to what was going on at home, but Tabitha always had a handle on things."

As he talked, an idea filtered into my brain, and I turned to Hudson. "Could he have been dosed with enough of the serum to make him suggestible enough not to look into the matter?"

Hudson paused a beat before looking at his father. "What was the purpose she gave you for the formulation she was putting together?"

"Adriana came to me saying that she thought that she was getting Alzheimer's or that her depression was so bad that it was affecting her memory. She seemed to think that there was a way to slow down the progression or make the brain more open to receiving new information to compensate for what was being lost," Chadwick answered.

"Have you dealt much with demon venom?" I asked.

Chadwick's eyebrows raised. "No, I can't say that it has been something I have spent much time working with. Once we figured out the basics of how to remove it from someone infected, there wasn't much reason to keep looking into it."

"Fair enough. But what if demon venom had been added to the formulation that you were creating with Adriana? Do you have a guess as to what that would have done?" I pressed, knowing I was on to something.

Chadwick looked stricken when he seemed to understand. "Oh God."

Quickly he pulled out his cellphone and called someone. They didn't answer right away, but he called them back immediately. "Denis, I'm sorry to call so late, but I need you to run down to my lab and see if the Day-Brite serum is still there in the fridge. Yes, call me back as soon as you get there."

Something about that conversation made my stomach sink. We all waited in silence, watching the phone laid on the coffee table between us all. When it lit up with Denis's name, Chadwick snatched it up to his ear. Whatever Denis told him wasn't what he wanted to hear, as he closed his eyes and dropped his phone to the floor.

"We finished the serum today. It was ready to be tested, and we made a batch of twenty vials. They're gone."

To be continued in *Liberating Water*

Elizabeth Knight

Elizabeth is an International Best Seller, originally from Illinois but now living in sunny Phoenix, AZ. Elizabeth has been writing for nine years and started out in YA Fiction but recently found herself loving the Reverse Harem genre. Like her favorite books, Elizabeth loves to write about strong women of all varieties. Not all strength is flashy or apparent at first glance—some lies just under the surface.
Don't Miss Out!
Be the first to know what is coming next by following Elizabeth's social media! You never know when or what will be coming next!
Facebook: Elizabeth Knight's Unicorn Queens
Instagram: elizabethknightauthor
TikToc: elizabethknightauthor
Newletter:
https://landing.mailerlite.com/webforms/landing/i0m1g8

About the Author

Elizabeth is originally from Illinois but is now living in sunny Phoenix, Arizona. Though she is newer to publishing, Elizabeth has been writing for nine years. She started in YA Fiction but recently found herself loving the Reverse Harem genre. Like her favorite books, Elizabeth loves to write about strong women of all varieties. Not all strength is flashy or apparent at first glance some lie just under the surface.

Don't Miss Out!

Be the first to know what is coming next by following Elizabeth's social media! You never know when or what will be coming next!

Website: ElizabethKnightBooks.com

Facebook: Elizabeth Knight's Unicorn Queens

Instagram: elizabethknightauthor

Newsletter: sign up here

ALSO BY ELIZABETH KNIGHT

Omegaverse

<u>Knot All Is</u>

Knot All Is Lost Duet - Complete

Knot All Is Ruined Duet - Complete

<u>Sunshine & Rainbows Omegaverse</u>

Bailey-Rose duet:

Clouds & Daydreams + Petals & Promises

Lyra/Eli duet:

Knot Now Knot Ever + Yes Now Yes Forever

Mafia Royalty Shared World

Caprioni Queen

Glitter & Guns

Blood & Heartache

Revenge & Truth

Love & Power

Gun Runner Princess

One For The Money

Two For The Show

Complete Series

<u>Hidden Empire Series</u>

Two Tricks

Three Tricks

Four Tricks

More Tricks

Our Tricks

<u>Hidden Empire Novel</u>

Harper's Renegades

[Read after Four Tricks for best series context]

<u>Omega Assassin</u>

Dual Nature

Hidden Nature

Perfect Nature

-

<u>Hope Series</u>

Hidden Hope

Claiming Hope

Defending Hope

Obtaining Hope

-

Standalones

Nicolette - MC Feline Shifter Story

Lying Lainey - Dark Omegaverse

Books Not in Kindle Unlimited

<u>Elementi Series</u>

Discovering Synergy

Refining Earth

Liberating Water

Taming Fire

Rescuing Air

Mercenary Queen Series

Birthright

Dragon Queen

Forgotten Throne

The Final Battle